BIRTHRIGHT

Julie
Enjoy.... whenever
you're not watching...
"The Young and the Rootless,"
Red Sox, Days of our Lives etc.

a novel

BIRTHRIGHT

BARRY AHERN

Tate Publishing & *Enterprises*

Birthright
Copyright © 2011 by Barry Ahern. All rights reserved.

No part of this publication may be reproduced, stored in a retrieval system or transmitted in any way by any means, electronic, mechanical, photocopy, recording or otherwise without the prior permission of the author except as provided by USA copyright law.

This novel is a work of fiction. Names, descriptions, entities, and incidents included in the story are products of the author's imagination. Any resemblance to actual persons, events, and entities is entirely coincidental.

The opinions expressed by the author are not necessarily those of Tate Publishing, LLC.

Published by Tate Publishing & Enterprises, LLC
127 E. Trade Center Terrace | Mustang, Oklahoma 73064 USA
1.888.361.9473 | www.tatepublishing.com

Tate Publishing is committed to excellence in the publishing industry. The company reflects the philosophy established by the founders, based on Psalm 68:11,
"The Lord gave the word and great was the company of those who published it."

Book design copyright © 2011 by Tate Publishing, LLC. All rights reserved.
Cover design by Kellie Southerland
Interior design by Lindsay B. Behrens

Published in the United States of America

ISBN: 978-1-61777-810-0
Fiction / Fantasy / General
11.05.12

Chapter 1

"Emotional Intelligence..." I looked to the ceiling for inspiration. *What on earth is that?* I thought. Mr. Crabtree had just announced the topic of the day. I had a familiar feeling I had come across the term before; however, as a thirteen-year-old boy, I still wasn't certain if this was something to be proud of. For now, I would remain tight-lipped. Situated firmly among all the other thirteen-year-old guys in my class, maintaining your masculinity was based on your ability to mirror the reaction of every other guy sitting around you. It was a game, a very difficult game, but with your reputation as fragile as a house of cards, this was the camouflage necessary for survival in the teenage world.

As I scratched my head, wearing an overly emphasized confused expression on my face, I suddenly remembered where I had heard of this "emotional intelligence." There were some girls talking about this kind of stuff while in line at the cafeteria a couple of weeks ago.

Largely, it all went over my head. All I could recall with certainty was that men did not have any emotional intelligence—*no, wait*; maybe they said that all men had too much emotional intelligence. Was this fact? I wasn't sure. Was I about to test the waters? *Absolutely not!* I would put whatever half-truths I had on this subject to the back of my mind with all of the other half-knowledge I had accumulated over the years.

In all, there were about fifty to sixty students in the class. Mr. Crabtree was up front, trying to generate some interest in this strange subject. I was sitting in the second from bottom row of desks, in between my two best friends, Bert and Henry.

"Zach, do you know what emotional intelligence means?" Bert said, with a scandalous undercurrent to his tone.

"No," I responded sharply, renouncing any memory of my cafeteria experience.

"Ya, it sounds stupid," he said decidedly, slouching back in his chair.

"Oh, completely." I laughed, sweating a little from the half-truth I was holding hostage at the back of my mind.

Bert had always been one of my best friends at school. He was short with ruffled, mid-length black hair and had one of the roundest faces you have ever seen. He was someone you would never really classify as being fat, but somehow he always seemed rounder than everybody else. Though he was a guy that did not lack confidence, he was very proud in how he presented himself, both in his words and his manly body language. But he wasn't a popular guy, not by a long shot, so this confidence did not come from a team of adoring fans and loyal minions. Instead I think he fed off how highly he thought of himself and tried to ignore everything else around him.

"I think it has something to do with girls," Henry whispered as he anxiously looked over his shoulder for fear of being over heard. Henry was innocent, tall, smart, and had a classic comb-over he had been sporting since the day he was handed a comb. He was the kind of guy I would trust with my life. He was the guy I would bet on winning a gold medal for mathematics or chess. However, outside of his comfort zone, he was like a porcupine in balloon shop—awkward and dangerous.

"At thirteen years old, we're allowed to talk about girls, Henry," Bert said dismissively.

"That's quite enough out of you, Mr. Albert Quirkley," said Mr. Crabtree.

"Sorry, Frank," Bert said flatly, failing to even look up and recognise Mr. Crabtree's request.

"For the last time, Albert, it's *Mister* Crabtree to you," Mr. Crabtree stressed quietly without raising his voice.

I often felt sorry for poor old Mr. Frank Crabtree. He was not the most respected educator in the school, though deep in our hearts we were all fond of the man. We didn't show it, but I think we all looked forward to his weekly religion class. It was a time when you would pretend to know everything and nothing about the subject matter (depending on what it was), all the while listening carefully to every little piece of information you could pick up. Quite often the information was regarding emotions, life, and well, religion. On the surface, this was exactly the type of material that could make you seem weird if you appeared knowledgeable or too interested in it. However, it was really all the stuff essential to your conversational arsenal if ever trying to pretend you are older than you actually are. To date, my record with the social elite of the school was dismal, and I was a far cry from their inner circle. Consequently, I was constantly stocking up on conversation material to unleash upon the elite in the unlikely event of an encounter. It wasn't that I *couldn't* talk to them; it was more like I didn't *interest* them. And the more you tried to appear interesting to them, the more desperate you appeared. Turns out, desperation is not an attractive feature to the elite. This is why I had reconciled myself to appearing quiet in their company but all-knowing about everything if asked for my opinion. It was a risky strategy, but as every other approach seemed to have failed so far, this was my new plan to climb the slippery social ladder.

One person who was most certainly in the inner circle of this special group was Beth. She was in our class and sat up front like a trophy on a mantelpiece. She always managed to show just enough disregard to the teacher to be considered cool but with sufficient portions of attention to qualify as respectful. She was slightly smaller than me with long, silky blonde hair and a smile that could disarm a small country. Annoyingly, her eyes were still a mystery to me, unfortunately I neither had the confidence or the poise to engage in conversation with this pretty girl, let alone look at her eyes!

"Mr. Gerbils," Mr. Crabtree said as he looked in my direction. "I want you to tell me all you know about emotional intelligence. Come on now, Zach. Stand up."

Goodness me, what am I going to say? I don't want to say nothing and look stupid… nor do I want to come across as the biggest girl in the class.

"Ahhh… are we getting a test on this, sir?" I asked, hoping with all my strength that this would be enough of a diversion to get Mr. Crabtree to pick on someone else.

"Well, that is the point; emotional intelligence is not something you can always measure academically, but it is a level of development that comes from the heart."

I could feel my body temperature begin to rise and my hands begin to shake as this nightmare slowly began to unfold. The information from earlier that I had taken hostage and pushed to the back of my mind was also becoming restless; it implored me to share my half-baked thoughts on emotional intelligence as it rattled the confines of my mental crypt, crying for its freedom like an angry inmate who questioned the very grounds of its imprisonment.

"Aaaaamm… but if you can't measure it, Mr. Crabtree, how do you know how much you know about it?" I said. *What a ridiculous response! If this buys me an extra second, I will be surprised.*

"Well never mind the detail, just tell me what you think," Mr. Crabtree replied.

Oh no, it seemed I had run out of padding. I had run out of questions. *Should I say something that makes a little sense or pretend like I know nothing in front of everyone?*

Mr. Crabtree's stare only increased with intensity. *Why is he picking on me today?*

"It means that if…" I mumbled nervously.

Ding aling aling aling! It was the bell signalling the end of our class; it was the bell signalling the end of hell! Alleluia, praise the Lord. I had been saved by a higher power; the awkwardness had come to an end. The panic was now over; I could get on with my life.

"We will pick this up again next time," said Mr. Crabtree.

"Sure we will, Frank," Bert said as he searched his area for his books and bag so he could proceed straight for the door in the hope of a quick exit.

Slowly, I returned from my upright state of panic to a seated position to gather up my things and replay the drama in my head. On a busy day, experiences like these get forgotten as soon as they happen, though on a slow, boring day, an event like this gets amplified out of all proportion. As it was only 3:30 p.m., there was still much of the day ahead of me. However, so far, my Mr. Crabtree cross-questioning had been the flash point of my day.

Still somewhat sweating from earlier, I began collecting my books, secured my bag on my back, and made my way to the door. Henry and Bert had disappeared, though as we always walked home together, I was pretty sure I would find them at the front gates. I always found the different social circles outside chatting after school intriguing. I had spent a large portion of my academic life trying to align myself with any one of these groups. Of course there were the elite, as well as the goths, the jocks, the smokers, the smart, the pretty; honestly, there was a clique for almost every social sector in the school.

When I was younger, I'd tried to spend some time with the goths. The main criteria included black clothes, a basic awareness of metal music, and a firm resentment of anything representing structure. I was not really sure exactly what this meant; all I knew was that I did not have to talk that much and still people seemed to like me. This was perfect, as I really wasn't sure if I had anything in common with them outside of the goth thing. Surprisingly, there were a couple of normal people in this group who I actually felt comfortable being silent with. Though after a while, the black clothes began to depress me. Furthermore, the constant hate and angst exuding from everyone became quite draining. I found myself angry at nothing most of the time and for no apparent reason. I was also introduced to the word "cynical," probably one of the only words I ever came across that actually looked angry! There were also a collection of guys in this group who wore eyeliner, and at a formative time in my life, I certainly wasn't comfortable enough in myself to start wearing makeup. In fact, I may *never* be comfortable enough to start wearing eye makeup.

To brighten my mood after this little episode, I then joined the smokers. Now this was split into two groups: those who smoked as much as their little lungs could contain, and those who liked to be seen hanging out with the smokers. The smokers always seemed bigger and better than the system. They would look down to the ground and exhale, smiling as they began to give their view on some random part of school life. They were never serious or uptight, but always relaxed and jovial with a superior, almost adult outlook on all things troubling to a conventional teenager. And why wouldn't they have an adult outlook? They were smoking! I got myself into the group by feigning an affinity for filling my lungs with smoke. This was nasty, but it allowed me access to the group. I found that we would sit around in circles talking about everything, having views on everything, wanting to settle everything, though no one was ever too bothered about *doing* anything about anything. It wasn't long before I also dropped out of this group; it wasn't for me. I always seemed to smell like an ashtray, and the irony was that their "unique," against-the-system views on life were so predictable it was becoming boring. For once it would have been nice to hear, "You know, *that is a good rule*. I think the school is right on that one." I will eat a packet of cigarettes when that day comes!

Like it or not, Henry and Bert were largely the only two people I hung around with at school. We were all desperate to be different so we could have our own peer group. However, it appeared that we were too normal to be different. If we could just have one odd pastime or habit, this would be the perfect level of partial abnormality that would allow us to fit into some group or gang. Depressingly, it just seemed that we were too *regular* to be exciting enough to fit in anywhere special. We were like old clothes, not shameful enough to throw out, and not hideous enough to stand out, we just blended in.

Regardless of my school social standing, the one thing I was sure of was that I wanted to be someone after I finished school. I was hungry to be more than just an ex-goth and ex-smoker. I wanted to be someone, and there had always been something within me that said I would be someone and I am different from everyone else. I have always had a kind of inner fire, burning with ambition, just dying to be set loose on something great. The problem was, I had no idea what this burning fire meant. What was I destined to become in life? It was like having the fastest, most powerful boat in the world but not knowing how to get anywhere. I was stranded, drifting around with my sacred, burning fire waiting for the opportunity or, more accurately, the inspiration, to set me free.

To add to the confusion, I also lived in a household that had very mixed views on not just what I should do, but on everything. In the red corner was my father, a hard-working man dedicated to his family. You set him a task, and he will do it; you ask him to do something for his family, and he will do it; you ask him to do nothing... well, actually, he probably wouldn't do that. The fact of the matter was, he was a worker, a committed, selfless, passionate man who would give you the shirt off his back if you needed it. Consequently, he had a very strong view that I should go get a job and start acting like a man as soon as possible. In my dad's eyes, tradition obliged me to do this, and there really was no other alternative. Although I was only thirteen now, the weight of this expectation sat heavily upon my shoulders as my teenage years started to count down.

Then of course, in the blue corner, was my mother. My mother has always been a positive person who is full of activity. Her view was that I should do what was in my heart and only pursue something that would make me happy. And this was my home environment, the place where I would develop my sense of clarity as I started to grow and mature into a man that knows his mind and can make decisions for himself. I wasn't sure how long this would take, but I may need more time than my teens!

This was a complicated environment. It was like a jungle of good advice, support, and recommendations, where absorbing the advice you were given was sometimes more dangerous than it first appeared. When I was nine, I expressed an interest to my mom that I wanted to be a painter. By the next day, my mother had bought a painting set, a blank canvass, and asked me to try and discover my inspiration. By day two we were on the verge of booking tickets to visit Paris to visit some galleries when dad discovered what was going on and almost had a heart attack. I was delighted with my painting. I wasn't sure I loved it, but I was having great fun. My dad didn't think painting was a real job, instead he tried to harness my enthusiasm for painting and turn it towards mathematics, swiftly smothering the idea of a trip to Paris before the idea could even breathe. I liked the fact that my parents thought differently on everything. It was funny, as long as you weren't in the middle! It also wasn't very comfortable when you were asked to be referee between them. This was neither fun nor funny!

As I made my way through the front door of the school, I spotted the guys waiting for me. They were both sporting their "cool" poses, Bert with his back against a wall and arms folded, Henry with both his hands in his back pockets, rocking back and forth. They soon spotted me, and I met them while walking in the direction of home.

"Did you see Beth today?" I said, trying to conceal the excitement in my voice.

"She was in our class, you silly nut," Bert said.

"Thank you for that reminder, Bert. I had noticed she was in our class, I was just seeing if you noticed her," I said, a little weary from Bert's childish carrying on.

"Oh, you are sad, Zach," said Henry, walking ahead briskly.

"I'm sad? I was only asking if anyone noticed a girl in our class…"

"I am far too busy at school to be wasting time on the immaturities of silly girls," Henry said dismissively.

"Sure, Henry. Well, I hope you and your school books will be very happy together," I said as if I had just put the scores on the board. Zach: one point, Henry: zero.

"Well," said Henry. "I think I will be happier with my books than you and your fake girlfriend," he said. I absorbed the reality of his statement. It seemed I was a little too premature on marking the winners and losers of that debate. Henry: one point, Zach: idiot.

"Tell me, do you think that you have ever been in love?" I asked with a little reluctance. Mr. Crabtree's

Religion class on "emotional intelligence" had left some horrible side affects. I wasn't too sure how the crowd would take this, but as the banter was good, I thought I'd test the waters. I thought that I was deeply in love with Beth and would do absolutely anything in the world for her. I would sell my soul! Not just to the devil, but to anyone who would buy it, if it meant one romantic evening with the girl of my dreams. When I was thinking earlier on what career I would want to do and why I want to do it, I realized that the only reason I wanted to get a good job was to impress the girl of my dreams. Honestly, all this education, going to university, great job prospects, are all for what? So I will have enough money to impress a girl. How I would have loved to have been around in the day of Adam and Eve. How much easier was it then? How wonderful it would have been to live in a place with food at your fingertips, surrounded by nature's finest décor and a good-looking lady who looked after the garden; the only downside would be the snakes. I hate snakes, though I do love apples.

"Yeah, I think I was in love once," said Bert. I stood back a little. I was surprised that the alpha male of the group was going to share his emotions. Maybe Henry wasn't the only mature one amongst us. "With your mother," Bert announced, laughing loudly at his own joke, nudging Henry to get in on the moment.

"That's hilarious, Bert. You are clearly a very funny, funny man," I said sarcastically. "No, seriously, you ever fallen head over heels for a girl?"

Bert wiped the smile off his face and tears from his eyes, still explaining to Henry that he was talking about my mother. He looked to the ground and said, "No, not yet, though probably when I'm older."

It's fair to say most people want to fall in love at some point in their lives, though why is it that we have to be a certain age to actually fall in love? Why don't six- and seven-year-olds fall in love? Is it that they are not intelligent enough to know what love is? Surely not. That would mean love is in some way dependant on a person's intelligence. That can't be right. Love should come from the heart, cutting through the non-sense, leaving you with a feeding of sheer excitement. No, it couldn't be that intelligence is linked to love; that's too depressingly scientific. Although, with all of that in mind, it does require a certain amount of knowledge and rationale to differentiate love from infatuation... to actually be *in love*. Can infatuation turn into love? Or is infatuation always doomed from the start? I looked at my own situation regarding Beth. Was I in love with her? Yes, I was infatuated with her, but love—I wasn't sure. It's scary that I could see absolutely nothing ever going wrong if Beth and I spent the rest of our lives together. It's probably because at that moment in time, I could imagine taking anything that Beth could ever throw at me. Maybe that *is* infatuation, failing to recognise a girl as a person and seeing her as a thing you can't have. The reality is that after a while, I would begin to discover that Beth is only human, and she would most probably annoy me like every other girl on the planet... no, that's not fair. Let me think for a minute... Actually, that does sound fair!

Chapter 2

Our trip home was predictable. As we came from the school gates and down Haricot Lane, we would pass the local graveyard on our left. The large, open graveyard was morbidly well populated. Of what could be seen, it wasn't very well kept, with long grass and overhanging branches at the bottom of the graveyard. At night, the overgrown branches looked like a giant hand clawing its way over the wall. Incidentally, I always walked faster past the graveyard at night.

After this stage, things would pick up a little and we would pass the ever-vibrant corner shop, Malkins. The shop itself was from the 1950s and run by the elderly Mrs. Malkin, hailing from the 1920s. She was an extremely old woman. Occasionally, if one of us had money to spend, we would go in there and do business with the old lady. Today was one of those days. "Hello, Mrs. Malkin," we said, pushing the door forward and ringing the bell at the top of the door. "You know you're going to have to get electric doors at some stage soon, Mrs. Malkin," Bert said as he eyed the loyal cowbell that would ring every time someone entered or exited the shop. "They're all the rage now, and besides," Bert said, looking over his shoulder, "the cows want their bell back. What farm did you steal that from?" She laughed and walked around to the front of the counter.

"I bet that bell will last longer than these electric doors, Albert," Mrs. Malkin replied.

She's probably right, I thought, getting horrible flashbacks of malfunctioning electric doors from a different shop closing on my nose when I was younger. How embarrassing. Bert also seemed satisfied and dropped his line of enquiry. As we parted with our hard-earned pocket money, we chatted with Mrs. Malkin. She was such a lovely woman. I could tell she was brimming with knowledge and wisdom but constantly holding back to let us have our stupid opinions. We waved as we hit the bell on our exit, embarking on the remainder of our journey.

Next, on the left, we passed a large, open park. The park was frequently filled with mothers and their children, as well as adorable old couples and, of course, those odd individuals roaming around all parks with no obvious intent. Today the weather was nice, the sun was shining brightly, the clouds were fluffy, and there was a beautifully calming breeze in the air dampening the vibrant buzz from the people scattered about the park. Amongst the masses I could see a new girl from our school; she had a particularly distinctive look. She had the darkest, shiniest, black hair I had ever seen, all tied up in a neat, pink bow. You really couldn't miss her. She was lying up against a tree, reading. How relaxing. In fact, the entire park looked so peaceful; it was almost like this real-life situation was choreographed with each person's position and movement in perfect harmony. I smiled to myself, enjoying the surroundings, until I spotted something a little off.

Suddenly, out of the corner of my eye, I saw a large dog begin to bark wildly; he was on a leash, but his wolf-like power and features seemed to be proving quite a challenge for his owner. It was startling, one moment I was feeling the gentle breeze brush over my face as the sunshine filled the park with joy and laughter, and then this sharp, aggressive barking shattered the serenity into tiny pieces. "What is the dog barking at?" Henry asked as he came up beside me and leaned on the wall looking in on the park.

"The other beast of a dog," Bert said, nudging in between Henry and me and pointing to an equally huge dog, also barking and growling and looking to break away from its owner.

"Oh man, there is going to be trouble here." Henry said nervously.

As both dogs barked and people in the area began to move away from the two dangerous looking animals, both owners began to come under more and more pressure to control their raging pets. On our left, the female owner of the dog looked like she was on the brink of letting go of the dog's lead. On the right, the male owner, a large, strong-looking man, looked like he had the measure of the dog as the two pulled in opposite directions. It appeared my real-life perfect harmony was quickly becoming a real-life drama unfolding in front of our very eyes.

Bert moved a little forward and turned to Henry and me with his back to the park. "You know that when a dog is fighting for territory, it doesn't see who or what it is harming," he said, more serious than I had ever seen him. "All the dog needs is a trigger to activate its primal want to fight and kill; the dog cannot be held accountable for what it does in this period. In this time-frame, the dog is not a pet; it is a wild animal. It will rip you apart with its teeth," Bert said as he looked back over his shoulder to the two dogs. "Well, let's hope these two stay as far away from each other as possible. If each is acting as a trigger for the other, each will fight like a wild animal if given the chance to transform into their beastly forms," Bert said anxiously.

As Bert looked back towards us, I could see something extraordinary occur behind him. The lady owner lost her grip on her leash, and the other man's leash on the other dog just snapped. Both dogs were loose and running frantically at each other. People screamed, ran, and scattered out of the path of the two beasts. When the two dogs met, they dived at each other, and there was a loud thud. This was followed by growling, biting, and a whole lot of blood spurting out onto the area where they were fighting. As the ferocious battle rolled across the park, a little boy's ball began to roll in the direction of the dogs. With the mother of the boy tending to her other two children, the young child ran after the ball, right in the direction of the dogs.

I froze. "The dogs are going to rip him apart," I said, not knowing what to do. Quickly we jumped the wall but then stopped. I don't know what Bert and Henry were thinking, but I was confused. I really wanted to do something for the kid. I wanted to be brave, but I couldn't. I was afraid. I didn't know if this made me a bad person or a selfish person, but I was terrified at the prospect of throwing myself at these animals. As I tried desperately to convince myself to do something, out of the corner of my eye, I saw further movement. It was the new girl from school; she was running from the other side of the park right towards the dogs and small boy. As she neared, one of the dogs was limping and a little less mobile than the other dog, so it was just snapping and biting. It was a dangerous situation.

At this point the mother noticed that her boy was running right towards the dogs. She screamed his name and held her face but didn't dare chase after the boy. Meanwhile both of the owners of the dogs stood at the periphery of the dogfight, calling the names of their dogs but both too afraid to try to physically stop the fight. The people looked on, gasping and screaming as we all prepared to see if this young kid would get mauled to death. But then the girl with the pink ribbon found herself at the side of the kid. She placed her hand on his shoulder and put herself between the kid and the dogs. She stood there, bold and defiant, moments away from a painful death.

As the dogs neared, they backed away from each other momentarily and took in their new joint adversary. They growled and barked while circling her until one of the animals lunged for her. The girl stood there unfazed as the dog jumped at her, going right for her face. Then as quickly as the eye could see, she flipped herself up in the air, allowed the dog pass under her and then landed behind the dog. She then put her hands on the dog's ribs and held it. The dog looked left and right sharply, knowing it had been outwitted; until it's visible heavy breathing began to slow and appear to come to a complete stop.

Meanwhile, the other dog was still growling and, like the other, lunged at the girl with its jaws snapping. The girl side-stepped the dog and grabbed onto its torso as it dived through the air. When it landed, the girl was still clinging on until, like the first, the dog's breathing began to slow until there was no more venom in its face. This was also the dog that had sustained an injury. Its left foot was up off the ground and suspended out of sheer pain. The girl approached the left paw of the dog. She appeared to rub its foot and then got up and started to bring the scared little child back to his mother.

Both dog owners were now willing to approach their respective pets and try to get them to go home. Order had been restored, people were clapping, and the mother embraced her weeping child as he cried on her shoulder. The police had just arrived on the scene with the fire brigade, and as they poured into the park people ran to them informing them of the situation. It seemed in the middle of the consternation people called everyone they could,

I bet the ambulance isn't far way. The girl, on the other hand, seemed already back to her book, where she bent over, picked up her book, and began to walk out of the park. She did not seem to want any adulation or praise for her heroic efforts. She had completed her good deed and wanted to leave the park. It was no longer a good place to read a book in peace. Bert, Henry, and I stood there in shock. Firstly, who was she? Secondly, how did she manage to do that? And lastly, what was she reading! These questions would have to wait.

Upon picking ourselves back up and jumping back over the wall, we got on the road again, where we would take a right down Denham Road, by far the busiest road of our little town. My dad worked with a company called Cube who manufactured cardboard boxes on Denham Road. They weren't a very big company, nor did they put much imagination into their name, but they produced the goods and had provided dad with work for the past countless number of years.

After passing through the tension of industrial mile, we found our local youth club, a busy, overused place in urgent need of restoration and cleaning. The furniture within the confines of our local hangout was openly flea-ridden, and sometimes, if we were very still, we could actually see the décor talking to one another. The general keeper at the club was named Wilton, an unusually uptight name for a man who appeared as flea-ridden as his furniture. His accounting and cleaning policy had a twist no one could even begin to understand, but he was a good man and always made us feel welcome. Along with

Wilton, there was often some wildlife roaming around in there: cats, dogs, and if you were lucky, a squirrel or some birds. If Noah's Ark had a local community center, this would be it. No one was turned away, and we just about had two of everyone and *everything*.

Just after the youth center, we finally arrived at the little suburbia where Bert, Henry, and I lived—the magnificent Bushel Grove. "I'll see you tomorrow," I said as I went towards my front door.

"See ya," they both shouted back as their voices faded into the distance.

Tomorrow was going to be a big day. I had to see the doctor about something private, something *no one* could ever know anything about. My plan was to go to school as normal and then later in the day disappear into town and make my way to the doctor. God, I was nervous about it, what if…

"Hello, my little Zachary," my mom said.

I wasn't little, and why my mother insisted on talking to me as if I were still eight was a mystery. "Hi, Mom" I droned back.

"We are having salmon fish cakes and broccoli for dinner. It'll be ready in one hour," and off she cantered back into the kitchen.

As I wandered about, I noticed that my little sister had beaten me home. She was eleven, though probably had more sense than the entire house put together.

"Hey, Miss Lucy, how was school?" I said.

"Great, today we learned all about…" Lucy began to ramble wildly through the insignificant details of her day.

Now this was something she was good at—talking! And something I was awful at—listening. But she never asked any questions, and so I always got away with it. Oh, I couldn't wait for dinner. *What are we having again?*

Ten to fifteen minutes into Lucy's very descriptive account of her day, I tried to lead her to the kitchen. It smelt good. My attention to Lucy had just decreased from fifty percent to ten percent. Food was now at the forefront of my mind. Thankfully, we were soon seated, and it wasn't long before we were ripping into Mom's fish-based masterpiece.

Many sticks of broccoli later, I decided to retire for the evening and go to sleep. I hadn't seen Mom sneak the full load of greenery onto my plate earlier, so I didn't get to fully negotiate the quantity of broccoli, sneaky tactics, but executed beautifully. Top marks, Mom. As a result I was very full, lying there in anxious anticipation of my trip to the doctor tomorrow. Well, this and the fact that six sticks of broccoli simply did not relax you for a decent night's sleep. I felt like a fat rabbit.

Then, as I lay there, digesting and pondering the day ahead, I heard a noise. It was something I had never heard before, so I got to my feet and went towards the window. As I approached the window, the noise got a little louder. It was like a very slow, weird echo of clicking noises. As I pulled back the curtains, the noise continued to grow louder. However, I could still see nothing. At this point, it felt like the noise was upon me. *Click... Click...* I looked behind me into the darkness of the room and began to sweat. For a second, I thought there was a person standing at the door. To my relief, I quickly realized it was only my robe hanging on the door.

Click... Click... Click. It persisted, getting louder and louder with no more evidence of where it was coming from. I was scanning the garden frantically while continuing to look behind me in case of an intruder. I was growing very uneasy and I felt like I was losing my mind. *Should I start yelling for my dad out of fear of an intruder?* Or should I just wait it out, as if I was losing my mind there really wasn't anything anyone could do for me now. Either way my heart was now racing as I waited for something terrible to happen. Then, just as suddenly as it started, it stopped.

I looked out into our garden, expecting this to be the calm before the storm, expecting a wild creature or monster to jump through the window at any second, though I could see nothing. It was very dark outside, and there wasn't a thing in sight. I wiped the sweat from my brow, leaned on the window, and rested my head on the cold windowpane for a moment, in the hope it would help return my heart rate to normal. The cold feel of the window against my forehead was the perfect antidote for my heated brow, as my breath fogged up the window, making it now almost impossible to see anything outside. Finally, with my body temperature and heart rate stabilizing, I pulled back from the welcome cold of the window and looked at the steamed-up windowpane. The only part that was not steamed up was the place where I was resting my forehead. Instead, there was a small little window within this steamed area, the only place I could still see through out onto the garden.

Focusing in on this little area, peeping out through the only place I could see through, I saw movement. It was a man. He moved his hand. I didn't notice him before because it was so dark and he was so still. He must have been looking at me all of this time. He was at the very bottom of the garden, standing straight with his hands down by his sides, looking towards the house. Shocked by what I was seeing, I went to wipe off the steam on the window for a better view. However, as I went to clear the area, the tall, dark figure stepped backwards into the depths of a thicker darkness disappearing from my sight. This time I think I would need more than the cold of the window to calm me down! My eyes were popping out of my head, and a cold sweat came from the core of my body as goose bumps began to cover the surface of my skin. This was really creeping me out. Who was that, and why was he in my garden? I was sure I wasn't dreaming, but I knew if I got dad, that's all he would say. So reluctantly I crept back into my bed, held the blankets tightly around me, pulling them on me like they had some sort of magical power, and tried to forget about what had just happened. As if I wasn't having enough trouble getting to sleep, I was now bloated, anxious, and terrified. Excellent! I should be asleep in no time! Now I feel like a fat, *anxious* rabbit.

The next day I rolled out of bed half-dead from sleep deprivation from the relentless state of fear last night left me with. I also felt like I was still digesting that flaming broccoli. I wonder how rabbits feel in the morning when they get up—bloated and tired, I suspect. As I came down the stairs, Dad was grabbing his coat and flying out the door with a piece of toast in his hand. Dad was ever the corporate soldier, galloping into battle as soon as the cock crows and signals the beginning of the day. In many ways I wanted to be like him, to be able to focus all of the energy and passion I could muster every day into a job, irrespective of how I felt about it. However, what I didn't want was the anxiety that went hand in hand with this daily penance. I would find a job that I loved so I would not dread attending to its needs. It wouldn't be a job or even a career, for that matter. It would be my calling! What an excellent plan. Now, to find this calling!

As Lucy and I left the house, I saw Henry and Bert up ahead. I didn't usually like walking my little sister to school with my male party, but Mom couldn't bring her today because she was busy.

"Don't forget to eat your sandwiches!" Mom yelled at me.

Oh God! So early and so busy, yet she still manages to find the time to make me feel like a thirteen-year-old baby. I was man enough to admit I wasn't afraid or too old for my mother's affections, but did she have to broadcast it to everyone who could hear? Luckily, Lucy reciprocated Mom's kind regards, and off we went on our merry way.

Ambling along to the tune of Henry's squelching sneakers, we were listening to Bert explain how he thought snails could eventually take over the world.

"They don't use that much energy, they don't eat much, and they have their house on their backs," he said convincingly. After a while I began to wonder why snails *wouldn't* take over the world.

As I listened on intensely to this extraordinary revelation, I began to hear that clicking sound from the night before again. As it had last night, it slowly increased in pitch and soon went from being a faint noise from the distance to a very distinct, infrequent clicking coming closer and closer. When I looked around, I noticed that we were coming up to the graveyard. I shivered to a stop as my imagination pulsed through the potential explanations of this eerie sound. Suddenly, things began to run in slow motion as I noticed everyone turn around and look at me with puzzled looks on their faces. *Click... Click...* The noise was definitely louder than last night, and if I ever thought something was about to spring up on me, now was that time. Would the mysterious man from last night now appear again? I hoped not.

My friends slowly turned their backs on me and continued to walk towards school. Could they not hear this? Were they not deafened by this abominable mystery? My heart was racing. Why was I the only one who could hear this? As I grimaced, searching frantically for an explanation, I felt something very soft brush up against my left hand. *Click... Click... Click*. The clicks were growing in power, coming closer and closer together. I braced myself as I turned slowly to see what had touched me. I was hot, panicked, and scared. Then, just as last night, silence... As I opened my eyes to see what class of creature I would find touching me on my left hand, I looked down nervously.

It was Lucy, staring at me as she tried to hold my hand.

"You look scared, Zach. Are you okay?" Lucy asked me as she gripped my hand firmly. In that instant my body was overcome by the most enormous sigh of relief; my legs went to jelly and my chest exhausted like a punctured tire. I felt a certain sense of temporary weightlessness. I was sweating furiously; this was getting quite unsettling. Though, admirably, I pulled myself together and, behaving like the ultimate big brother, reassured my little sister that I was perfectly fine.

As we began walking again, Lucy began to ramble about her first class. It was a very comforting background noise that slowly allowed me to feel safe again as I continued to recover from my near...something...experience. I hoped to God it wasn't another part of becoming a teenager. I still wasn't entirely comfortable with everything else accompanying my teenage years. What a completely unnecessary, embarrassing part of life. I wondered if all the guys at school heard this clicking noise. Surely not, but there must be a reason for this recent audio weirdness I was experiencing...there just must be.

Math was first on the agenda today. I quite liked math when I could do the sums. However, usually if I could do the calculations, so could the entire class. This would always take a little away from my personal victories. I almost needed other people to get things wrong to feel good about getting it right. On reflection, this seems very wrong, but I didn't have many victories. It was good feeling that you are not the same or worse than everyone in the class. Miss Hanchen was our teacher, a very dreary-looking lady in her early thirties. She always had her hair tied back in a bun and had the most symmetric face in the world. It was like her face was manufactured to a certain standard. Weirdly, I sometimes felt quite attracted to Miss Hanchen, which confused me. I certainly didn't fancy her, and I didn't like math that much. So why the hell did I occasionally feel like I was drawn to her? Today was one of those days when my mind was battling to stay awake, yet my hormones were all over the place. I hoped Miss Hanchen did not think I fancied her. I hoped I was in no way *behaving* like I fancied her. With this confusion in the front of my mind coupled with the fact that I spilt some Coke all over my pants at the start of the class, I was going to have to remain very still until I heard that bell.

"Did anyone get 55.25y?" Miss Hanchen said in her usual, dull tone. I looked at my page and saw 55.25y. Quickly I threw my hand up in the air and waited for the class to join me. Incredibly, only three other people put their hands up in the air. What do you know... I was actually *learning*. "Well done, Zach," she said as I lay back in my seat, trying to make as much eye contact with the people around me as humanly possible. *Enjoy the moment, Zach, enjoy the moment,* I said to myself as I put my hands behind my head and grinned smugly. "Would you like to come to the board and show us how you did it, Zachary?" she asked. *Oh, she can't be serious!* My grin quickly disappeared, and my hands came from behind my head and up on the desk again. We have a problem. We have a big problem.

The spilled drink stain was all over my pants, and I didn't just spill it on myself. I *covered* myself in the stuff. *Okay, think... I can't refuse to go up because I did get the sum right... Ugh!*

"Zach, we're waiting..." Miss Hanchen said impatiently. Yep, just in case everyone wasn't looking at me, I pretty much had the gaze of the entire class now.

"Ah, I have a sore hand, Miss. I won't be able to write on the board," I said.

"Oh, in that case, Zach, take yourself down to the nurse; she will have a look at it," Miss Hanchen said decidedly.

To hell with you and your kindness, Miss Hanchen. "No, Miss, I can wait until after class," I said, panicking.

Miss Hanchen began to smile at me. She looked from side to side and started walking over to my desk. As she arrived, she gracefully caught the back of her skirt and positioned herself on the side of my desk. I had never seen Miss Hanchen so... *un-dull*. What was going on? I never wanted to get a sum right ever again! Miss Hanchen put her left hand across the desk and leant on it. She crossed her legs, put her other hand on her face, and said, "I think I know why you don't what to go to the board."

I think my heart stopped. My sweating quickly returned to panic as I began to question how on earth she knew what I was thinking. And that being so, what was going on now? Was she now somewhat flattered? Was she flirting with me? Was she going to ask me out? She stared at me, smirking with this sort of devilish innocence. I didn't know what to say. There was far too much anxiety in my head to even begin to know how to judge this situation. Then slowly, like a cat about to purr, she leant in a little closer to me. Though I could now quite clearly smell her perfume, I was preoccupied with a sick, anxious feeling. As she continued to move towards my ear, she uncrossed her legs and whispered, "Do you think I'm stupid, Mr. Gerbils?"

Jumping to the floor, she began roaring, "How dare you come in to my class and be dishonest? Do not lie to me, Mr. Gerbils. If you cannot do the questions, try, but do not—and I repeat—do not try to make me look like an idiot. Do I make myself clear?" Oh God! I was so relieved. Granted, I now had a different type of fear and panic. However, this was the fear and panic I was far more familiar with and would do my reputation no harm. I had to be careful not to look so relieved as she roared at me.

"Of course, Miss. I'm so sorry," I said with as much sincerity as I could muster.

"Oh yes, they are always sorry when they are caught, but I tell you, Mr. Gerbils, if..." And on and on she went. So she thought I was a cheat. I was a bit disappointed I couldn't claim the credit for this one act of mathematical fortune, but if this disgrace would save me an embarrassment of mammoth proportion, then I would take my punishment. Maybe this is what they mean by the tortures of genius. I was never putting my hand up ever again.

When the bell went we all began to gather our things and make our way to the science lab. Science was taught by a quiet, nervous little gnome named Mr. Finke. I liked science, though I found it really hard to concentrate in his class. He was a very clever man, but he would typically teach at a level just above everyone's head. If you worked hard enough, you could keep up with the little dynamo, but usually there would come a point during class when I would imagine him with a rod in his hand with a big red hat. Though as quiet as he was, if today's shenanigans with Miss Hanchen were anything to go by, maybe Mr. Finkle would also bite my head off. I mean, I had never seen Miss Hanchen so angry in my whole life. Fortunately, I didn't intend on going to Mr. Finkle's class today. This was my chance to disappear into town and have my private doctor's appointment.

As my cover, I decided to pretend to go to the nurse's office just so I would have an alibi. As I approached the half-glass door of the nurse's office, I peered in through the frosted glass to see a girl. The nurse was raising her arm up and down slowly, then going to a notebook and writing things down. It's amazing the amount of drama you have to go through every time you see the nurse. And almost every time, despite the findings, her conclusion was the same: "Let me give you something for the pain." Honestly, if just once she *didn't* give someone a painkiller, we might think she actually had an idea of what she was doing.

I recognised the girl in the nurse's office; it was the new girl I saw in action at the park the day before. I could not mistake her jet-black hair down to the middle of her back and the pink ribbon that kept it in check. Even through frosted glass, this defining feature was clearly noticeable. You don't find many black-haired girls with pink ribbons. Usually, this class of ribbon was reserved for the blonde contingent of the school. As I backed away from the door, there was a still silence in the hallway. This was the perfect stage for my getaway. If caught, I would say I was waiting for the nurse and I went to wait in the men's bathroom to keep off the corridors... brilliant; they wouldn't be able to prove a thing. Here I come, Labbledon.

Smiling from ear to ear, without the sound or sight of one person, I walked slowly down the hallway congratulating myself for such a good plan. Maybe I should be a ninja warrior when I am older? I may have to get tougher, faster, and braver, but surely good planning was a part of what was needed to be an effective ninja. I could start by eating some protein bars; I think they are meant to make you strong, all of the sports guys at school seem to snack on them.

With the end of the hallway only feet away, there was a sound from behind me. I turned quickly to assess the urgency of the situation. It appeared one of the handles of a door from behind me just turned; I think it was the nurse's office. Startled, I consulted my ninja skills for guidance. Unfortunately my ninja skills had not yet fully formed so I ran the remaining length of the hall like a girl running from a spider. As the voices from the nurse's office increased in volume I pushed out the exit door and let it slam behind me. I was puffing. It seemed that becoming fit should also be something I put on my list if I wanted to be a ninja. Thank goodness, the danger had been dodged; I was once again back on track. Still puffing, I cautiously made my way to the front of the school to walk the short road in to Labbledon. Technically I wanted to get there as quickly as possible to avoid being seen and missed from school, but that last sprint really exhausted me. I was so unfit!

As I stepped outside the front gates, I got myself onto the footpath and looked ahead for the sights and smells of the heart of our little community. Today my slow walk to Labbledon would turn in to an even slower walk, as the glorious sunshine put its hot hand on my head and seemed to push me backwards every time I tried to step forwards. I only hoped I would make my appointment, today I was travelling to a part of Labbledon that I had never visited.

Labbledon was a reasonably sized town. It had all the amenities and facilities of a large town with a population of about twenty thousand people. My objective was to find the office of a Dr. Reggie Philips. I was going to see him about something that had been troubling me for the past couple of weeks. No, not my aptitude for math, but something else entirely. There was something wrong, something not quite right that I was very uneasy about. Believe me, if there had been another way of solving this in a less embarrassing way, I would have taken it, but it seemed this was my only option.

I had once confided in Bert a year or two ago about a personal matter. He'd found it all quite amusing, and a little after he'd picked himself up off the floor from laughing, he rose to his feet and started calling me a girl. Although I was grateful for his contribution, I did not achieve what I wanted from the conversation. Upon review of his guidance, I questioned what the hell I'd thought I would achieve from asking him in the first place. This time it was going to be different. I thought of asking my parents, but then thought absolutely not. A complete stranger would do absolutely fine. I needed to get into town and get this over with as soon as possible. I hated feeling like this.

So let me see, 44 Thairwood Road. I wiped a little dust off a brass plaque on the wall. "44 Thairwood Road." This was where he practiced. I took a deep breath and approached a big, old, traditional, wooden door. From its age, size, and appearance, I felt like even the door was judging me. Quickly, I pushed it open and entered into the main hallway. The hallway was a narrow passage that almost compelled one to break stride towards the large, bright red sign labelled "Reception" at the end of the corridor. As I walked I could feel the walls pushing me forward in opposition to the resistance of my nervous, heavy legs. When I reached the end of the hallway, it opened up to a wide, expansive space. The ceiling was about ten stories high and the width of the place as far as the eye could see; this was not helping my nerves.

To the left of the large, red sign there was a middle-aged lady with short, auburn hair, pretty for her age, waiting for my first words. She was the receptionist, dressed in pure white behind a pure white counter, looking out through a purely white-framed window. I tried to swagger towards her in an effort to exude a confidence that said, Yes, I may look a little bewildered, but I know what I am doing. I also tried to wear a kind of indifferent look on my face, taking my surroundings in as if I was distinctly unimpressed and had seen this kind of place many times before. I was about five strides into my indifference when I realized the auburn-haired lady was much farther away than I originally perceived. It was at this point I evolved my movement into an indifferent swagger of reasonable speed. It appeared I swaggered very slowly!

Finally I reached her; I made eye contact and laid my arm on the window frame like a cowboy about to order a drink at a bar.

"Can I help you?" she said, still waiting for me to speak. Goodness me, I had invested so much energy into my walk over to her I almost forgot why I'd walked over here in the first place.

"Yes, I am looking for Dr. Reginald Philips," I said loudly. The lady looked down and began sifting through some paper, scrunched her face, and said "Ohhh…hmmm…I am afraid the doctor had to step out on a family matter. Can you reschedule?" she said with a sincerely apologetic tone in her voice.

Great, I thought, *just great, all this anxiety and angst for nothing.*

"Well, if you want to think about it, I advise you to go up to his office and sign the book outside. That way when you do decide another time, you will not be charged. The doctor will want your signature as evidence that you turned up," she said perfectly.

The lady smiled at me, as if we were on a date, as if something good was happening, whereas I just stood there puzzled, thinking, *You are the one who cancelled on me, why do I have to prove myself to the doctor! Why do I have to prove that I turned up? If he were here, I wouldn't have to prove anything at all!* "Ahh yes, I will go and sign his book. Where is his office?" I said, a little defeated.

"Floor four, second last door on the right. You will find the book outside," she said. The lady was still smiling at me. I found this annoying. Smiling is meant to be a positive expression, and I find nothing more annoying than an expression being used out of context. In this situation there was nothing for anyone to be happy about; it was out of context. Why was she smiling at me, and why was I smiling back?

Annoyed, confused, yet still smiling for some unknown reason, I turned around and made my way to the stairs. This was like no other place I had ever seen. The stairwell was not just a way to ascend, but all of the way up the stairs, there were doors into different offices. It appeared that this was not just a medical location but a place where space was leased by a whole load of different types of people and businesses.

After climbing the first two stairwells, I made my way up the third sequence of steps. I noticed from the distance that there was a doorway halfway up these stairs with no door. Instead, there was a man standing in the threshold of the doorway with his arms down by his side. *Perhaps it is a mannequin,* I thought as I eyed up the oddity in my spiralled upward movement. As I neared the tall figure, I realized it was no mannequin; it was a tall, thin man. He had a friendly smile on his face and thick, black-and-white hair on his head—strangely not grey but pockets of black and white with a charcoal beard covering most all of his face from his nose down.

"Zach," he said, extending his right arm and waving me towards him. "I thought I missed you."

"I thought you were on the fourth floor, and I thought you were out," I said, confused.

He smiled, walked towards me, and put his hand on my shoulder. "I take it you met our new receptionist. A delightful girl, but she has been struggling greatly with everyone's office; I do apologize. Please, won't you come in?" he asked.

"Over the past two weeks, Jessica has misdirected approximately twenty to thirty patients on me; in fact, it has become such an issue I now wait at my doorway. I hope I didn't startle you? Please sit," he said calmly. So far full marks for Dr. Reggie.

His office appeared clean, organized, and well kept. The walls were a warm peach color with yellow ornaments in different parts of the room. There was a yellow pot with a flower on the left on his desk and a small collection of yellow and white rocks scattered to the right of his desk. "So tell me, how can I help you, Zach?" he asked, looking at me. These were the words I had been dreading to hear all day long. I began to shift nervously in my seat. "Are you feeling ill? Do you have pain? Have you sustained an injury? What seems to be bothering you?" he asked.

I looked towards the calmness of the plant on his desk for comfort. "I feel scared. I mean, I'm *not* scared, but recently I have had a number of episodes where I feel I have lost complete control over myself, but then during this experience, I feel this energy pulsing through me. More recently I am even hearing noises... clicking sounds. I don't know why this is happening, and I can't seem to control it. What can I do?" I felt so strange saying this. Most people go to the doctor for a sore throat, a cough, or a cold, but not me. I was there for something abnormal. I hated feeling like this.

"I am glad you came, Zach, and yes, I have seen this kind of thing before. Now, how can I explain this? Do you play cards, Zach? Poker?" the doctor asked.

"Emm... Well, I know the rules, and I have played a couple of times, but I am no expert," I said honestly.

"I play poker, Zach, and I can tell you, it is one of the most enjoyable games you will ever play. It is a game of chance, a game of cunning, and a game where you need the awareness to know when and when not to play. However, there is a great danger in this game, and the moment you feel you are bigger than it, the game will end you. You may have the best cards in the pack, but unless you respect the fact you are just a part of this much bigger, variable process, you may end up in trouble. What

I like most about the game is that when the cards are dealt, on the surface, everybody's hand of cards looks the same. None stand out; they all look the exact same from the back. However, there is that very rare occasion when you receive an invincible set of cards, a hand so powerful that you know you cannot lose Zach…you are this rare hand of cards. You may feel and look like everyone else, but there is another side to you that contains so much potential that you may be uncomfortable with what you find. Do you understand?"

No, I thought to myself, *what the hell is he talking about? Oh, I hope this is a medical doctor and not psychiatrist. I should have checked his credentials better before I decided to see him.* I looked at the floor and then back to the doctor. "No, I don't think I do, Doctor. What do you mean?"

The doctor smiled. "Let me show you."

He got to his feet and walked around to my side of the desk. He sat on the desk in front of me and reached for the pile of rocks to his side. He picked up a yellow rock and a white rock and turned towards me.

"I want you to put out your hands, palms up," he said. I put my hands out and opened my palms. He placed a yellow rock in my left hand and a white rock in my right hand. He then wrapped his hands around each of my hands, closing each fist around each rock. "I want you to close your eyes and think back to when you last felt this feeling of vulnerable powerlessness. I know this will feel like a horrid task, but please, I beg you to trust me," he said.

He was right; I didn't want to do it, but he was the doctor, and if I had any chance of beating this, I needed his help. Frankly, I was not hopeful I could induce the experience in the first place, but I would humor his direction.

"Now I want you to say the letter *V* if you begin to get that feeling, and I will give you a further instruction," said the doctor. His voice was actually soothing, and though this was not what I had expected, he did seem to know what he was doing.

After a couple of minutes, I began to feel like it would never happen. I thought back to my most recent experience, but nothing was happening. Then suddenly I got that tingling feeling, the clicking started, and I found myself inducing this horrible reaction.

I shouted "*V!*" as the whole experience began to get uncomfortable and painful. I expected a voice to come from straight in front of me where the doctor was sitting, but instead I heard a voice from about ten feet behind me say, "Open your palms." I opened my palms. The rocks he had placed in each hand seemed almost weightless.

Quickly the clicking and the pain began to dissipate, and soon I began to feel like myself again. The voice from behind me said, "Open your eyes."

I opened my eyes to an empty doctor's seat in front of me. I heard his footsteps come up behind me, and he said, "Look at your palms." In each palm there was a pile of dust. The pile of dust in both hands had both yellow and white dust all mixed together.

I smiled, wanting to know immediately how he had done this very cool trick. He placed his hand on my shoulder again, and said, "Before you ask, I was standing by the doorway the whole time." I laughed in response as I leaned forward and placed the messy little piles of dust on his desk. "Whether you do or do not believe me, Zach, what I wanted to show you is that you do have the power to control this; you have the power to induce it and stop it."

"But how did you get the rocks out of my hands, replace them with dust, and then scatter all of the other rocks on the table?"

The doctor walked towards his desk and sat down. "That is the most irrelevant part of our session today. What is important is that you recognize that you are different and that you have the power to control what you are most unhappy about. Next time we meet, I will tell you how we turned the rocks to dust." He smiled. "I am glad you came to see me here today, Zach. Thank you for showing me your uniqueness," he said as he began signing something on his desk. "Why don't you call back same time next week, and we can pick things up from there? I will inform Jessica, and she will call you to firm up a time. How does that sound?" he said, still smiling.

Although I would still have to get out of school for the appointment, it was worth it; I hadn't felt this good, this comforted, in a long time.

I left the doctor's office feeling a lot better. I felt he had seen my symptoms before, and he appeared to know exactly what to say to put me at ease. This was such a huge relief. It was so comforting to share something I was deeply worried about with a stranger and get precisely the sympathy and guidance I had wanted. There was a smile from one side of my face to the other. Upon reaching the bottom of the stairs, I heard the auburn-haired lady, Jessica, call my name. I began walking in her direction. Normally I would have been very angry for that kind of mistake, but because I was so happy with my consultation, I decided I would take it easy on her, correct the information she was incorrect on, and let it go.

"Hi, Jessica," I said boldly. "About earlier, I was on my way up to Dr. Philips when I actually bumped in to him right outside his office, which is, in fact, located in a different place than where you indicated." I smiled sensitively as she looked back at me with a confused and simple expression. "I understand you have not been here that long, so I completely understand the mistake. I just wanted to let you know he is actually located off the third stairwell," I said.

The girl looked down at her papers again and began sifting through the mountain of paperwork in front of her. She didn't mean any harm, but how annoying it must be for everyone who relied on her.

"Mr. Gerbils," she said after me as I walked away. I turned back in her direction, though not venturing one step closer. Whatever she had to say, she could say it to me from where I was now standing. She looked up from her papers with a slightly stressed look upon her face, tilted her head to one side, and said, "My name isn't Jessica. I have been working here for thirteen years," she said calmly. "And the reason I called you over was because Dr. Philips called. He said he should actually be in shortly and could see you then if you are prepared to wait," she said, still wearing a slightly confused look as a result of my earlier speech. With that, I felt a tap on my shoulder.

"Mr. Gerbils, I am Dr. Philips. I apologize for stepping out without prior notice. I trust Sarah has explained the situation?" the doctor asked.

The auburn-haired girl looked at me anxiously. "Yes, I just informed Mr. Gerbils." I was confused; this wasn't the guy who just saw me. What was happening? Was this guy an imposter?

"Yes, please lead the way," I said suspiciously.

As we made our way up the stairs, we began to near the office where I just had a consultation. This time there was no man at the door. As we passed, I stopped and looked in through the doorway. Everything was exactly as it had been moments ago: the vase, the rocks; the only thing different was the paperwork was gone from the desk. I stood at the entrance, looking into the room in sheer disbelief.

Dr. Philips stopped and asked, "Are you okay?"

I wasn't sure. "Who is usually in this room?" I said to the doctor.

"This room? Why this is the show room for the complex. There is no door, no plaque, just a perfectly furnished office … as if any office can be like this." He laughed as I silently choked on the series of lies that stranger had just fed me. "Are you coming?" he asked anxiously.

"No, Dr. Philips, not today. I will reschedule. I am sorry."

And without even making eye contact, I went straight back down the stairs and exited out through the front of the building in an effort to get some air. I wasn't sure what had just happened. *Who was that man I just spent the last hour with, explaining my problem to, and how did he know me?* He did not ask for money and didn't even bother to write down any of my details. *What did he want from me?* There was something very strange going on, and I couldn't help but feel there was someone watching me.

Chapter 3

"Leave me alone...please..." a voice cried in the distance. The fear in the cry woke me from my walking daydream. Ever since I'd left 44 Thairwood Road, my mind had been in another place; I could have been walking out in front of traffic, and I doubt I would have even realized it. Thankfully there seemed to be no traffic on the road today, which left me in very safe surroundings, but the silence allowed my mind to constantly revisit the strange consultation I'd just had with that fake doctor. Who was he?

"Please stop...Please," shouted the voice again as I got a little closer. I was walking down a road out of town towards the school. I was on the right-hand side of the road. There was a black, metal fence on the left side of the road and a tall wall running along the right side of the road. Up ahead there was a gap in the wall where the boy's cries seemed to be coming from. I approached slowly and peered carefully around the wall to see what was happening. Unsurprisingly, it was some of the kids from school beating up another kid, bullying in its rawest form.

I hated bullies, but since I wasn't that popular at school, I never really helped anyone else out. I was too scared for my own safety. I didn't want to draw attention to myself even if I did feel bad for the person getting bullied. Well, this time it was going to be different. It was time to stand up and be a man, I thought, terrified, hiding behind the cover of the wall. I hoped I would be as brave without the wall!

There were three perpetrators: the fat one, the scrawny one, and of course, the crazy one. This was the nominated spokesperson for the group.

"Are you an idiot?" asked the mad one.

"Ah ... no," said the frightened kid.

"*What*, are you calling *me* an idiot?" the maniac replied.

"No ... no ..." the kid said, backing away from the mad guy.

"What ... you calling me a *liar*?" The crazy guy said. He followed up his statement by landing a substantial thump on the arm of the scared kid, which seemed the trigger for the other guys to join in.

The boy who was getting beaten up seemed small, and as they hit him and beat him, they pushed him about recklessly around their triangle of abuse. The last thump he received had him lose his balance and go flying into a tree, where he dropped to the ground. The horrible trio surrounded the boy as he tried to get to his feet. By an even more unfortunate stroke of luck, the boy's hand landed directly on top of an anthill. Usually these mounds are brimming with activity as the traffic of moving little black masses continue to march tirelessly in and out of the ants' lair. Strangely, in this instance, where there at first seemed to be thousands of ants, suddenly there wasn't an ant in sight; it was empty.

Although the boy was distressed, he got back up on his feet to face his attackers. This time he seemed more composed; he now seemed fearless. He stood there tall and proud, almost daring his attackers to make their next move. The fat guy went to punch the boy in the stomach. He wound up for an almighty punch and delivered it mercilessly to the cheers of his two fellow bullies. Surprisingly, the boy didn't even move, while the fat guy backed away and fell to his knees, holding his hand in pain.

"What the hell do you think you're playing at?" the crazy guy roared at the boy.

"Nothing, but if you try to hurt me again, I'll hurt you," the little kid said as he stood there courageous and defiant.

"Okay … now you are going to get it," the crazy leader said as both the remaining two guys moved in on him. It was time to put my plan in to action. I had to do something to save this poor kid from this continued beating.

I took a deep breath, looked through the gap in the wall briefly and walked past it quickly. This was all part of my fearless plan. I looked back again to the area of the bullies through the gap in the wall and prepared to shout at them. I looked at the boy who was getting beaten up. I took a deep breath once more. I waited. I poised myself, but nothing came out. Instead I just slowly exhaled the lungful of air I had just taken in and stood there like a fool.

I felt like I tricked myself in to thinking I was brave, and I fell for it. Truth is I couldn't do it; I couldn't knowingly put myself at risk for this boy. It wasn't that I didn't care; it wasn't that I didn't want to help, but I was terrified. Who am I but a misfit at school with so little special about me that I didn't even fit into a special group! I had two friends. Together, we made sure we stayed out of the spotlight. To do this would thrust me to the very center of the heat of the spotlight and invite people bigger than me with more friends to be my enemies. I mean, why would I do that? The fact was that I was too small, too inferior a human being to have the guts to make a difference and have such powerful enemies. Unfortunately there was nothing I could do. I felt like I was in a plane, spiralling towards its doom, standing side by side on board the plane with the boy who was getting beaten up. The unfortunate thing was that I had the only parachute. And although I wanted to share my parachute with the boy, I needed it for myself; I needed my anonymity to keep myself safe.

Resigned to the fact that I was too weak, too frightened, too useless to do anything about this horrible situation, I stepped in to the gap of the wall a little more to watch what was happening, and so I could perhaps help the poor guy getting beaten up after the bullies disappeared. Disgusted, I watched on as an older boy passed me on the footpath; he must have been eighteen or nineteen, well dressed with glasses.

"That is horrible," the guy said as he passed the gap in the wall and continued walking.

"It really is," I said, embarrassed with myself for not helping.

After I replied, I heard the keys of a car jingle as the boy, who was parked just beyond the gap in the wall went to sit in. Mesmerized by the horror unfolding in front of me, the jingling behind me stopped. Until, suddenly, without warning, I heard a voice from behind me roar over the wall.

"Hey, you, fatty...yeah, you with the stupid leather jacket and Green Day T-shirt. Why don't you and your two girlfriends come out here, and I'll give you a proper fight!"

Shocked by the taunting, the bullies all turned in my direction and pointed at me.

"You want some of this, popstar?" the crazy guy said to me.

God no, I thought to myself pointing frantically to the guy in the car on my side of the wall that they couldn't see. "It wasn't me," I said trembling in a tone so low that I could barely make out what I said.

"Oh, well, that's okay then, why don't we just talk about things then," he said, smiling as he and his two friends began to run in my direction.

Still shocked, I looked to the guy who just roared at the bullies; by this stage he had started his ignition and was proceeding to vacate the area. I don't think these guys really wanted to talk, unless talking meant punching me in the face! So with my entire body shaking from this case of mistaken identity, I looked towards the direction of the school and ran like the wind. I was travelling over these grey paving stones as if I had taken flight. My heart was beating wildly. I was petrified.

As I approached a bend in the road, I stopped and looked back. The stupid gang of three were in hot pursuit. Puffing and panting, bent over in two with my hands on my knees, I smiled briefly at the success of my escape so far, but then panicked at the prospect of having to run again. These guys may catch me. My race horse style exit from the danger area was fuelled by pure fear, I really hadn't considered how long I could run this fast! I suppose I assumed because they were wearing leather jackets that they were smokers. *Good Lord, they better not be fit, otherwise they'll kill me!*

Fifteen minutes of slow running later, my frantic gallop had turned in to a desperate jog as I approached the gates of the school. This would be my safe haven. I was pretty sure the terrible threesome would not set foot on such holy ground. I was going to be okay. Quickly remembering that I had snuck out of school, I took myself out of sight and tried to enter the premises as covertly as possible. I must say I felt very good about myself. I saved a boy's life; I managed to lure away a bunch of apes from a boy that could not fend for himself. I felt like a hero, like a real-life Robin Hood. As I embellished my false bravery beyond the actual facts, I quickly forgot how much of a coward I was. I focused on the result of actually causing a successful diversion, even if the only reason I lured them away was because another guy yelled at them and they thought it was me. Truly I knew I let myself down, but I was glad that I ended up helping in the end.

As I walked along, a small bit taller and a small bit prouder than usual, I noticed how quiet and still the school corridors were. It was the last class before school ended, so I decided to tuck myself away and hide somewhere. No point in disrupting class. Usually the music room and main hall were vacant, so off I went to find a place to hibernate for the hour.

Music was a real love of mine, both listening to it and playing it. My weapon of choice was the guitar, which I'm sure my parents regretted ever buying me. At the end of the month, which was also the end of the term, there was a show where I was going to both play and sing a song. This was something I most definitely did not want to do, but something that my music teacher insisted I should try in order to *develop* myself. I found music a very personal thing. I was not entirely comfortable with a public demonstration of how I invested myself into my music. I'd tried to get out of it, but I was getting tired of creating excuses I couldn't back up. Though as it was one of the last days of school, I thought that if worse came to worst, I could hide myself away for the summer.

As I sat there thinking over the day's events—my future, the doctor, and my new heroic status—time seemed to disappear. It turned out school had ended a long time ago, and it was now dark outside. My parents would probably be wondering where I was, though

I still had another hour or two before they began calling every neighbour in a ten-mile radius. After a great deal of searching, I eventually found a way out of the school through one of the male toilet windows. It was a cold night. The air was very still, and the darkness had an eerie glow about it. There was a full moon lying low in the sky, fighting desperately to lift the evening's black strangle on the day.

As I cleared the school property, I soon approached the graveyard on my left. I hated passing this place during the day, let alone in the still of the night. Consequently, my aimless amble soon turned into a focused march until, unexpectedly, I heard the sound of a branch break behind me. I stopped, looked around, and saw nothing. Now, with an even more determined spring in my step, I turned back to the direction of home, where my walk soon graduated into a scurry. Then again I heard a couple of branches break. Although petrified, I stopped and turned again to get some sort of clue of what was causing this sound. What was it about wanting to understand the unknown that overcame all levels of fear? I wished I didn't care about these random, unexplained noises, but I did. Cautiously, I moved a little closer back in the direction of the graveyard to see if I could piece together any evidence that would explain the odd noises. Gently and quietly, I tippy-toed back, my heart racing, and my curiosity wet with intrigue.

Is it something supernatural? Is it a cat? Or is it one of the deceased? As I squinted over the dimly lit collection of graves, I heard the noise again. However, this time I realized that it was not a branch breaking but a very loud *click*. It was the same sort of clicking that I had noticed the evening before and on the way to school that morning. Although this was an unknown that I was curious to identify, there was a certain pain about this clicking that exceeded my curiosity. Nervously, I turned again in the direction of home and began running. I was very afraid, and the faster I ran, the louder this incessant clicking became. I was becoming breathless and dizzy, and the noise was beginning to give me the most horrendous headache. It felt like my brain was about to explode. My sprint soon dropped to a jog and my jog turned into a walk until finally I was reduced to my knees.

What on earth is this? I curled into a ball on the road, clutching at my head until slowly, everything seemed to fade. It was like my brain was swelling inside my head, and the pressure became unbearable. As I grimaced helplessly, the pain began to lessen, and I soon began to get very, very sleepy. That is all I can remember from that night until...

Still curled up in a ball, I slowly began to regain consciousness. There is a short period between unconsciousness and consciousness where your senses begin to tune into the environment just before you open your eyes. For me, this moment seemed to last forever. The first thing that struck me was the smell. It continued to change and change. It seemed as though I was moving, but I didn't think I was moving.

Even still, the smells seemed too different to encounter on the same trip. Smell was never really a sense I paid much attention to, but now that it was getting abused, I was more aware of this powerful sense than ever. What was even stranger was that as the smells changed every couple of seconds, so did the temperature of what I smelt. Some were ice cold, almost hurting as I inhaled, while others were so hot I had to gasp again in order to intake more air. Where on earth had I ended up?

The relentless clicking that had brought me there had stopped. It was replaced by a mixed flood of sounds. I felt like my mind was replaying all of the sounds I had ever heard, one after another after another. And maybe that's exactly what was happening, every moment, every smell, every sound I had ever experienced being recounted as if everything up to this point in my life had led me to this moment. In fact, I still wasn't entirely sure I wasn't dead. Maybe that's why my life seems to be flashing before me. If I were dead, there would be good news and bad news. The good news being that it doesn't feel that bad, which is excellent; the bad news being that I was now lifeless, which is not so excellent. It was time to find out where I was.

When I opened my eyes, I was surprised. I was lying in the corner of a triangular room. There was a corner about twenty feet to my left and twenty feet to my right. The walls were maroon in color, about ten feet high, and had a very dark black, thick liquid flowing down them. I was lying on a pitch-black, soft surface, not that I could see it very clearly. All I could see was a black type of smog covering the surface of this apparent floor. The ceiling, alternatively, was a bright, white sort of fog. I couldn't see the ceiling either. All I could make out was the fog.

After a while I began to notice that the black liquid was not gathering on the floor; it was just flowing down the walls. As I got to my feet, I noticed one of the walls becoming completely covered in this liquid. When this happened I found it was even more difficult to imagine the shape of the room. It now looked endless on one side of the triangular room. However, the flow of black liquid soon began to lessen again on this wall, and the wall emerged once more. Strangely, this time it emerged as a mustard color. It's odd. Had I not been so mesmerized by this amazing little place, I think I would have been absolutely terrified, but as it was so intriguing, I was glued to its every move.

"I know you," a girl's voice said calmly. It was at this moment my intrigue and enthusiasm died a sudden death, and I was back to being terrified.

"Who said that?" I said, shivering in fear.

"I'm over here," the voice said, which seemed to be coming from one of the corners. As the dark liquid began to flow a little less, the wall soon got brighter, allowing me to see a small girl in the corner of the room. As I focused in on her face, I soon realized that I didn't know her. Even in a place completely removed from reality, this was an awkward situation. I wondered if you get embarrassed when you're dead.

"You don't recognise me, do you?" she said. Before I responded I took one final look. She was a pretty girl, with long black hair and was roughly my age. She was also in her school uniform, yet I still couldn't place who she was.

"Who's there?" a boy's voice whimpered from the other corner. Good God, another voice! This time it was a boy. He sounded even more nervous than I was. As the other corner started to get a little clearer, I began to make out the boy's face. He was a little smaller than me, a little chubbier, and had short yet wavy brown hair.

Wait a minute—it was the guy I saved from getting beaten up on my way back from town that day. "I know who you are," I said as he looked me up and down. Unfortunately, he came to the same conclusion that I had arrived at when I looked at the girl; he didn't know who I was. How embarrassing. Whoever planned this stupid affair must be having a good laugh at us.

It was time to start setting things straight. "I'm Zach. I'm from Labbledon. I know who you are because I saw you getting beaten up when I was going back to school today. I ended up being the diversion, even if I didn't mean it, that allowed you get away. However, you, Miss, I'm not sure we've ever met," I said unconvincingly. The boy took a step forward in response to my nervous speech.

"My name is Bala Eltree. I live in Labbledon too but was raised in New York all my life up until last year. I think you are a year ahead of me at school, but you probably don't see me much." I think we're probably the same age, but because of his move from New York, maybe he'd had to stay back a year at school. Heaven knows I was scared, but this guy was terrified.

"Nice to meet you, Bala," I said in an effort to comfort my new friend.

We both turned towards the girl as she moved a little to the side and said, "My name is Wen Ung. I moved to this country from Beijing when I was a baby. My mother is from Beijing and met my father while he was working there. After they had me, they moved back to this country," she said sadly. Just as she said this, she turned her head. It was a large pink bow.

Hang on... long, black hair... pink bow... it was the girl from the nurse's office today. It was the girl from the park who'd saved that kid from the savage dogs. "I know you!" I said enthusiastically. "You go to our school. I noticed you today when you were in the nurse's office," I said with the smile of success on my face.

"What were you doing looking at me in the nurse's office?"

Suddenly, I felt not so smiley and not so successful. "No, I was looking 'cause... well... I wanted to see if I could go in and..." I was rambling, and I wasn't even making sense to me.

"*What?*" Wen said with disgust. This wasn't going very well. I tried to explain a little more, but the more I tried, the more things spiralled out of all control. My second impression had better be good.

"Why were you at the nurse's office today? Are you okay?" Bala asked; what a kind, caring question. Now that is how to make a first impression.

"Oh, it's nothing, really. I think it's just..." She paused and looked at the ground for a while. "Well, it's just that I have been hearing this sort of clicking sound recently, and it's really scaring me," Wen said with a sense of embarrassment.

My jaw dropped. Never was I so relieved at another person's pain. God, maybe she was right not to like me; that's a terrible thing to think. Before I could answer, Bala said, "Are you serious? Because I have been getting these awful headaches recently, all set off by this incessant clicking that no one else can hear. My dad thinks I'm going mad. My mother thinks I'm saying it to get out of going to school. It's horrible." He was also looking to the ground as if it had caused him some serious concern. This was all way too coincidental to be by chance. It seemed that for some strange reason, we had been selected, but the questions were *by whom* and *for what*?

"This clicking," I said. "I too have been hearing it. What do you think it means?"

We all looked at each other, no one knowing what to think or say. I hadn't noticed, but since we all started speaking, there had been an absolute still, and suddenly we could smell nothing. There had been a change; instead of us listening and tuning into our surroundings, it seemed like our surroundings were now tuning into us. As the three of us looked to the floor, wading around in our own paranoia, I noticed that the black smoke began to move away from the center of the room. Then, bit by bit, a very bright sphere of light began to rise from the center. Its shine was almost blinding; however, it was surrounded by a thick, white cloud, which suppressed its glare just enough for us to look at it. Once it was positioned right in the center of the room, it stopped.

"What can you see, Bala?" the sphere of light said to him. Goodness me! The shining sphere talked with a very deep, male voice.

Bala, visibly terrified, replied, "What?"

The white sphere paused. "What do you see, and why do you think you are here?"

Bala looked around the room nervously. "I see a triangular room with two other people in it." So far so good; he was doing just fine. Poor guy... it couldn't be easy. "I see a black ceiling, white clouds flowing down the walls, and a bright red floor... and then there is you... a large, black sphere rotating in the center of the room."

I was puzzled. Yes, I too saw a triangular room, but all of the colors that Bala named were completely different from what I could see.

"Do you see the same objects and colors, Wen? How about you, Zachary?" the sphere asked me.

Wen was pretty quick to answer. "Ah... no."

Followed shortly with my support. "Hmm... no."

"The truth is that the three of you have always seen things differently. Why? Because you are different from everyone else you have ever met. Now answer me my first question: Why do you think you are here?" the sphere said. It was all so real, yet at any moment I felt like I was going to wake up from this strange dream.

"Is it because you want to kill us?" Bala asked. The thought had never even crossed my mind, but now that

Bala had mentioned it, I wanted to hear the answer! Maybe for some odd reason we *were* there to get killed.

"How do you know you are *not* dead already, Bala? In fact, while you were *living* on earth, how did you ever know that you weren't dead? Death as you know it is defined as the end of your time on planet earth, but have you ever thought that your time on earth was the time spent dead from *another* life? What if before you were born on earth, you were living a different type of existence up until you died from that life and arrived into your current world? For that matter, how do you know that your time spent on earth is not preparing you for a better existence... unless of course, life is perfect on earth... *Is it perfect?*"

"Ahh..." Bala said, still not sure if the sphere was saying he was or was not dead.

"Life on earth is not perfect. It is full of evil, greed, and hatred; and this, friends, is part of the reason you are here," the sphere said.

Bala was still staring at the sphere nervously. "I'm not sure what you just said, but just to be clear... you're not going to kill us, are you?"

"On the contrary, Bala. You are far too special. Let me explain," the sphere said calmly. Bala and I breathed a sigh of relief, but Wen never even seemed that bothered about the whole thing.

"Once every one hundred years in each universe, every star and planet arranges into a particular configuration. When this occurs, it induces a magnificent explosion of energy that travels through the stars and goes directly to each planet where there is life. Earth is one of these planets. Three people are then selected to receive this almighty power for each planet. In your case, the energy was split between America, China, and England," the sphere said. It seemed to address all three of us.

Though I was still waiting to wake up from this odd dream, I soon began to realize that this, in fact, might not be a dream but actually happening.

"But why were we picked? And why don't I feel any more powerful?" Bala said.

"No one knows how the *Viscents* are selected; some think it is your destiny and some think it is by chance, while others believe that the sole purpose of your existence is to be a Viscent."

"A Viscent. What's a Viscent?" Wen said curiously.

"The *vis* comes from visionary and the *cent* comes from century," said the sphere. "Every one hundred years, each world produces three Viscents, who are all born on the exact same day at the exact same time. Initially the budding Viscents are unaware of their birthright; however, as they are called upon, they are given the opportunity to become who they are destined to be. Every Viscent of every generation also has a unique power within them that they inherit from a fallen Viscent that has since passed, and of course, Viscents cannot die of old age."

"What," said Wen. "How can someone *not* die of old age?"

"Viscents age just like everyone else, and although they may look like they are aging, and although they may look like they are slower, typically they are as fit as they were at twenty years of age at every point in their lives. All that really changes is wisdom."

Bala was scratching his head. "But if Viscents can't die of old age, how do they die?"

"Let me tell you about your predecessors, the three Viscents in your position before today. Your predecessors were tremendous. They saved this planet from chaos more times than you could imagine. They each developed their own special powers and used them with deadly effect," the sphere said.

"So will we get to meet our predecessors?" I asked with a schoolboy's enthusiasm in my voice.

"I am afraid Wilbur, Zanthe, and Enid have since passed. Zanthe died around forty years ago from a battle in a different world that almost took the lives of all three Viscents. This is where Zanthe was assassinated." Suddenly the gravity of what was happening was beginning to hit home.

"Enid and Wilbur were devastated but continued to fulfil their roles until one night, Wilbur was ambushed by an unknown assassin and was murdered here on earth. Enid was very upset and hurt, and although she was then on her own, she continued to be the world's only Viscent. Recently Enid took on a fight knowing she could not win. Enid was killed in this battle. After this gruesome fight, I found a note from Enid stating, 'I know this fight is too big for me, but sometimes you have to do what is hardest, to do what is right. Please wish the three new Viscents all the luck in the world. They are in my heart.'"

We all looked at each other, trying to decipher what this meant. Then softly the sphere stated, "You see, the next three Viscents cannot be informed of their birthright until the previous three have passed. Enid knew that she would be killed in battle, but this is what she wanted, to make way for the new Viscents. Enid will be remembered as one of the most deadly Viscents ever to walk this earth. Her humanity was only ever matched by her power against those who deserved the full force of her wrath," the sphere said respectfully.

I felt a tear well up in my eye for such commitment, such selflessness. I wished I had what it took to be a Viscent. "To date you have felt things, you have seen glimmers of your power, but if Enid had not died, unless all of the Viscents before you passed, then you would never fully develop your power. It would always be there just below the surface," the sphere said.

"Hang on. So you are saying that now that all of the Viscents before us have gone, we are the new Viscents, and I will get these pains in my head forever with weird visions and a new power? Are you serious?" Wen said with a little rage. She must have been in shock. I know I was in shock. I could barely breath this was so terrifying.

"You are in part correct and incorrect. You are correct in that yes, you are proposed to be the new Viscents of your world and you all have a power hidden within you waiting to be developed. However, where you are incorrect is that, now that you are in that state where your body is trying to realize its Viscent power, you are getting pains in your head and seeing these visions. So as long as you choose to be a Viscent, the pains in your head and visions will soon discontinue. They are only a product of the turning stage you are currently experiencing," the sphere said, which was a little comforting. For a moment we all thought about what the sphere had said, until once again Wen tilted her head took a step closer to the sphere.

"So what do *you* do? Who picks you?" Wen said, visibly shaken by all of this information.

"I am known as Evall, or The Core. Each planet in each universe has an Evall and three Viscents. The Evall and Viscent community is known as the Oranthium; we have rules, responsibilities, regulations, and as you will grow to learn when you visit, we have a language. You will not need to know how to speak it, but there are words for things like your power, your classification, that are all based on ancient Oranthium script. The Evall's role within the Oranthium is to control our own Viscents, inform them, and support them. Together we ensure a balance to each universe, a peace in our own worlds, and when required, we help each other. However, the Viscents you meet on other planets could be of any age. They could be your age, as they would have received the same energy you received on the same day you were born, or any other age up to five hundred years old if not older. If a Viscent doesn't get killed, the next generation will never get the opportunity to become Viscents. As I mentioned earlier, each living Viscent has a unique power. They use their powers together to protect their own world and help keep each universe in balance. The Evall is the communicator between the planets. Sometimes there are missions where a number of Viscents are needed to team together. Sometimes there are specific missions where a particular Viscent is asked to fulfil a certain task in their world or another. You are the Viscents of your world."

"So how often do you Evall get replaced?" Wen said rather coldly.

"Though your mind is not allowing you see me now, I am just another person on planet earth. I am standing here before you, but all you can all see is a sphere of some color rotating in front of you. When I die, the succeeding Evall will automatically step into my position, so although they do not know this yet, as soon as I die, my wisdom and experience will travel to them. As I mentioned before, you are all presently in this turning phase which is why you cannot see me as just another person, your Viscent abilities are immature and weak, but when you master your own Viscent power you will all just see me as plainly as I stand before you," said the sphere.

Wen, Bala, and I were looking at each other, around the room, to the floor, and then at each other again. We were taking in an awful lot of information. For a couple of minutes no one talked; we just stood there thinking of all that was just said.

"I hope you do not mind, but shortly after you were all born, I arranged for you all to live here in England. On your own you will only realize a fraction of your abilities, but together you have enormous potential. The more time you spend together, the more powerful you can become," said the sphere.

"But why England, why here?" Bala asked, a bit annoyed at this part.

"Bala, I appreciate that you have come from New York, and Wen, you have come from Beijing. Seemingly, both of your parents' lives have led you to live here. I had to make sure that happened."

"That is so unfair!" Wen said. "Why did my 'position' have to affect where me and my family lived? It's not fair."

"You were brought to this particular place because this is where Zachary was born. As he is the strongest of the three of you, this was picked as the collection area. You must to spend time together," said Evall firmly.

Oblivious to the frosty stares of both Wen and Bala, I had temporarily become fixated on Bala's sneakers and could not help admire the striking pattern along the sides. However, after realizing that everyone now hated me and that I now seemed to be the one with the most responsibility, I promptly returned to the strange conversation we having with the mysterious white sphere, Evall.

"Hang on a minute. I'm not the reason Wen and Bala are here, and I don't have any magical *powers*."

"On the contrary, young Zachary. You have the strongest ability, and you must work closely with Wen and Bala if you are to succeed on this very special mission," Evall replied.

"Mission? What mission?" Bala said, reverting back to his quivering tremble.

"You need to earn the right to be a Viscent. You need to earn the right to use your power. You need to find your power," Evall said flatly.

"So what are you going to ask us to do? Is it dangerous?" Wen said anxiously.

"You will be sent to three different worlds. There will be a task in each world that you must satisfy before you return. You will not be told the tasks; you will need to discover them. You will have at most one week in each world to undertake what you are there to achieve," said Evall.

"It seems pretty tricky," I said, trying to stay calm as my heart thumped uncontrollably inside my chest.

"So how does it work? What will the worlds be like?" Wen asked practically.

"I can't tell you what you may be asked to do, but I can tell you that *you* get to choose the *type* of world you will be sent to," said Evall.

I scratched my head. "What do you mean, *type of world*? How do we know what types of world are out there?"

"There are more worlds and life forms in the multiple universes out there than you could possibly imagine. You may not know which ones are good, but you know what is wrong with your own world. For instance, you could wish to go to a world where there are no weapons or you could wish to go to a place where they do not record time; all of these places exist. You need only to tell me the type of world you would like to visit, and I will make it happen."

Wen was looking at the ceiling, thinking, tapping her foot on the ground like we were running out of time.

"So if I asked to go to a world where there is no light, you would send us all there?" Wen asked.

"Yes," replied Evall.

"And would we have a place to stay?" Wen queried.

"It is Oranthium law that if you are sending your Viscents to another world, you check with the governing Evall of that world. As long as it is okay, the visiting Viscents will occupy the bodies of the resident Viscents of that world, or if that is not agreeable, you will be given a different body," Evall explained.

"Weird," Bala said. "So if we do assume the body of a Viscent of another world, while we are occupying their bodies and living their lives, where do they go?"

"Their Evall will arrange for them to occupy your bodies in your world," said Evall.

As I proceeded to get more and more freaked out, I thought to myself, *If I am in the body of another person in this other world, how on earth will Bala and Wen be able to recognize me? Actually, how will I recognize them?* I was beginning to sweat.

"So how do we recognize each other in this new world?" Wen asked before I had a chance to get the words out.

"I want you to listen carefully, I want you to take your left hand, take the tips of the two fingers next to your thumb and touch your face with these two fingers, to the side of your left eye, below your eye level," Evall said to us clearly.

Like the clumsy oaf I was, I tried to do exactly as the Evall explained; I took my left hand, found that place just to the side of my left eye and touched it. When I looked over to Wen and Bala to see how they were doing, I was surprised. Each of them had a mark on their faces. Each had a bright light coming from the underneath their left eye. It was no bigger than a thumbprint, and as they were also touching this part of their face the mark was slightly covered, but the marks shined magnificently with a bright silver glare from both Bala's face and Wen's. Like me, Bala seemed to be noticing the same thing as he pointed at me excitedly, and then pointed at Wen, in disbelief at what he was seeing.

"As you have probably all worked out, you all have the Viscent birthmark slightly to the side, underneath your left eye. It is not visible to anybody but fellow Viscents, and you can only see this mark on other Viscents if you touch your own birthmark. The birthmark is a symbol from the Oranthium that represents the power that you will go on to develop when you become a Viscent. So as you embark to these worlds, identifying each other will not be the issue, the completion of the task should be your principle concern," Evall warned once more.

God, this was confusing. "So what if we do not complete the task, or worse again, fail to discover the nature of the task?" I asked anxiously.

"I regret to say that if this occurs, you will be provided with another body to occupy in that world. You will be stripped of your gift and trapped in that world forever," Evall said severely.

There was a silence. At thirteen years old, the weight of responsibility in the decision I was about to make was more than I could ever dream of. This was such a big opportunity with devastating repercussions if things went wrong.

"Do we have to do this?" I asked.

"No. If you do not choose to do this, you will return to your world as if this never happened. You will be stripped of your gift and your planet will have to wait another one hundred years for their next Viscent. People have refused to do it before and I imagine will refuse to do it again. Do what your heart tells you to do," Evall advised.

I looked at Wen and Bala as they glanced back nervously. "As your powers are currently weak, you need to develop them and reach your potential. If you reach your potential and you earn the right to be a Viscent, you will be branded on the underneath of your right arm. This branding will not shine like your birthmark, but it will be visible to everybody. It will be a permanent mark on your body. This branding relates to the part of the Oranthium that represents your category of power. There are three categories of power at the Oranthium. Once you are branded, you have been accepted into one of these categories. In addition to becoming a Viscent at the end of these trials, you will be granted one wish to be used for the benefit of your world. But for any of this to happen, all three of you must be successful in all of the three worlds and achieve your tasks. It is only at this point the three of you will be granted one wish between you for your world and achieve your branding. This wish could change or shape your own world in whichever way you all deem appropriate. It is time for your decisions," Evall demanded.

Wen was staring at the floor while Bala was now grimacing. It seemed like he was going to make a decision one way or another.

He stepped forward and said, "You know I'm sick of being picked on. I am sick of feeling bad about myself because others want to be nasty. I want to make a difference. I want to do something that means something. I hate to think that I may never see my family again...but...but...this is what they would want," he said with a conviction that we were all a little shocked by. Goodness me, Bala had a lot more courage than I could have ever imagined.

"I don't get picked on." Wen smiled sympathetically to Bala. "However, I don't have a social life. I don't have any friends, and perhaps if I didn't go home, not many people would even notice. I've never been good enough at anything to be anyone. This is an opportunity to be someone. Yes, the stakes are high, but so is the reward, not just for me, but for anyone I can help...I would like to put myself forward," Wen said as she looked across at Bala.

I couldn't believe the other two signed up for it with so little thought. I was beginning to sweat. Looking up and down and around in the hope of inspiration, I eventually said, "Well...I'm not sure about this...I mean, my family, my friends...I'm really sorry, but..." I thought about the people I cared most about for a second, the people that were stopping me from doing it. Ironically,

I then began to realize that these are exactly the people that I should be doing this sort of thing for.

I thought a little more and said, "This is a mammoth responsibility. I mean, trying to complete tasks we don't know about in worlds we have not seen…I just…I just…I'm just scared we'll not get to see our families again…" I continued to pause for a while. The longer I delayed, the heavier the weight of everyone's expectation. Suddenly I began to feel the pressure of what we were being asked to do. I mean, I didn't really get bullied, I had friends, I led a normal life…and maybe that was the problem. I wasn't afraid enough to have to do something nor ambitious enough to want to do anything different. I lived my life in the shadows, and I didn't want to change that, in fact I was terrified to do anything that would change any part of my current life. I was scared of becoming a Viscent. What if I couldn't do it? What would happen if I let them down? Wiping the sweat from my forehead, I looked at Bala and Wen; yes I was more scared than I have ever been in my whole life, but I knew what the right thing was to do. "Okay, I'll do it. Anything else would be selfish. I want to help. I want to make a difference…Yes, count me in," I said nervously.

Bala and Wen both looked at me with a shared sense of pride. I felt we were doing the right thing; I just hoped we could do it. I hoped that I wouldn't fail them.

"Very well, my young Viscents. In that case, it is time to send you on your way. Bala, you will have the first opportunity to choose what type of world you would like to travel to. After you make this request, you, Zachary, and Wen will pass out and wake up in that world. You will not wake up together and will need to find each other in order to achieve your task. You will return here in one week. At this point you should have achieved what you were there to achieve, otherwise I will return you to that world in another body, where you will spend the rest of your lives," said Evall.

"What will we have to do when we get there?" Wen asked.

"That is for you to discover; I can give you no guidance. Finally, I would like to commend you all on your bravery and wish you much luck over the next three weeks. Now, Bala, think carefully. What world would you like your first task to be in?" Evall asked softly.

God, I thought, *what is he going to say? In fact, what am I going to say? In about ten seconds, we are going to be in a place completely of Bala's doing. Think, Bala, think. Make it a good one.*

"I wish we weren't always chasing money all of he time. In fact, I wish no one chased the evil of more money. Perhaps if there were no money, happiness would come first every time. Money wouldn't be a problem. Yes, maybe this would be a better world. Yes, I know what I am going to request. I want to go to the world where there is no money."

Excellent choice, I thought. *What could be bad about a world where everything is free?* I smiled. I wondered what it was going to be like. A heavy drowsiness began to set in, my eyelids started to close, and then *bang*. I was out. This was getting annoying.

Chapter 4

When I began to regain consciousness, I felt safe and secure, as if I had been sleeping for a very long time. I questioned whether my time in the twilight zone with Bala and Wen was all just a dream. When I opened my eyes, I soon realized that I might not have been dreaming after all. Although I was in a bedroom, things were very different. The entire room was green—different shades of green. I was wearing green pajamas, and my bed sheets and carpet were also green. *What the hell is this?* I got out of my bed and heard a woman call. She must have heard me. As I stared at my green attire, I stood in disgust. I looked ridiculous. I decided to get a change of clothes from my green chest of drawers. When I pulled out the first drawer, I noticed that every other single garment I owned was also green. I hated the color green. It reminded me of sick. I proceeded to check the second, third, and fourth drawer; however, as before, everything was green. There was a slight dash of white in some of the clothes, but largely they were all green.

"Breakfast is ready," a woman called again. Well, I had just about learned all there was to know about my room, so I decided to answer the woman's calls and proceed out of my new, weird room. When I came out of my room, I wandered into a hallway until I came to a room with a lot of noise. As I leaned in front of the doorway, I found three faces staring back at me. It was about now I was remembering that Evall said that when we go to another world, we would take the body of a Viscent from that world. I must be in a body of another Viscent. This must be this Viscent's mother, father, and little sister… they were having breakfast. In that brief second, there was so much going on in my mind.

"Where are the stairs?" I asked as if I were talking to a group of strangers (which I suppose I was). Everyone laughed, which I didn't appreciate.

"We live in a bungalow, silly. Oh, Lawrence, you are a kidder sometimes. Come sit down," the mother replied. *Lawrence.* That's not my name, though at that point that was the last thing on my mind. When I approached the table, the dad was on my left, my new mom on my right, and my little sister right in front of me. The man pulled out a chair and said, "I almost ate your eggs." I smiled back to him. Ironically, I had so many questions I was practically choking on them, so eating my eggs for me would be fantastic. I hoped he wasn't joking. The strangest thing was that everyone else in the room was also wearing green, and every color in the kitchen was also different shades of green. Again, there were some items with tints of white in them, but largely it was all green, just like my room. I felt like we were sitting in a field.

I also noticed that we all had the letter *G* on our sleeves, backs, and fronts. "Put the kettle on again, love, will you?" my mother said.

"Ah yeah, sure... oh and actually, why do we all have the letter *G* on our clothes... Mom?" Again everyone laughed. I was glad I was providing so much comic relief to everyone this morning.

"Are you okay today, Lawrence?" my new mother said.

"Yeah, I'm fine, I just didn't get much sleep," I replied.

"Okay, love, and as if you don't already know, the reason *G* is written on our clothes is for the color-blind, of course," she said, preoccupied with about three other things as she responded to me.

"Of course," I replied, knowingly nodding my head, even though really I was thinking, *what does that mean?*

"Are you sure you're okay?" the lady said with genuine concern.

"Sure, honestly, I'm fine. Maybe when I eat something, I'll make a little more sense," I said in an effort to reassure her. The lady smiled and took her eyes off me and back to her morning routine.

Thinking deeply about my new mother's odd response, I concentrated on putting more water in the kettle. In doing this, I got a reflection of myself in the kettle. I didn't look the same. I tried to get another look at myself in the toaster. Yes, I definitely did not look like this yesterday. I was beginning to freak out about looking different. I knew I was in the body of another Viscent, it just felt a lot stranger than I had anticipated.

It was all so weird. I felt like I didn't know myself anymore. Sitting down at the table again, I asked nervously, "What time are we leaving for school?" At last a question that didn't have everyone rolling around laughing.

"You and Winnie will be leaving in ten minutes, now eat up and get your bag." Winnie? What a funny name. That appears to be the name of my new sister.

I ate up as quickly as I could; the whole situation was really weirding me out. Upon fetching my bag and getting Winnie to pick out what I needed to wear for school, we made our way towards the front door. As I spotted the strange man, *Dad,* still in the kitchen, I asked, "Where's Mom?" Even if we were in another world, I wanted to say good-bye to my new mom.

"Your mother is gone to work, Lawrence. Are you sure you're okay?" he said, looking up from the table. It seemed like he actually did go on to eat my eggs; he wasn't joking after all.

"Yes, of course, I'm fine... I suppose... I'll see you later," I said as normally as I could muster. *I can't believe that my mother is working,* I thought as we made our way to the front door. When we stepped outside, Winnie walked in front of me, asking if we could hold hands on the way to school. While I was nodding in agreement, my senses had been hijacked by the extraordinary sights all around me. We were living on a slight hill surrounded by a number of other green bungalows. Everyone's car was green, and even the road was green. Clearly there was a massive significance to the color we wore and lived in, but what could it be? As we walked towards the edge of the estate, high, iron fences soon came into focus. The fences were at both sides of our green road and green footpath. At the other side of one fence, there was a red road, and at the other side of the other fence, there was an orange road.

Thankfully, as Winnie and I were holding hands, I wasn't paying the slightest bit of attention to where we were going. On the side of the orange road, I saw tall blocks of apartments in the distance, colored in bright orange. On the red side of the red road, I saw large, two-storey houses with each house a definite shade of red. It seemed like I was in Legoland or in some giant game of Monopoly, but in fact this was real life, a life seemingly without any money. This was of course because Bala asked to visit the world without money! It was time to ask some questions. Yes, I appreciated that my little sister was only about five to ten years old—God, I was so bad at putting ages on people—but if she was half as clever as my Lucy, this should be fine.

"Winnie, do you want to play a game?" I asked playfully.

"Yeah sure, I love games," she replied.

"I want to see how good you are at explaining things, so I suppose this is actually more of a test than a game. Are you in?" I said, smiling.

"Oh yes," she said excitedly. It seemed she was decisive; this was a good sign.

"I want you to pretend that I know nothing about this world, like I am an alien or something. Now, what I want you to do is explain how this little planet works, assuming I know nothing. Think you can do that?" I asked, hoping she would play along.

"Yeah, sure. Where do you want me to start?" she said in anticipation.

"Greetings, little woman," I said in a pretend yet brilliant robot-type voice. "Why do you have so many colors in your world, and what do they mean?"

Winnie giggled. She seemed to be enjoying my fake game, as was I. What an amazing robotic voice. I surprised myself.

"Well that is a very good question, Mr. Spaceman. You see, a long time ago there was something called… what is it called again? Bartering, that's it, where everyone would swap things with each other. You give me five lollipops, and I will give you two sherbet dips, because roughly five lollipops are as good as having two sherbets. Though sherbets always make me so sneeezy." She laughed, showing me how she would get the sherbet on the stick and shovel it in to her mouth. Her explanation was good, and similar to how I understood history in my own world, except I don't think they were swapping sherbets for lollipops!

"However, after a while, people needed to barter more, and the more they bartered, the more fighting there was. This was when bartering became bad, Mr. Spaceman. One man would say, 'I want fifty lollipops for my two sherbet dips,' when really his sherbets weren't that much. That would be just silly, but everyone was doing it. So the rulers at the time decided not to focus on the value of the items, like sherbets and lollipops, but the value of the *people*."

"What? So the rulers could swap people or something?" I asked, trying to keep up. This twist was distinctly different to the history in my world.

"No, you silly spaceman, so the people would not need to play swapsies anymore with their things," she replied skipping along, laughing. I tried to reciprocate the laughter, but I was so confused.

"I don't understand," I said in my robotic accent again, trying to disguise the fact that I was actually completely lost.

Winnie smiled. "You see, the rulers decided to put a value on the service each person could give to society. The value of these services became color coded. The value of a person is defined as a combination of the service they provide and their competency and potential," she said, still smiling.

"That's impressive, Winnie, I can't believe you understand all of this," I said.

"I don't really understand it. We had to learn that stupid definition as soon as we started school. Oh it took me ages to remember the word combination." She frowned, bobbing her head from side to side.

"So how does it work then? Do you know that?" I asked, hoping that an example would make this easier to understand.

"That's easy. So we're green, Mr. Spaceman. That means we always wear green, we live in a green house, and we can go into any green shop and get whatever we want. There is a shop near we live that have the best green apple-flavoured gum-drops. I always get them. I could eat them forever. Once my friend Anne and I had a race to see how many we could eat in a row. This was a stupid idea, Mr. Spaceman," she said, rubbing her stomach.

"So you mean that we are color-coded as green people and go to green places…and I am assuming these two roads either side of us come from red and orange places," I said.

"Yes, Mr. Spaceman…You're funny, Lawrence." She giggled again as I came to the realization that Bala had gotten his wish; this *was* a world without money.

"So why are there fences up separating the three roads? Surely we could use the same road?"

Winnie squeezed my hand tightly. "You know, Lawrence…oh, I don't want to play this game anymore; can we play another one?" she said with a sense of fear.

"Is it because they don't like differently colored cars on the same road?" I said, smiling.

Winnie looked up at me anxiously and said, "Yes, and the fact that each color hates every other color. The fences between us seem to make people so angry and sad, and no color is allowed to spend time in another color's area. The penalty is death. There is only one place where people can choose to meet, but I've never been there. Usually, as long as you stay in your area, you don't see that much trouble," she said in a low, soft voice.

"So why do you feel so afraid?" I said, feeling sorry I was putting Winnie in this position.

"Because I don't like feeling like people don't like me when I haven't done anything to them for them to think I am bad." A tear came running down her face. "You know, sometimes I feel like doing bad things, not because I am a bad person, Lawrence, but I think that at least if I act bad, I mightn't feel so bad about people hating me," she said, looking at the ground in front of her. I didn't know what to say. How awful. I never thought about it like that before. Maybe she was right; maybe people do behave more like how they think they are viewed than how they view themselves.

"Well you know what, Winnie? I think you are the loveliest, green-suited little girl in all the land."

She looked up at me and smiled with a thin layer of tears coating the surface of each of her eyes magnifying them to the point that she would have made a newborn puppy look mean!

"And you know what? These people don't hate you or me; they hate the world they're stuck in," I said, trying to reassure her, though it would have sounded a whole lot better in my robot voice.

Up ahead there was a massive, horrible monstrosity of a building in bright green.

"School," Winnie said as she ran off in front of me, waving. I could see that she felt safe there. God knows how I would've found the place if I was on my own. I wondered if I would find Bala or Wen. I so hoped they were also green people.

Following after Winnie, I embedded myself in a wave of other students and allowed them to carry me into the school. As I was growing to appreciate, everyone was wearing green, but not just green clothes—the exact same clothes. *Uniforms,* I thought to myself, *how utterly pointless.* I would have imagined just wearing green clothes would have sufficed as a uniform. I noticed that the children were all quite well groomed, and listening into some of the conversations, they were also quite well spoken. I was afraid to open my mouth.

Pouring in through the front door of the school, I suddenly got a strange feeling. My heart began to beat a little faster, my focus began to blur, and then *bang*... my awareness of my surroundings disappeared, and all I could see was the shape of a brass eagle. Then once again, as suddenly as it occurred, I found myself back walking in the center of this swarm of students. The good news was that I hadn't passed out—something I was getting quite used to recently—however, the bad news was that I had no idea what that image actually meant.

As I pondered the significance of my vision, the bell went and people began to disappear into their respective classes. My swarm of counterparts soon began to disappear, leaving a tall, well-dressed lady at the end of the hall.

"Lawrence, you are in career guidance now. Now move along," the lady said. It sounded and looked like Miss Hanchen, and as she quickly closed in on my position, I found that I felt the exact same about this Miss Hanchen look-alike, afraid and kind of excited. However, this was neither the time nor the place to be making such observations. "Did you hear me, Lawrence? Please make your way to room 2B," she said firmly. *This is not good*, I thought. *A location; now, if only I knew where the damn room was.*

"Come on, follow me. I'm on my way there anyway to introduce your speaker for the day," she said strictly.

As we walked side by side, I felt a certain closeness to the green Miss Hanchen, almost like we were husband and wife marching down the corridor to the altar. In real life, I'd like to walk a little slower so the music could keep pace. She actually looked quite good in green. "Tuck your shirt in, Lawrence," she said. *Well, that kind of attitude will have to stop when we are husband and wife*, I thought to myself. *What will everyone think?* I laughed to myself.

"And keep up, Lawrence, stop falling behind," she ordered. *Well you know what, this isn't going to work. I am afraid our future potential wedding is off. No, no, Miss green Hanchen, you blew it, with all your whining and moaning… You, my dear, are going to have to find yourself another Lawrence.*

"Here we are, 2B." The green Miss Hanchen opened the door for me, and I walked into a sea of green, tired students. I took my place within this green blanket and waited for the show to begin. The green Miss Hanchen took center stage.

"Good morning, class. Now today is a very special day. You get to have an insight into your future; you get to have a preview of what you might be doing for the rest of your lives. As you are all aware, when you are about to finish school, you select a career, and you are assessed to see if you are eligible to fill that role, and if so, how much potential you show for the role. For some of you that might mean that you will move up the color banding to a blue or a red; however, for others it will mean that you may have to move down to lower-classed colors such as orange and yellow," she said flatly.

"It is a difficult time for all of you, I understand, because as soon as you get selected for a different color, you move out of your family's home, move across to the color of your new home and settle for the rest of your life. Of course you can get to meet your family again but when this does happen, it will happen in the designated communal area shared by all colors. What we do not want happening is people putting themselves in green roles so they will stay in this color area. You are encouraged to excel where you have the ability; however, if you choose to underachieve, it is your own decision. So without any further ado, let me introduce to you our very special guest. He will be on the panel that decides what you become, and he will be on the panel that assesses you if you ever choose to apply for a change in color. Please welcome the distinguished Winston Wardock," she said like a presenter on television.

Everyone clapped as a tall, sour-looking, elderly man floated into the room with an almost monastic feel about him. When silence fell upon the group, he looked up and held our attention. He was an intimidating man. He was a powerful, commanding, angry-looking man. As the *golden* silence wore off, Mr. Wardock stood still and eyeballed the class. He was wearing a long, white robe with the letter E written on it. What did the E stand for?

"Good morning, boys and girls." *Oh, how condescending; we're not babies.* "You all know me as one of the five emperors that rule this region. We decide when you finish school and what color you become. When you are in society, we decide if you should drop a color. If you want to progress yourself and move to a higher color, you apply to us, and we decide what you will be. We are the masters. As you are all greens, this will mean that both of your parents will have qualified for this color. Green is a good color; it is third from top and five above the bottom. If you..." he continued.

Green is third from the top. Wow, I wonder what my new mom and dad do. A question for Winnie on the way home, I think.

"So, boys and girls, all you need to remember is to be confident, strong, and willing to appreciate your value. Thank you," he said robotically.

An unconvincing, muffled clap then followed as the ghoulish Mr. Wardock, and his power robes left the stage. The green Hanchen climbed up after Mr. Wardock left so she could address us again. She too was clapping, and she too was unconvincing.

"Okay, before you break up for classes, I want to make a couple of announcements for the week. The two main events this week are the entertainment trials and the Medofoth finals. Firstly, at the entertainment trials on Wednesday, all of this class will be asked to sing a song or undertake a dance. If you show exceptional talent, this may be a consideration for you and your future career.

If not, you will be asked to stop singing or dancing and return to class," she said.

"The second event is one we have been waiting for all semester. The Eagle's Pirch Medofoth finals, a competition that every orange, blue, and regional school entered at the start of the year, but all of them have been beaten, leaving just two schools in the competition. It has come down to the Evanisgart Greens verses The Hoilago Reds," the lady said with a tiny bit of excitement in her voice. I realized that this was a massive event, and though I had not been there for any of it, the green Miss Hanchen was really revving it up.

"We are very proud of the two students who have gotten us to this point, and we hope that you will all join them in their quest for glory tomorrow. It is a game of concentration, poise, and timing. It is a game that demands not only upon one's physical agility, but one's mental agility as well. It is a high-pressured affair, but we have no doubt that our two contenders will have no trouble conquering their opponents. So can you please join me in wishing the very best of luck to our two Evanisgart Greens finalists, Miss Fidelma Garrick and Lawrence Constabin." All heads turned to me. My heart sank. People slowly began their obligatory clap as the pieces of my world began to fall to the ground in perfect tune with the generous applause. I had figured out this morning that my name was Lawrence, but I prayed to God that my last name wasn't Constabin. "Come on, stand up," the green Hanchen barked. I looked around me and then pointed to myself while looking at her. "Yes, Lawrence, yes. We haven't got all day," she said impatiently. I rose slowly to my feet, not that my stature would define me much better amongst my fellow greenery. In doing this, I also noticed Fidelma shyly rise to her feet. She was like an angel. She was composed and calm and seemed completely at ease. For the slightest second, I felt a weightless sensation come over me as I imagined the prospect of spending time together with this Fidelma—what joy; however, this was quickly trumped by the fact that I hadn't a clue what I was doing.

Every class that day was frightening. It seemed that the Viscent whose body I was occupying preformed quite well in this school, hence I was really struggling to live up to expectation. This Lawrence guy was clearly quite a good student. By the end of the day, I had to take on my biggest task yet—finding my way home. I searched desperately for Winnie; I could take my chances and follow the green brick road, but I knew I would feel much safer if Winnie was with me. "There you are," I said with an enormous amount of relief.

Winnie looked a little confused. "Yes, here I am, are you walking me home?"

"Yes, of course I am," I said with a twinge of desperation creeping in to my voice.

"Great, we haven't walked home together for ages," she said with a big smile on her face.

We soon set off walking and began speaking about the day's events. She told me of her successes in the classroom, and I told her of my Medofoth event later in the week. Of course she already knew; the whole school was talking about it apparently. From the other talk we'd had earlier in the day on careers, I was eager to find out more about this elitist panel and what exactly our parents did, but before I could get anything more from her I had to hear about this guy she had a crush on.

"He gave me his wigglybob today," she said blushing.

"That's nice... though what's a wigglybob?"

"Ha ha, you are so old, Lawrence. It's the wiggly thing you put on the top of your pencil," she replied, searching her bag for her pencil. "Here it is. Isn't it cute, Lawrence?" she asked, handing it to me.

"Ah, it's a green head with crazy hair and big crazy eyes. Ah yes, it looks great, I suppose." It looked weird, really weird.

"He said it is so he can see me at my desk all the time," she said blushing, taking the pencil back from me staring at it like it was his crazy head and crazy eyes. "Maybe tomorrow I will ask him to marry me," she said suddenly, smiling as if that was a great idea.

"Hang on a second, Winnie, hang on. Look, he seems a nice guy, his wigglybob is cute-ish, but you should try and just play games with him, get to know him. Do you think Mom would have got married to dad the first time he gave her a wigglybob?" I asked, trying to make her think of her parents.

"Oh, I love that story, Lawrence, and I love the way dad tells it. I love the way that they were both born in the yellow area, but when it came time to get assessed it looked like Mom was going to get recoded to a better color, green, but dad was struggling to qualify to get out of the yellow. So it was only with Mom's help that dad ended up in the green area, and they lived happily ever after," she said smiling. What was interesting was that when you are color-coded everyone around you is somewhat equal to you, which I suppose it great, as you will have more in common with people. But what if the person that you love is in the orange area, or the gold area? That seems unfair. It seems tough that there are such tough constraints between colors.

This elitist panel that Mr. Wardock seemed to be on was also fascinating. After Winnie's reflection on Mom and Dad's romance, I said to Winnie that Mr. Wardock suggested the elitist panel could be changing, but without revealing details I asked Winnie how much she knew about this. Of course, Mr. Wardock didn't mention anything about changes; I just wanted Winnie to tell me what she knew about the panel without me having to ask about something I should already know. The Spaceman game wasn't going to work a second time!

"Well there are five of them on this committee; however, there is only one leader. His name is Bronson Keel. Even though he is a small short man, he makes me so nervous, with his long, black hair and that mark on his right cheek that looks like a permanent, red bloodstain. He is a mean nasty man Laurence, and is probably one of the big reasons there is so much anger between colors. He scares me. I dread the day I have to stand in front of him when I need to be classified at the end of school. Hey maybe they are asking him to step down from his position because he is so mean. Maybe that's the change," Winnie said as she looked at the ground.

Annoyed with myself that I had upset Winnie again, I pretended to tell jokes in my robot voice for the next part of our walk. I soon got her laughing from my antics as we skipped home together until we noticed a large cluster of people in the distance. "Where are they all going?" I asked curiously.

"That is the meeting area where people of different colors meet. Mainly it is families that meet there when children get sent to a different color based on their abilities after they leave school, but sometimes because of the mix of colors, bad things happen there," she said anxiously. I felt a strong urge to go and investigate, but put it down to curiosity. There was still so much to learn about this place.

The next day was a very special day at school, not because of school, but because of what I was asked to do. As I seemed to be one of the top boys in the class, I was given the honor of going into town and collecting a book that our English teacher, Mr. Bufont, had ordered. How exciting! This was, of course, like asking a horse to go and pick out a tennis racket. The point being I didn't even know where town was, let alone where he ordered the book from! I wasn't exactly the most qualified for this job.

Fortunately, thanks to the help of some strangers, I soon found myself in the middle of town. It was so weird. The only positive thing about this entire stupid place was that everything was free. Clearly, as I was in a green area, all the shops were green, so I could take anything I wanted. I saw a shop on the corner that had food so, feeling the hunger a little, I went in and had a look around. After a while I picked up a sandwich and some milk and then left the shop. I felt like such a thief, though the irony was that because of this strange setup where everything was free, crime was probably very low, if it even existed at all. What a way to stop theft! Allow theft, and everyone only takes what they need. I wondered if they had much trouble with waste, with idiots taking too much and not using what they take.

Although the streets were thick with people dressed in green, I could also make out the odd person dressed in white. At first I thought it was one of the regional emperors, but as one of these gentlemen approached, I saw he had the word "Guardian" written across his chest and back. These were probably the police of the area. The poor guys were probably bored stiff. Upon spotting the shop I had to visit, I ventured in, collected the book, and walked out. Again I felt incredibly bad doing this, but to everyone else, it was entirely normal. It was the world without money; they probably don't even know what money is.

On my way back to the school, I set eyes on that communal meeting place again, except this time, I got a bad headache and again felt compelled to go in its direction. When I got a little closer, I saw all of the differently colored passages from each area channelling into the meeting place. It was like a rabbit's burrow. At this time of day, it was nearly empty except for a girl standing under a large monument. After closer inspection I realized that the monument was a large, brass eagle, the one I had seen the day before in my vision on my way to school. I was getting a bit freaked out by these occurrences, but I still wanted to move closer to get a better look.

"Zachary," I then heard from the distance. *Where did that come from?* When I turned around, I saw a boy in a gold top come towards me. The boy seemed to have his left hand up by his left eye and smiled as he walked faster and faster in my direction with his right hand in the air holding up three fingers. Suddenly I remembered what our Evall said, only Viscents can see the birthmark of other Viscents, but to be able to see this birthmark I had to touch my own birthmark. So just as our Evall explained, I put my left fingers on the left of my cheek to the side of my left eye. Just like before, I saw that silver glimmer of light to the side of the left of eye of the guy coming towards me. It seemed like it could be Bala.

"Bala, is that you?" I asked, guessing it was Bala, but I suppose it also could have been Wen.

Still puffing and panting as his brisk walk turned into a slow walk, he said, "Of course it's me. Didn't you see my shiny silver-looking symbol thing when you put your hand up to your eye?"

"Yes, I did, but I was just checking, I thought maybe you could be Wen," I said to Bala.

He came to a complete stop, looked me up and down, and said, "Are you serious? You confused me with Wen? Oh my goodness, Zach; that is so insulting. I am a man, you know," he said, pumping one of his biceps.

"I know you are. I just wasn't sure. All I could see was that the shiny symbol under your left eye, but why were you holding your right hand up with three fingers?" I asked, suddenly realizing that it made no sense.

"Because there are three of us, so I wanted to show you the number three, with my fingers, so you knew it was me," he said with a well thought out explanation.

"But I could see the glimmer under your left eye, I didn't need—"

"God, Zach, give me a break. I found you didn't I?"

"Actually, how did you find me? How could you tell it was me earlier? Have you just being going around with your hand up by your left eye all the time?" Bala smirked at me.

"That day you acted as a diversion for me when those bullies were beating on me, well, I also ran to the gap in the wall after the bullies left me, and when I did, I saw you running off in the distance," Bala said laughing again.

"I don't understand," I replied.

"Well, you kind of run like a lizard, Zach, and sometimes you even have a hint of that lizard movement in your walk, so when I saw this guy with a movement very like your own, I took a chance, and what do you know, I was right," he said, clapping his hands.

"I do not move like a lizard, you cheeky... wigglybob," I said with embarrassment.

"What's a wigglybob?" Bala said, not knowing how offended to be. I stared back at him, wondering if I had the energy to explain what this stupid piece of school equipment was when Bala spoke again.

"So coupled with your lizard movement, and the fact that you were in this area, an area that I have been having visions of ever since I arrived here, I thought if anyone else could have been having these visions it would be you and Wen," Bala said, pointing to the eagle I had also been seeing visions of, right over by the girl that was crying.

When we started walking a bit closer to the eagle, we realized that the little girl dressed in red that was crying was now looking right at us. Almost at the same time we both realized that this may be Wen, so together we put our hands to our faces, and sure enough, the bright shine from under the person's eye lit up. It was Wen, and just as we identified her, she identified who we were.

"Wen," we both said, running in her direction. She quickly jumped to attention and ran to embrace us.

As we neared, Bala held his right hand up with his three fingers but then stopped just short of Wen to tie his shoelace. I continued and opened my arms and gave her a big hug. "I knew you would come. I just knew it," she said, wiping the tears from her face. "Is that you, Zach?" She said, pulling away from me.

"Yes, it's me, Wen," I replied.

"I knew that was you, Bala. I saw that three finger thing and thought, that's got to be Bala. What does it mean?"

Bala sighed, still on the ground with his shoe, "It means there are three of us, so I was showing you it was me by—"

Wen interrupted. "But I knew it was you guys with the glimmer thing under your eyes," Wen said confused.

"I think he thinks it's a kind of secret handshake or something," I added.

"Okay, okay, can we get past my three finger gesture? God, so what are you doing here, Wen? Have you been seeing this brass eagle?" Bala said as he proceeded to tie the biggest, most useless knot ever.

"Yes, I've been seeing it constantly ever since we arrived. I have been here for around three to four hours. I didn't know what else to do or where else to look. To be honest, I hoped one of you would know what to do," she said as her defeated tone lowered.

Bala rose to his feet. "Yes, of course. We have to complete this task," he said, scratching his head. There was a nervous silence as we all stood there not knowing what the next step was.

"Don't worry," I said without explanation. "We'll figure it out." Again I went to hug Wen, as did Bala as he placed a hand on both of our shoulders. Upon doing this there was an enormous flash of blinding white light that appeared and disappeared in a matter of seconds. "What was that?" I said in shock.

"This just gets weirder and weirder," Bala said, grimacing.

Then breaking away from both of us, Wen said, "I saw something." She walked over to the direction of the eagle and sat down.

"What did you see?" Bala questioned softly.

"I saw a little boy and his father. They were playing hide-and-seek in their garden. The little boy had big smile, thick, curly hair, and was counting with his father as his mother went and hid. They all seemed so happy. The woman was a tall lady with shiny brown hair and the man was well groomed but with a nasty bloodstain on one of his cheeks," she said with her eyes glazing over.

Bronson Keel, I thought to myself. *But why was Wen dreaming of Bronson Keel and his family?* Suddenly I remembered a vision from the flash of bright light.

"Actually, Wen, I too have a brief recollection of something I saw in that second. It was that same man with the bloodstained face, but instead of being happy, he had his head in his hands and was holding a picture of his wife and child and crying, '*Why?*' It appeared that the wife and child you saw with him were now gone, maybe even dead," I said, confused. It didn't quite fit with the vision that Wen had seen. It was like putting the pieces of a puzzle together. Bala had now focused his attention to the ground again. When he does this it's difficult to know if he is thinking or just spacing out. Just as I was about to prompt a response, he said, "I saw the boy. Yes, though he isn't little anymore; he's our age. His name is Shavil, and he was dressed in red. He is alive." Bala looked up from the ground.

We all moved from our position, trying to think of everything everyone said.

"Okay," I said. "Let's review the situation. Firstly, I believe the man with the stain on his face is Bronson Keel. My new sister in this world described him to me earlier and told me he had a red bloodstain on his face. He is the lead emperor who decides people's color classification. He is meant to be a mean, nasty man, but from what Wen saw, he was once a very happy man. It seems that for some reason, when his family was taken, he became a different person. Though, if what Bala saw is true, if we could find the person who we think is his son, Shavil, and reunite them... Maybe there's a chance we could make some sort of difference, you know, make the nastiest man in the land a little happier. It can't hurt."

"No wonder you're the leader," Bala said. "I was happy enough to have had a vision. I didn't know we had to put them all together." I smiled a little at the compliment.

"He is only guessing, Bala," Wen said, which was completely true. "But unfortunately, that is the best we've got."

"Right. Then here is the plan: Tomorrow night I am in some Medofoth competition where we are taking on the Hoilago Reds. Wen, are you going to be there?" I asked.

"Yes, they mentioned it today. Apparently, you are in for a severe beating," she recited from her day at school.

"Thank you. Now if we can spot Shavil at that event, Wen, can you try to get him to meet us here tomorrow night?" I asked.

"Yeah, but how will I know him?" Wen replied.

Bala walked over to Wen. "Shavil has long, shiny red hair, bright blue eyes, a scar on the right of his neck, and a slight limp," he said.

"That's impressive," I said as Wen and I stared at him.

Wen scratched her head. "In my vision the kid with Bronson seemed to have the same red shiny hair and piercing bright blue eyes, but he didn't have a scar or limp," Wen said frowning.

"Look, we have to assume all of our visions are linked. We have to assume it is the same boy. What do you think? You think we can take this Shavil kid to meet his dad?" I said.

Bala then chipped in again. "Now although I know that this Bronson chap lives in the gold area, I'm not sure I can bring Shavil to Bronson all on my own. If Bronson's son is living in the red area, and Bronson lives in the gold area, we can't just walk his son over to him."

Wen turned to Bala. "How about you bring some of your gold outfits here tomorrow night, Bala. Maybe we can work something out then," she said with a little urgency.

"Right, then. We have a plan. It may not be the right one, it may not even be the right task, but what else are we going to do?" I said. "Let's get Shavil here tomorrow night after the Medofoth finals. Let's bring him to his dad," I said in desperate hope that our half-formed plan may half work.

"Zach, I will see you at the Medofoth finals tomorrow, and Bala, we will see you here tomorrow night," Wen said, moving in the direction of her red road.

"Okay then, good luck," Bala and I both said as went our separate ways. I was nervous and anxious but somehow relieved to have met Wen and Bala again. Maybe we were one step closer to becoming what we were destined to be.

The next day there was an almighty buzz about the place. There were banners, posters, and well-wishers galore patting me on the back and wishing me good luck. Slowly, the atmosphere was absorbing me, or I was absorbing it. I was beginning to feel like a schoolboy celebrity. However, I did get the feeling that half of the people wishing me well didn't even know who I was; let alone what I was doing. It seems that people can get caught up in idolization very quickly. I didn't care though. I was going to soak it up for as long as I could. What was strangest was that there came a point when I even felt my walk change a little. Instead of my regular, reasonably understated, straight, functional walk, I developed an open-footed swagger. Honestly, in about ten minutes, my head swelled up beyond all belief. Perhaps this is why I had developed the swagger; maybe my head had become so heavy my legs were struggling to keep me in a straight line.

Meanwhile, Winnie was still walking by my side. She looked so proud of me. It was a great feeling to see someone I cared about look at me and be sincerely happy for my success. Admiration wasn't something I was used to (clearly, from how I was responding), but this certainly made me want to achieve more. I wanted to have this feeling again.

"I think Fidelma is looking for you. She's in the school cafeteria," a strange-looking well-wisher called as they gave me a passing pat on the back. Suddenly I was terrified again; however, I wasn't sure exactly why. Was it (a) because I would have to speak to Fidelma or (b) the fact that this Medofoth stuff was for real? My swagger quickly returned to a conventional one-foot-in-front-of-the-other walk as I tried to find my way to the school cafeteria.

When I opened the door, Fidelma was sitting gracefully at a table on the far side of the cafeteria with books everywhere. I walked over slowly and tried to work out what I would say by the time I got over there. Damn it! I'd arrived already and I hadn't thought of anything.

"Morning," I said in a muffled, low voice. She looked up and stared at me silently. "*Morning*," I roared at her. I almost gave myself a fright. It seemed I had lost the ability to control the volume, tone, and clarity of my sounds... Well this should be fun.

"Morning, Lawrence. Now, I have looked over a lot of the potential angles of tonight's game, and I think you should read over the following. I also think..." she continued. It is great when you are speaking to someone you really fancy as you have full entitlement to stare at them until they are finished talking. The trick is to look like you are paying attention and then add the occasional comment. "Which is why I think we should spend more time on this. What do you think, Lawrence?"

I hadn't been listening to a word she was saying; however, I had successfully established that she had blue eyes. This, unfortunately, might not come up tonight, but it was an important fact nonetheless.

"Absolutely," I said convincingly, though again I said the word "absolutely" too quickly and too indistinctly.

"Now, we shall be leaving here at 6:30 p.m., so do not be late, okay?" she said rising to her feet. "See you later."

"*Bye!*" I boomed again as she passed me. This was getting embarrassing. *Pull it together, Zach.*

Later that evening, a busload of people had assembled at the school to travel with us. Some were excited about the event, while others were voicing their passion for victory for the entire world to hear. I wondered if people got beaten up in this world. As we piled into the bus, we took our places quickly. We were on our way to the communal playground. *Weird*, I thought. "So are we doing this outside, then?" I said to the person beside me.

"No," he said, staring back at me blankly. *How very informative*, I thought as I continued looking back in his direction.

"So if it's not outside, will there be a tent?" I asked as he looked over at me again.

"No," he said. This guy was beginning to annoy me. As I continued to stare at him, I could see the communal area in the distance. Then something extraordinary began to occur. The whole area was rotating upwards, revealing a massive arena on the underneath of the communal area. Slowly, the playground flipped, rotating its playground area underground and bringing the new, big building above ground. It was spectacular. It was a large, white building, but it had a number of different jets of colored water shooting up into the air, splashing off the white walls, and flowing into a moat below. The strangest thing was, as we passed over the moat, I noticed that none of the colored jets of water were mixing. Each was remaining completely immiscible. Consequently, the moat appeared to have differently colored stripes in it.

When the bus stopped, there were lines of armed guardians everywhere. A line of guardians flanked each side of us as we were led to our auditorium. I was surprised by the amount of guardians that were there and confused at why it was so heavily guarded. As we entered the auditorium, we saw all of the reds. They were caged off, and upon seeing us, they went absolutely wild. There were literally thousands of them; clearly there mustn't have been much to do in the world without money on a school night. On the other side were the greens, who were roaring equally as loudly but in a positive way. The atmosphere was raw, live, and deafening. I wanted to get back on the bus. Suddenly, I didn't feel so brave. Fidelma came up behind me and held my hand for a second and said, "We can do it." It was at that moment when most of my anxieties were temporarily lifted, and although I really didn't know how we would do, her touch and comfort were just enough to give me the confidence that I needed.

It was a massive, circular arena with many tiers. We occupied one half of the arena, and the reds had the other half. However, each and every tier and color was caged off. The circular arena was looking down on to a square floor, like a chessboard with many more squares. Along the sides of the arena, each row was lettered from *A* to *U*, and each column along the top and bottom was labelled one to twenty one. It was a phenomenally big playing arena. As I took in the playing area one last time, I disappeared into the changing rooms to put on my costume. There was a large man in a white guardian outfit outside my door. Without explanation he opened the door, and I entered. To my abject disappointment, I was soon to learn of the nature of my costume. There it was, waiting for me on a chair. A black helmet, good; black boots, good; black gloves, good; and a tightly fitting, green Lycra body suit... *What?* It had a black *G* on the front and a pair of short, black pants that would be worn on the outside of the green suit. It looked tight... it all looked very tight. I picked it up and further inspected it in the hope to find some additional spare material in the costume hiding from my first impression; no, it appeared it was going to be exactly as tight as it looked.

With a jungle of supporters chanting outside, I decided not to waste too much time and began trying to figure out how to get into the thing. Ten minutes later I had managed to get one of my legs through one of the legs of the costume and managed to put one of my boots on. It was the other leg that was causing me the problem. I had both hands on the garment, pulling desperately when the door opened. "You all right, Lawrence? Oh... sorry..." Fidelma said as she stood there like a rabbit in headlights. The shock of the intrusion caused me to lose my grip, and quickly I found myself flying backwards onto the ground. I landed on my back with one leg still in the costume and the other leg of the costume lying across my other bare leg, mocking my futile efforts.

"Yeah... yeah... I'm fine," I said, groaning with pain and embarrassment.

"Do you need any help?" Fidelma said.

"*God* no, thank you, but no," I replied. What could be more embarrassing? I sat there defeated by my tight costume before the contest had even started. Come on; time to get going, time to get my game on *and* this bloody costume.

Ten minutes later, I emerged from my dressing room. Fidelma had been waiting. The snug fit of the costume seemed to compliment her figure far better than my own. I felt like an idiot. I was dressed like a superhero, a superhero in a costume that felt a size too small.

"You ready?" she said looking at me intensely.

"As ready as I'll ever be," I said as we hugged and then made our way down to the end of the corridor and out into the arena. I was terrified, and I couldn't stop thinking about how ridiculous I looked. These blasted black, short, snugly fitting pants were not comfortable. The only consolation was that I at least understood how the game was played. From the reading material that Fidelma had given me, there seemed to be three parts to the game: movement, attack, and objects.

Movement is key. When a player is on a square of the giant style chessboard, he or she can move eight different directions from his or her square. Each of these directions is represented by a color: forward is red, to the right is yellow, diagonally forward left is pink, and so on. If a player saw one of these colors, he or she could move one space according to that color. If he or she saw that color with a black dot in the center, then he or she could move two spaces in that direction. In all there were sixteen different signals for the player to respond to. At the start of each game, five of these signals would flash on a board on each wall of the enclosure. All of the lights then go out temporarily and the player would move in accordance with any two of the signals he or she saw appear on the wall. For instance, if two of the five signals were red and yellow, that would mean that the player would go forward one space and then to the right one space. The opposition will also do the same; they will get five different signals and then while the lights are out, they move in a combination of any two of their five signals. When the lights come back on, the players are prompted with five new, different signals, and they repeat the same process again. The players have to move according to the combination of two signals every time the lights go out, but they get up to five signals to choose from. Players have to think fast!

Now if that wasn't hard enough, there was also attacking to be done every time the lights went out. Each player gets a large stick; the stick has the numbers one to twenty-one on it and letters *A* to *U*. Now just before the lights go out, I am also to look at my opponent's five signals. Although I don't know which two they are going to pick, I have to make a guess. Whatever movement I guess they will make, I need to quickly note which space my opponent is going to end up on. When the lights go out, I press, say, *D* eight, and if my opponent ends up on *D* eight, the square disappears and my opponent falls through the floor with a puff of flames in their wake. It's as simple as that. In short, you have to anticipate the square they will move to and then ensure that the square will disappear when they get there.

The third and final thing to remember is that there are objects. Often there could be a number of balls floating around or mechanical little creatures. If one of these touches the player, that player loses one of his or her signals. He or she goes from having five signals every time the lights come on to four signals. Each time it happens, it makes it easier for the opponents to predict where the player will go as he or she will have fewer signals to choose from. As this was my first time playing, and it was a final, I wasn't feeling confident. It's hardly an easy game; I barely understood the rules.

As Fidelma and I walked into the arena, the place erupted. People were chanting and shouting like their lives depended on it. I took my position on *E* seven and Fidelma on *E* fourteen. She put her right leg stretched out, her left leg bent in a crouching position, and her left hand palm-faced on he ground. She was ready. The sound of the audience was deafening, and without thinking, I just adopted the same pose as Fidelma; I thought it best to at least look like I knew what I was doing. Then there was a voice:

"Good evening, ladies and gentlemen, and welcome to the final Medofoth game this season. I think…" As the man spoke, a runner came over to me and gave me some earphones. I noticed that both my opponents and Fidelma also got these headphones. Without direction everyone immediately placed their headphones on and looked ahead. Similarly, I took mine and decided I would try to do the same as soon as I figured out how to put them on.

"So without any further ado, let us begin the game: twenty, nineteen, eighteen..." and then loud, fast music began playing that seemed to drown out the crowd. The atmosphere was crazy. Eventually I figured out how to put on the earphones, and like Fidelma, I placed them over my ears. Suddenly there was silence. These earphones were good! I could see thousands of people around me, screaming and shouting, but I could hear nothing. The whole place was vibrating. I looked at the wall in front of me. There was a countdown to tell us when the lights would first go out. This was it. Our opponents looked athletic. They were occupying the same spaces as Fidelma and I but on the opposite side of the board. Three seconds to go, and my first five signals would go on the board with my opponents'.

Three, two, one: I looked at my five colors. The combination I would chose was going to be pink and red—struggling massively to recall what these colors represented I thought anxiously about where I needed to move to as soon as it went dark. Then the lights went out, and I scrambled for my life. Suddenly I saw three massive explosions of fire rise up from different squares, one very near me. I had forgotten to predict where my opponent would go. This was even harder than I thought it would be.

Fifteen to twenty minutes of this kind of game play later, I was exhausted. Things had been frantic. Every couple of seconds I was looking at colors, moving, guessing their colors, and all the while seeing the crowd out of the corner of my eye, fist thumping the caging containing them and creating a noise so loud that I could feel the vibrations through my tight costume. It was a miracle that my opponents hadn't knocked me out yet, and an even bigger miracle that I ended up in the right square every time. There were flames flying up from squares every couple of seconds and there were balls going over and back across the arena, some rolling and some bouncing. There were also little mechanical creatures all over the place. It was like a war zone. I just didn't know where to focus my concentration.

Although I was beating off whatever came my way with the stick, I did manage to get struck twice. I was down to receiving three movement signals, while Fidelma and the other boy and girl were down to receiving four movement signals. I was hot; all of this movement and fire was really heating the place up. Fidelma was doing brilliantly. Her movement was swift and decisive, and our opponents never even seemed to get near her.

Then, unexpectedly, the lights went out, and amidst the many surges of flames, I made out the face and figure of one of the other team as she fell through the floor. *Wow, we may actually win this; there goes one of their players.*

The removal of the other player from the game was thanks to Fidelma. She was good at this. When the lights came back on, I found two mechanical-type spiders coming towards me. As I battled to get them away from me, the lights went out before I could determine which direction I needed to move. Then without warning, the floor opened, and I was swallowed by the fire and slid into the basement. I was furious with myself. The principle rule in this whole game is that if you don't move you will be removed from the game. I didn't move, so, unfortunately, I was done. I had let Fidelma down.

I brushed myself off angrily and made my way to the exit. I was eager to see the end of the bout between the reds' remaining man and our very own Fidelma. When I got to the end of the corridor, I saw the girl from the other team that had been knocked out. I took off my earphones. "Well done," I said.

She turned and looked at me and said, "Thank you." I was surprised at such a civil response from someone who should hate me. As I focused back in on Fidelma's powerhouse performance, I spotted Wen in the crowd.

Though she too was mesmerized by this amazing exhibition, I managed to catch her eye. Cleverly, she had managed to sit herself next to Shavil, the boy we were looking for, as she pointed discreetly to the person beside her. He was exactly as Bala and Wen had described, shiny red hair and clear bright blue eyes I could make out even from where I was standing. Though I wasn't sure how we were going to manage to get this guy to do what we wanted. If the past twenty minutes were anything to go by, I thought he would rather shoot me than listen to me.

While pondering a number of potential plans on how to capture our man, there was a magnificent roar. I looked out on the arena, and Fidelma was there, standing on her own. She had done it. She dropped to her knees and put both palms on the ground. She had backbone; I'll give her that.

The loud voice appeared again, announcing, "Ladies and gentlemen, though I think you will agree the performance for the Hoilago Reds was a strong, convincing demonstration of strength, grit, and determination, the victory this evening goes to the iron-willed tenacity of the Evanisgart Greens. So can you please join me in congratulating this year's champions, the Evanisgart Greens!" Fidelma ran over to me and gave me a big hug. I wasn't sure for what; she pretty much eliminated the opposition all on her own. She did well, and I was delighted to be a part of it. Like me, she was exhausted but had a smile going all across her face. As the crowd began to get a little wilder, I began to question our safety for the trip home. Thankfully, the guardians were close at hand, and we were quickly ushered to our buses so both sides could be kept apart. This I found very relieving. I wasn't really in the mood for a fight. I barely had the energy to get out of the Lycra suit! Unfortunately it would mean that I wouldn't be able to meet up with Wen and the guy we needed, Shavil. I was also concerned about Bala. We promised to meet him at the communal area tonight. Well, that's where we were, but the communal area was under us. I hoped Bala was okay.

Chapter 5

The next day at school, I was once again the living legend of the Evanisgart Greens. I adopted my swagger once more and walked around with a very superficial level of confidence. This was a feeling I would enjoy; never in my life had I felt so popular. Briefly, I began to think what school *was* like for me back in my own world. As I was now one of the popular people at school, I didn't even dream of looking to other kids that may have had a more normal status. I was too caught up in my own popularity. I felt a little ashamed. Although I was lapping up this extra attention, I was also quite aware that I might have been acting differently because of it. I was becoming the kind of person the real me in my real world would hate. But perhaps that's the way with all kids or people that get fame or notoriety over a short period; they behave like pumped-up fame junkies because they are not used to the attention.

With that in mind, I tried to be a little more aware of my body language. I tried to sit humbly and began to think if I would meet Wen and Bala in the park that night. I was aware we agreed last night, but as it didn't work out I could only hope that they would appear tonight. A skinny, well-dressed, happy man then bounced into the room and asked us to be quiet in a very friendly way, smiling and raising his eyebrows. We soon responded to his request and awaited is guidance.

"How are all you lovely people today?" he said. *What on earth does this joker teach?* "As you already know, we are going to test you this week to see if you have what it takes to be an entertainer. Well, boys and girls, I am your evaluator, so put away those books, shake out those arms, and clear your throats; it's time to have some fun!" Ah man, I was not in the mood for this so early in the morning.

"I want everyone to move their desks to the back and sides of the room and then stand in a circle around me," he said as he clapped is hands like a performing seal. It was then that I noticed how big the room was and how few desks there were in the room.

"My name is Mr. Carmic, or Chesza, to my buddies—that's you guys—and today I will be testing you on your voice and dance. Those of you whom I select shall proceed to the next level of examination. So, my little pumpkins, are you ready to do it?" he said as he punched the air for no apparent reason. To be frank, I wasn't ready to start doing anything with Chesza. Why was he asking us to call him by his first name? I hated teachers like that. It was like they wanted to be your friend. Chesza had turned on some music and everyone in the circle was looking at one another as if we were about to get shot. Chesza was trying to initiate a warm up before we started doing anything. Boy, could he smile; I wasn't sure if he'd stopped smiling at any point since he'd entered the room. We clapped, we lunged, we jumped, and of course, we exhaled. Watching Chesza lead us was so entertaining. He moved like a friendly lizard, very sharp and distinct in his movements, but yet very gentle. I thought this was funny until I remembered Bala suggested I moved like a lizard. Surely I'm not like Cheza,

"Okay, it's about time we got our first *funster* out here and see what they've got." *Oh, this should be good. I can't wait... though, what's a funster?*

"You, yes, you with the little smirk on your face, come on. I know you want to," he said. *Good God, is he talking to me?*

"No, I'm fine, thank you," I said quickly.

"Well, if you don't come over here, I will fail the entire class, do you understand?" Now, he said this with a smile on his face! I mean, how could he? Clearly smiling was an action of Chesza's that he did not associate with being amused or happy. It was just an expression he was comfortable wearing *all the time*. As I approached the center of the circle, Chesza moved to the side and began clapping for me. Oddly, as depressed and embarrassed as I was, I found it hard to stay mad with this friendly lizard-man. Now standing squarely in the middle of the circle, Chesza said, "Now, I want you to dance to the music. I want to see how good you are; just forget we're here." *Ohh* yeah, no problem. I'll dance away, will I? Like no one is here. Come on, Chesza, this is ridiculous...

I began by swaying my torso from side to side. This was subtle, though at least we had movement. I then began clicking my fingers and moving my arms up and down like I was playing the drums standing up. Though I was quietly pleased with my little set, everyone looked on in sheer disgust. Unfortunately, the acute awareness of my surroundings was having a detrimental impact on my performance. It seemed that my legs were not going to move today. It was like they were too embarrassed to join in. I thought, *One more minute—one more minute and it's over.*

"Florence," said Chesza. *Oh, thank God*, I thought. *I can sit down.* "Why don't you get up there and join him," Cheza ordered. *What? Join me? No, no, no... this is horrible enough on my own.*

Florence was a very large girl. She had shaggy, brown, greasy hair and a dress as large as a reasonably sized tent. As she approached, our nervous eye contact said all there was to say. She may as well have said, "You dance like a baboon, like a jungle animal," while I was thinking, *Goodness me, you're going to crush me with your hands, Florence.* As soon as she was close enough, Florence got right down to it. It seemed like even though she may dress and behave conservatively, she was dancing and moving like a true performer. She had one hand behind her head, her eyes were closed, and she was moving those hips in perfect harmony with the music. Oh yes, she had just taken ownership of the floor. Meanwhile, my legs decided that they wanted to join in and began to shuffle from side to side. Yes, we had full motion—arms, hands, and legs. Unfortunately, although Florence and I were opposite each other and dancing together, it looked like we were both dancing to different songs.

"Now we're getting funky. You, the guy with the red hair, how about you get up there?" Cheza said, willing yet another person to join the embarrassment. As if Florence and I didn't provide enough of a freak show, up bounced this little mini Chesza. In no time at all, this guy was body popping, head jolting, and crotch grabbing—all of the time looking and smiling at me! Now I wasn't an expert on dancing etiquette, but surely this was wrong. It felt like he was trying to hypnotise me with his sharp jolts.

Thankfully, the song changed, and we all got an opportunity to readjust to the music. I didn't recognize what the next song was, but there was a hell of a beat to it. Florence saw this as a song that required her to put both hands at the back of her head, again all of the time with her eyes closed and bobbing up and down. And on the other side of me, very much inside my invisible circle of personal space, I had mini-Chesza smiling hard and thrusting in my direction every couple of seconds. I was uncomfortable. I was *very* uncomfortable. Fortunately, at this point I was far too involved and frustrated to manage my inhibitions, so I too closed my eyes. I thought maybe, just maybe, doing this would reveal me to be the dancing mastermind I might be. It seemed to be working for Florence. So with a little belief in my blind-dancing prowess, I proceeded to do a fancy turn for the crowd. In my head I was as graceful as a swan, though in reality, as I turned, I managed to slap Florence right in the face.

Oh dear, this felt embarrassing. I opened my eyes immediately and saw her drop her hands to her side and begin shouting over the music, pointing her finger at me. I thought she was going to beat the hell out of me. What was also strange was that when I opened my eyes, I realized that the water in the fish tank at the bottom of the class was moving—moving and gushing in tune with the music. I thought this was unusual, though as Florence's finger came within inches of my face, I crashed back to reality and put the fish-tank concerns to the back of my mind as I stood there, motionless, awaiting some form of imminent retribution. To my relief there was no retribution, but to my surprise, the water in the tank at the end of the class suddenly became still. There was no more gushing. So with Florence ranting and mini-Chesza still thrusting relentlessly, I stood there questioning whether this class would ever end. So far it was not looking like I was going to make the cut as an entertainer!

After a lot more embarrassment, evil stares from Florence, and happy smiles from mini-Chesza, the class ended. It took me about three classes to recover from that dancing class. I kept replaying those stupid moves in my head. In fact, after that class, the rest of the day flew by, and before I knew it, I was off home again. Winnie was not with me because she left early with another girl—something about a school trip. Hopefully I could find my way home.

Setting off on my journey home, I was eager to go to the park. I knew that we had not formally agreed to meet there, but I had missed Wen from the night before and I was hoping that somehow we would all think to go there today.

When I got closer to the park, I saw a golden figure. Could it be Bala? I ran with hope in the direction of the mysterious figure. As I neared, my suspicions were confirmed. "Bala, it is so good to see you. How are you?"

"Me? I'm fine. We get treated like kings over there. I'm eating like an absolute pig," he said as he rubbed his stomach. At that moment I noticed he had a bag.

"What's the bag for, Bala?" I asked.

"Well, as we agreed the night before last, I brought another golden outfit so we could smuggle Shavil across," he replied.

"Why yes, of course. Excellent, Bala. Have you seen Wen?"

"No, I think I have been here for about an hour, and no one has turned up," he said, looking around him.

"How have you been here for an hour, as school has only just ended?" I asked.

"School?" Bala laughed. "I don't go to school on a schedule. I get up, eat a lot of food, and go to school when I want to go. The teachers are amazing, though. They almost make me want to go to school."

"Wow... that is cool, though no wonder you're putting on a few pounds," I said.

Bala took a breath in. "It's this gold suit. It makes me look fat."

I laughed as Bala smirked back, seeing if I was buying his story, which I very much was. It was only last night I too was wearing an outfit that didn't bring out my best points. I then noticed Bala look over my shoulder and squint. I looked around and saw two red figures walk towards us. It was Wen and that guy Shavil from her school.

"*Wen!*" Bala roared into my ear. It hurt, but it was an accident, and Bala didn't mean it. "*Wen!*" He did it again, once more in the same ear. Now that, I *am* holding him responsible for.

"Zach, Bala…" She smiled. "This is…well, this is Shavil…Shavil White." Before Wen had said this, we were all smiling with an almost tangible air of excitement and relief between the three of us. However, the gravity of this for Shavil suddenly dawned on me. He looked up briefly and acknowledged us but just stood there the rest of the time looking at the ground. He didn't look like a shy type of guy. He had strong features, well-groomed, long, red, shiny hair, and a reserved yet evident confidence that he did not feel like boasting at this particular time. Wen must have told him that he had a father, though we still weren't sure if she had said his father was Bronson Keel.

"Okay, so here is the plan," Wen said, quickly whipping us back into the moment. "Bala, did you bring a spare pair of golden clothes?"

"Check," Bala replied.

"Okay, what we need to do is get Shavil into these gold clothes, and then you must take him through, Bala," Wen instructed.

"Whooa, me? Hang on, I am just the provider of clothes," Bala answered.

"Look, we will be doing well enough if we mange to get Shavil into golden clothes without the guardians seeing. It has to be you who makes sure Shavil gets into these new clothes," Wen repeated.

Bala had not banked on having such a prominent role in the little adventure. He looked very anxious.

"Zach," Wen said as I stared at Bala's reactions. "There are guardians on every gate of this park to the different colored areas—on the gold, green, red, orange—and we simply will not be able to get Shavil into these clothes without a diversion, do you understand?"

"A diversion!" I said with the same nervousness Bala had when he was getting his instructions.

"Yes, and not some little diversion, but a big diversion. Only then will you draw the attention of all the guardians for long enough. On my count you will go towards the fence and start climbing it as if you are trying to get into another color's area," Wen suggested.

"Right," I said calmly as I fought back the need to shout, *Are you crazy, Wen?*

"So I propose we do this now. Bala, get ready to get the clothes out of the bag. Zach, start making your way to a part of the fence," she said as she pointed the way for me.

I turned slowly in a deeply confused way, wondering how on earth I got this job and why I was going along with it. I looked back and saw the eyes of three poised, dependant people cast all of their hope in my direction. No pressure then, no pressure at all. When I reached the fence, I looked at the closest guardian, put my hand on the fence, and began to climb. The guardian looked at me but said and did nothing. As I climbed, more and more guardians started looking at me, but why were none of them doing anything? Were they robots?

When I reached the very top, I said, "Hey, look at me! I'm going over the fence!"

Again nothing. Looking back at my comrades, I shrugged my shoulders. I could see their hopes begin to evaporate as my chance to divert attention was failing miserably. Determined to try and yield some sort of response, I continued to shout, slagging off the different colors in an attempt to try and provoke one of the guardians. While doing this, one of my legs dangled in on to the other side of the fence. Just then a massive alarm began to sound, and I fell off the fence into the golden area. *"Kill him!"* All of the guardians began to yell as I felt bullets whiz by me. In the stroke of a second, I had gone from drawing no response to having the entire park's guardians come in my direction. This was not the plan!

I began to run quicker than I ever had in my entire life. Luckily, I was in a wooded area, so I was still somewhat covered; however, I could feel those guardians on my back. *Think, Zach, think. What should I do?* I quickly thought of potential solutions—throw stones at them, call them names, dance—but none of my ideas seemed to be giving me the answers that I needed. Then suddenly it struck me: If I take off my green clothes, they won't know that I am trespassing. Granted, I would be indeed naked, though better be a live naked man than a dead dressed one.

Frantically acting on my new plan, I tore off my clothes and continued to run. I felt like Adam in the garden of Eden, except instead of having Eve, I had a group of snakes chasing me with guns. Thankfully, in the depth of this wooded area, I stumbled upon a very large, impressive house, and right outside the house were golden clothes hanging on a clothesline. I quickly grabbed something to preserve my modesty and then continued to run as fast as my legs would carry me. As I ran and ran, I began to notice that either the woods were beginning to become a little less dense, or I was getting larger. *Oh no, it couldn't be.* Yes, it seemed that I was now exiting the wooded area, and very quickly, all of the trees were at my height and getting smaller and smaller until they were completely gone from sight. And there I was, standing with my hands in the air and a large ring of guardians all around me, pointing their guns at me and roaring.

"You are surrounded; do you have any last words before we shoot you?" a large guardian said gruffly. *Yes, I have a lot of words.*

"Yes," I said nervously, the weight of the situation suddenly hitting me. "I have a message for Bronson Keel," I said.

"Right, then," I heard from the distance as a burly, brutish-looking man came running towards me. His expression was hard to make out from the distance, though as he came closer, I could see his anger. In fact, the closer he came, the angrier he looked. Well, this was a terrific plan. I don't think we had thought as far as me getting caught, losing my clothing, and having a number of guns pointed at me!

"This better be important, otherwise you will have a slow and painful death, my friend." My sentiments exactly; this better be important!

"Can you tell Bronson that I have news of his son," I said as clearly as possible. The guardian laughed.

"You really are desperate. Emperor Keel does not have a son. Kill him," he ordered.

"No, wait. Please, can you please just ask him, please? And if I am wrong, you can kill me as many times as you want," I offered as consolation.

The guardian got on his radio and whispered something while staring at me. The guardian smiled. This did not amuse me. He walked over, stood in front of me, put the gun in my face, and cocked the trigger. The two barrels of the gun were resting on my cheek; they felt so cold. I leaned hard on the barrels of the gun to relieve myself of both my weight and the life I was soon to lose.

He smiled and said, "The Emperor wants to see you."

I backed away from the gun and wiped the involuntary tear from my eye. Never had I been so terrified and relieved in all my life; it's odd how such extreme polar emotions seem to travel together.

The guardian handed me white guardian robes. "Put them on; you can't see Mr. Keel like that, you are not worthy to be in golden clothes." After I put the robes on, he went behind me and put the gun to the middle of my back as the rest of the guardians involved flanked me on both sides, marching to my every step. I tried to think this was a good thing, though it certainly didn't feel good. As we approached a large, golden building, all of the guardians stopped marching and provided a path for me and the brutish guardian to walk all the way up to the door. The building was odd. It was about sixty stories high and two football fields wide but only had one large window in the very center of it. In fact, this window seemed to be on every side of the building; what a poor design. This window was about the size of one football field, so it was a very large window.

Then there was a loud noise as an object—what seemed like a bullet—shot out the top of the tall, golden building soaring up to the heavens. Everyone stopped and bowed down. I was confused. It soon became clear that this was no bullet, but an actual man. In a matter of seconds, this man began plummeting towards the ground at a frightful speed. It was only then I noticed that the figure seemed to be falling in my direction. I panicked. I was going to run, but I was surrounded, and I would probably be shot. Helplessly, I remained poised for impact. The figure was quickly growing in size as it fast approached us. Faster, louder, nearer... *Dear me, I am about to be flattened.* I hunched up and closed my eyes until *bang*; this massive, tight sheet extended about forty feet from the man's back. Then, just as the man was about to fly back up because of the massively tight sheet, he quickly cut himself from it and opened a tiny little parachute to bring him the remaining couple of feet he had to travel to ground. Now that's an entrance … a bit complicated, but impressive.

The man landed right in front of me. It was Bronson Keel. He looked angry, tired, bitter, and, above all, evil. I wasn't overjoyed that all of my hope of living now rested in this man's hands. He stood there with his hands behind his back, looking through me, when he said with a sinister sense of calm, "Who has the insolence to refer to my son?"

"It was me, ahh…" I tried to remember what my name was in this place. "My name is Lawrence Constabin," I said with relief.

"I don't care who you are. Why were you referring to my son?" he said.

"Because, Emperor Bronson, your son is alive," I said, frightened to death of what he was going to do to me.

He looked at me, and though he was suppressing how this made him feel, I could see his emotions gush about inside of him like a river that had broken its banks.

"How dare you! I appreciate that not many people know I had a son, but for those… For you that choose to disrespect me with this information is simply intolerable. You will have a quick death—I want you dead from this world," he said dismissively.

"*Please!*" I cried; things couldn't end this way.

The guardians loaded their guns.

Bronson turned, bitterly shaken by this confrontation, dropped his head, and began to walk towards his golden building. With a dead silence commanding, a whisper in the crowd braved the only word that could defeat this deathly still.

"Dad..."

Emperor Bronson froze in his tracks. He raised his head, brought both hands to his face, and turned around to face the crowd. It seemed like the first time in his life Bronson was reduced to a mere shadow of himself. He stood there with a suspicious vulnerability, looking into a sea of faces, waiting for this earlier uttering to be confirmed. It appeared his damaged heart had come back to life, desperately wanting his hopes to be realized.

"It's me," the voice whispered.

A parting in the people ripped through the crowd to reveal the source of the peculiar mystery. Bronson's son looked to his dad. At this point all the son was going on was what Wen had told him earlier that day. The son was hurting, tears welling up in his eyes, and waiting for this man, Bronson, to accept him. Bronson stared at the boy. A strangled smile slowly began to emerge amongst this flood of emotion until both Bronson and Shavil ran to each other and cried, "*My son*" and "*Dad.*" Bronson Keel and his son embraced each other for a few seconds as the crowd looked on and witnessed a side to their dark, evil leader they had never seen before. They were hugging each other tightly, as if now was the release of all the bitterness and pain that had built up over the years. Up until now, Bronson had been the man who split up families, who rejected people's applications to rise to a better color band. In effect, he destroyed any happiness that came his way. More than that, he made absolutely sure the different colors were strictly cordoned off and had nothing to do with each other. So all things considered, how could a man that carried out such heartless deeds suddenly be reduced to tears?

Bronson turned from his son periodically and looked at me. "Where? How? Thank you." He turned back to his son. "I thought you were dead," he said as he looked sorrowfully at his long-lost son. "Exactly eight years, two hundred forty-one days ago, I had the worst day of my life. Your mother and I were travelling back with you from a day out in the local park. You had always loved walking, running, exploring. You were the energy that kept us on our feet. On our way back from the park there was a crash, and our car went straight through the fence line into the red zone's territory. When I woke in the hospital of our golden town, they told me that you had both passed away in the accident. This was the day I wept bitterly about the carefree happiness in my old life and gave birth to a new heartless, cold existence. The pain was so suffocating. I knew that I could not survive another event that could crush me that much, so I made a decision to cut intimacy out of my life and to interfere with everyone else's happiness to prevent them from the same inevitable disappointment of losing what they love most about their lives. It's strange; although everyone is their own individual, independent self, in the end, your happiness, contentment, or love is completely invested in other people. In some ways this renders you vulnerable with little control over how you will feel. My aim was never to become the monster I have grown to be, but after a while I began to act like how I was viewed. All I wanted was to prevent people from the kind of heartbreak I had to suffer." He looked at his son again and embraced him. Bronson's son was beginning to feel more and more emotional as his father spoke. They were like two pieces of a puzzle that had finally found each other.

The boy then put his dad at arms' length and looked at him, saying, "While you were waking up in that hospital back in the golden area, I was waking up in a hospital from the red zone. They told us you were dead."

"They told us...." Bronson said, looking shocked, interrupted. "Who was this 'us'? Did your mother survive?" Bronson was on the verge of breakdown once more.

His son looked back calmly and said, "Of course she is still alive, though she has never been the same since the crash. I think a part of Mom also died that day." Bronson fell to his knees, placing his head down and putting his arms around his son. Amazingly, throughout all of this excitement, the crowd was still completely silent. There was a sort of reverent fear evident amongst the masses. Bronson took to his feet, stood proudly, cleared his throat, and said, "There are going to be a lot of changes around here. I want to review policies, I want to review my decisions, and I want to apologize for any of the heartache I have caused. From this day forward, I am no longer your master whom you have to cower to, but your leader who will lead you to a better life." The crowd gave a polite cheer and began speaking quietly to each other.

Bronson turned to Wen, Bala, and me and said, "How can I ever repay you?" We looked at each other, smiling, when without warning, Bronson's expression changed. His eyes flickered over and back, and he looked stressed once more when he said, "Who decided to send me and my family to two different hospitals? I know we went over the fence line, but there is no explanation for what happened. Someone interfered with the accident investigation. Someone deliberately broke me and my family up."

Maybe Bronson was right; maybe someone did try to split up his family. It is possible that whoever sent them to different hospitals wanted this hatred between the colored regions to get much worse when Bronson came in to power. Bronson may have just been a pawn in an elaborate, well-conceived, malicious, evil master plan. As Bronson slowly began to picture his revenge, a dark shadow passed over his eyes; however, thankfully it was followed by a hug from his son, who said, "It's good to have you back, Dad." Bronson then turned to his son, parked his suspicions and want for revenge, and hugged his son affectionately.

As I looked at them, I thought about what Bronson said. Someone, some evil force or person did decide to split his family up. Why and who? Was this our next task? I then began to hear the clicking sound. I looked to Wen and Bala, and it seemed they too could hear this increasingly loud noise. It wasn't long before we passed out again and awoke in the mysterious place once more.

Chapter 6

As before, I saw that we were in a triangular room. It had the same smoky, black floor, a smoky, white ceiling, and a white, revolving sphere in the center. This extremely weird place was actually starting to appear normal to me. I looked across the room, and to my comfort, I saw Wen and Bala climb to their feet.

"Well done, my aspiring Viscents. You did it," Evall said.

"Did what?" Wen said impatiently. I had a feeling Wen didn't completely enjoy that world.

"With your gifts combined, you were given clues on how to unravel and build a better future for the world you were in. You succeeded. You identified the main reason people were unhappy, and you began to understand the problem. Upon doing this, with little regard for your own safety, you approached the problem and discovered it was not the man that was evil but the world that had made him this way. You have done well," Evall said.

We all put a slight grin on our faces, wilfully accepting this praise and looking humbly to the ground. Though really I hadn't fully taken in what we had just done yet. I mean this time last week the biggest adventure of my day was trying to survive school, which wasn't easy at the best of times. But now I am a Viscent, who is about to develop my very own power. And I have just spent time in a different world, a world without money, and got to see how other people live and how their world works. This really is so cool, but where should we go next?

"Now, for your next world. What do you choose, Zach?" Evall asked.

I had become so used to being called Lawrence I almost didn't respond to Zach. It was at this moment I realized that we would have to do this all over again, and it was me who would decide the type of world we would enter. I wasn't ready to do this all over again, and I didn't know what kind of world I should request. Clearly from the last world, if I wished for something that I hoped would be positive, there would be side effects. I looked over at Bala and Wen, who seemed physically exhausted, yet their eyes were glued on me, hanging on my every word. Their eyes were popping from their faces in anticipation, as if we were playing musical chairs and they were waiting for the music to stop. I needed to wish for something safe, something that would definitely give everyone a better standard of life … and then suddenly it hit me. I had it … If I had to wish to go to a different world, I think had an idea.

"Yes, I am ready to make my request," I said confidently.

"I wish for a world where everyone is equal," I said nervously, hoping that this really would be a safe request. I mean what could be that wrong with a place where everyone is treated the same as everyone else?

With that, as before, we all fell to the ground and passed out. We didn't spend as much time chatting this time; it was straight to our new world.

My next memory is opening my eyes slowly. It seemed as if I had been out cold for a very long time. I felt completely refreshed. This time, unlike before, I was well aware this was going to be an entirely different world; therefore, I could prepare not be so disoriented at the environment I was about to discover. As my eyes opened a little wider, I realized that I was in bed. It was very dark in the room, and I was eager to get to my feet and have a snoop around. As I shuffled in my bed, I heard the sound of deep breathing. There was someone else in here with me. Though I had just reminded myself that I should not be shocked, when I discovered that there was someone else in the room with me, I suddenly found myself in a pool of sweat, second-guessing what on earth I should do.

The breathing was consistent, and the only half-positive thing I could derive from the situation was that the breathing did not seem to be moving. Well, I sure wasn't going to fall back to sleep, so I lay there wide-eyed and fully awake, strangling my pillow in blind fear. Then, oddly, the breathing seemed to change; the rhythm altered. *Goodness me, what were they thinking? Was I about to be murdered?* The tension was torture. I felt that my fragile life hung in the balance. However, the tension was then shattered as a deafening siren flooded the room, alerting all within that something was wrong. Though this certainly raised my heart rate a couple of notches, I was relieved that something was happening that perhaps would allow me to assess the situation and identify the source of this creepy breathing.

The lights in the room then illuminated, which was followed by the siren cutting out and a computer's voice stating, "Please proceed to wash." With the lights now on, I sat up from my resting place and took in my surroundings. Truly I was not alone in the room; in fact, there were five other people in the room with me. There were three beds in a row on the other side of the room and three beds in a row on my side.

My adrenaline was pumping. *Am I in jail?* This didn't feel very equal to me. Then almost in perfect synchronicity, the other five people got up and proceeded to walk towards the door. They were all guys who appeared around my age and all with shaven heads. Observing this odd sight, I put my hand on my head and found I too looked like the other five guys. What worried me the most was the fact that they all seemed to have scars on their arms and faces. Some of these wounds were distinct red lines on their faces and arms while others were a lot less obvious. These cuts and bruises were making me nervous.

Fearful of looking out of place, I followed my five new friends, and on I proceeded after them to wash. As we entered the washroom, there were six washbasins in a row. As anticipated, each of the five took to a specific basin, which left me the one that was second from the left. It appeared the first thing we all did was wash our faces, and in harmony with the other guys, I too let the tap on the right run until the basin was full. As I washed my face and listened to the splashes of everybody else. I looked ahead of me to see if there was anything of any interest. Directly ahead there was something that looked like a giant poster stuck against the wall. At first I wasn't clear what it said, and some of the words didn't even make sense. But after considering how it was put together, it quickly struck me what it was. It looked like a timetable. Illuminating the poster, there was a spotlight perched right above it, casting light upon all that lay below. The room was dark, and although the poster was difficult to read in its entirety, I think the main headings read:

>   CAST
>   Rise
>   Wash
>   Exercise
>   Eat
>   Travel
>   Learn
>   Eat
>   Learn
>   Travel
>   Work
>   Travel
>   Eat
>   Sleep
>   Replenish

A "Cast," like the actors in a movie? How does a cast come into it? There was also a lot of other writing below and to the side of each of these headings; there were also times against each of them and durations. Though at least it seemed to make sense so far; we had been woken from our beds, we were now washing, so I suppose the next thing on the list is exercise. I was nervous. I was useless at sports, and I bruise easily. My success in the last world was just beginner's luck. Please, no more sports or tight black shorts! With the entirety of my focus on the poster, I realized that everyone was finishing up; it was time to return to our bedroom.

As we re-entered the bedroom, I observed that in contrast to the definitive scars on each guy's body, the walls were all just bare, plain, smooth, concrete surfaces. The floor seemed to be concrete, and the ceiling was just... yes, concrete. Now I have never classed myself as a guy with any taste or style, but for goodness sake, this was completely unimaginative and devoid of any sort of character. *Do we all have to have horrible houses to be equal?* I thought. *Well, actually, maybe we do.*

When I returned to my bed, as in the washroom I noticed that each of the guys was standing opposite their locker. Of the six lockers in a row, there was one with nobody at it. This must be my locker. Walking swiftly over to my locker, I looked inside. My locker contents were not going to turn heads. I had black pants, brown shirts, and grey warm-looking things to wear over your shirt. They were dull but they all seemed to go together okay. Thank God I wasn't wearing green anymore. Black and brown never felt so refreshing. However, instead of donning these items, all of the other guys were putting on robes. And what was stranger again was that they all had different colored robes, yellow, black; I grimaced as I thought to myself, *Not another color-coding experience!* I looked inside my locker again. Amidst the many, many sets of bland clothing, there was a red robe. Like the other guys, I decided to get the robe out and put it on. As I tied the strap around my waist, I noticed another strange feature to my locker—there was a small collection of knives, swords, and staffs. It struck me as odd that in a place that seemed so controlled there would ever even be a need for fighting. As I absorbed the significance of the killing contents of my locker, I stood there, not knowing what to select when a neighbour said, "You're going to be using the staff today." Startled by the sudden interest in my arming, I followed my neighbour's instruction and held it firmly for whatever was about to occur.

As my conversationless, armed, robed "friends" finished dressing, I proceeded to follow them with my staff. We went upstairs into a very wide, long room. There were no regular shelves, lockers, or furniture. Instead there was a soft floor lined with a soft material with a number of different obstacles and objects in the middle of the floor. There were ropes hanging from the ceiling and types of climbing frames scattered throughout the width of the room. It was like an adult playground. All of the guys ahead stopped, lined up, and stood facing the entire room in front of us. At that moment we saw six other guys enter the room from each corner. They all had corresponding colored robes on, and similar to my group, each lined up parallel to a wall facing the center of the room. There were now four perfect lines of six guys. Each line had six robes that were different, though each group of six contained the same set of six different colors. Each group of six also had a different weapon. Our group had the staff, the line opposite us had swords, and so on. As I looked at the focused, militant look on the faces of each group, I stood there anxiously and nervously clutching my staff. There was silence. Each guy was poised, and with a thick, palpable tension polluting the area, I had a terrible feeling something was about to go down.

A siren sounded, upon which everyone moved. I tried to observe what was happening... Everyone was scattering. What were they doing? It was at that moment I realized what was happening. The four guys from the four different groups of six with yellow robes assembled; the four guys with black robes assembled. My task was clear. I needed to find the three other guys with the red robes from the other three groups of six. This way our group would have four guys of the same red-colored robe, but we would all have different weapons. This was happening so fast that in about twenty seconds, there were six color-coded groupings of guys assembled and ready for the next step. As I presumed, each guy in our red group had a different weapon. I was the guy with the staff. Perhaps I was to fight all of the guys with the staffs? That would mean I would be fighting all of the guys from my house—*how awkward.*

"Good morning," a robotic voice sounded overhead. "Welcome to your daily exercise. Exercise will stop when each of the twenty lights going along the center of the ceiling goes dark or if one color attains surrender from all of the other colors before the lights go out. To attain surrender you must get handed the surrender slip from your opponent. This is inside the right breast of your robe. The lighting along the center of the ceiling will be your principal lighting. As time passes by, it will be more difficult to control your offence, hence surrender becomes more difficult to attain. The number one aim is exercise; the number one rule is that no one is to die. You are not allowed to take life. The games will begin in five, four..."

That was it! I was about to have my life taken from me! I looked at what I had in my hand, and suddenly my expression went from a deflated, beaten frown to a mildly optimistic smile. I had been a part of the school band for years, but not as a person who played an instrument—as the person who would throw the baton up in the air and catch it. This wasn't the ideal training for combat, but the point was that I was very familiar with the movement of a baton and it just might pay off.

As I stood there in desperate hope of optimizing my intuition, I saw someone run towards me. It was one of the guys dressed in green. He was angry and came at me like a wild dog. Quickly I stepped out of the way. He proceeded to keep running up the wall and then somersaulted back to ground again. My confidence in my baton skills was diminishing by the second. Once again he ran at me; however, this time I decided to put my skills to the test. When within range I used the length of the staff to jab him sharply on the forehead. I then dropped to the ground and followed through by taking his legs from under him. He fell backwards on is back. I was never so happy to see pain inflicted on another person.

Although he rose to his feet immediately, my renewed confidence in my own skills assisted me in my combat with this guy and anyone else who challenged me over the next couple of minutes. I decided to stay where I started from and just defend as necessary. As I scanned the area, it resembled a cross between a playground and a war zone. I commonly heard screaming and yelling and saw bodies flying through the air at the hand of some of the most amazing moves I have ever seen. These guys really were trained professionals. It was a mystery how I was even managing to keep them at bay.

Then out of the corner of my eye, I saw three guys beating up on this one guy. What was strange was that the three were a complete mix of different colors. There was even a guy in a red robe beating on that one guy.

Without being able to explain it, I began making my way over to this tussle. Something told me there was something that wasn't right. As I neared it seemed it was worse than I thought. They were not looking for this guy to surrender; *they wanted to kill him!*

There was a guy in a red robe and a guy in a yellow robe holding the fallen fighter up as a big guy dressed in a black robe pulled back his sword and proceeded to drive it forward, straight through the injured party. Thankfully my movement was swift, and just as he put his arm forward, I hit his sword and sent it flying away from the body of the beaten guy. The red-robed guy then reached out to me and said, "Comrade, this is not your fight."

I looked back at him and said, "If this is wrong, then I am afraid this is my fight; we just may not be in the same team." I wasn't sure if it was the adrenaline, my baton skills, or my cleanly shaven head, but this was not like me, and I was suddenly realizing I may be biting off a lot more than I could chew. I was frightened, just like when I saw Bala get beaten up that time, but this was different. I knew I had to do something. The three abusers laughed a little until the guy in the black robe turned to me and said while rubbing his blade, "Predictable, I thought you would never join us." All three then focused on me. It seemed my good deed would have consequences. "You see, we are to follow the guidelines. We are just pawns," the man in black said as he prepared his weapon and locked eyes with me.

All three were now surrounding me. I was dead. But before the first guy could take his first lunge at me, another guy in a black robe came to the forum. He jumped and somersaulted into the center of the circle with me and said, "You are not alone." I didn't know what this meant, but with a beating from three trained fighters looming, I would take all the help I could get. It was three against two, a yellow, red, and black against a red and a black.

What followed was a gruesome exchange of hand-to-hand combat. We fought and we fought until it was me and the guy in black against the other guy in black and the other guy in red—a red and a black robe against a red and a black robe. From afar this did not make obvious sense, but you could see in the whites of our eyes what we stood for. By this stage all of the lights in the battleground had gone dark apart from one remaining light in the center that allowed us to continue battling in the shadows. As the final light began to flicker, the other two fighters began to drift outside of the remaining lighting as my black-robed opponent dropped his weapon to the floor and extended his hand. The large room, once filled with screams and violence, was now almost silent apart from the efforts of the other red and black fighters in the shadows.

He said, "I am sorry."

I looked at him, taking in the large outline of his massive frame and how his muscles seemed to bulge out through his black robe as the spotlight of the only remaining light in the room rained down on him. Sceptical but impressed at his maturity, I began to reciprocate this gesture by dropping my weapon and following my opponent's lead. I too extended my hand. What happened next came by complete surprise. The black-robed fighter stood on both of my feet, preventing me from moving. He grabbed my right wrist with his right hand and forced my right hand across my body. Then he flicked out a small knife in his left hand and said, "Goodbye, *Viscent*." I could not defend myself. My left hand was stranded. He was about to plunge a knife straight into my rib cage, and I could do nothing about it. Then just as he was about to stab me, just as the final light was about to go out, someone emerged from the shadows and dived on my assassin. The room went black. After what seemed to be an eternity, the lights came back on. There was another fighter lying on the black-robed fighter, holding him down with both of his arms. The black-robed guy on the ground was laughing and said, "Next time, my friend, next time."

I was shaken, very shaken, as I watched this guy on the ground stare at me in anticipation of our next encounter. The fighter who saved me turned around. It was the fallen fighter from earlier that I had jumped in to save. He approached me and, quietly, before we had to go our separate ways, said, "I don't know why they were after me today, and I don't know why that other guy in the black robe jumped in to help you. This kind of stuff never happens. But you saved my life, so I was only glad to help in saving yours." He then tilted his head and said, "I have also heard of your kind before, and I am guessing that you will become far more powerful than I could ever dream. We saved each other's lives in a very obvious way today, but remember in your greatness that you can also save people's lives by doing the smallest things. Good luck, my friend."

I was thankful that he saved me and surprised he knew what a Viscent was, but what was most alarming was how the black-robed fighter also knew I was a Viscent. Suddenly I felt very vulnerable. It appeared that an opposing force knew of the Viscents and wanted to hurt us or kill us! I wondered who that evil, black-robed fighter was and why that group was trying to kill that guy from earlier that I was trying to save. I wondered if the black-robed fighter was a bad Viscent. I wondered if the group from earlier was trying to kill me or trying to kill the Viscent whose body I was occupying. I began to remember the warning that Evall had given us before accepting our challenge—the warning that there were other dark Viscents and worlds out there that wanted us dead, that wanted us to fail. It seemed like I just had my first introduction to this dark force. As my mind continued to race, the guy in the black robe, still on the ground, got to his feet and eyeballed me as he walked away. "There will be a next time, Gerbils," he said, walking away from me, smirking over his shoulder. The hairs on my skin stood up straight as my heart began to seize up in utter shock. This guy knew exactly who I was and how to get to me. It looked like earlier was a trap. Stiff with fear, I turned towards my exit. I had to put this to the back of my mind, otherwise I would be too afraid to do anything. This was a frightening welcome to the world of equality.

As I tried to pick myself up from the drama of our morning exercise, we went back to our respective dormitories, changed in to different clothes, and walked down a long, concrete staircase where four ladies proceeded to show us to our seats. In the middle of the floor there was a large, concrete table with wooden benches going up and down each side. When I took my seat, the four ladies kept bringing us food until a siren went again, signalling the next announcement, which stated, "Transport shall be leaving in ten minutes." Everyone rose to their feet and went back into their respective burrows. Where was this transport going to take us, and more importantly, why couldn't I finish my breakfast? You can take my dignity, sanity, and self-respect, but not my breakfast... This must be the "travel" part of the timetable.

Upon returning up the concrete pathway that we had all just poured out of, I found all the other guys. They were all busily getting ready as quickly as they could with a distinguished sense of calm. When I am rushing, I am like a storm, overturning everything and anything in my path. These guys seemed to organize as they rushed. What a skill! It was strange that no one was talking. I wondered if we were allowed to talk or if this place had some weird vow of silence. Sure there were some words exchanged on the exercise battlefield earlier, but that did not seem like the norm. Though oddly, as we all looked the same with our clothes, shaved heads, and footwear, there was a real sense of belonging. When you look like everybody else, you feel like you fit in with all around you. It was funny that the principal reason I was fitting in was because no one was talking, so I wasn't sticking out. As I too began rummaging calmly through my stuff and trying to find and arrange all of the things like everyone else, my mind drifted. The only downside to fitting in is that you find it more and more difficult to remember what you stand for. As I looked around for the second time and noted how alike we all were, I suddenly realized that some of the guys looked a lot more alike than I first thought. Were we all related? I was a little panicked by this discovery and consequently began to abandon my preparation and leave my usual mess in my wake, one step at a time.

Again, the siren sounded. Everyone lined up and began to walk down the stairs. To say I was having fun would be a lie, but to say I was curious... Well, I was intrigued by the little place. Onwards we marched through the kitchen, the place where I'd befriended and left a beautiful breakfast behind me, and on through to a long hallway, where we stopped at a large, metal door. I was now with twenty-three other guys, and we were standing in a row, waiting to be let loose. I wondered what was outside those doors. The colored world was interesting, but after a while it got a bit boring. I wondered what was next. I wondered what the world of equality would look like outside. So far my idea of equality wasn't panning out the way I had intended; so far it was pretty confusing and dangerous!

As we all stood silently, one of the ladies from the kitchen pressed some buttons, and the giant, metal doors began to part from the middle, opening as gently and as smoothly as the finest silk curtains. When I tried to look out to see what was outside, I was met with a bright light, preventing me from focusing on anything. I was perplexed. What could be so important that we all had to line up for?

The guy that was first in the line then stepped forward. The lady strapped a sort of keypad onto his chest, and she punched in some letters or numbers on the keypad. After this, he stepped out, and he was gone. The second guy then had the same done to him, and the third guy and the fourth guy. What did this little keypad do? For a brief second, I thought I was a robot. I then felt my arms, legs, and torso, and well, at least I still appeared to feel human. My relief was short lived because I was the next one up in line. Like all before me, she grabbed me roughly, attached this sort of keypad thing, keyed in something, and gestured me towards the door. I looked back like a child on his first day of school; however, instead of sympathy, I was met with an impatient stare quite clearly making sure I understood there was no sympathy to be found here. I conceded, took a deep breath, turned towards the blinding light, and stepped into it.

"*Woo, wowooo...*" I wailed as a force picked me up from my standing position and propelled me forward. I was moving; what a weird sensation! I was standing up, raised slightly off the ground, and moving in a forward direction at what seemed to be about one hundred miles per hour. About fifty to eighty feet ahead of me was the guy that had been in front of me in the line. To my left side—concrete, to my right side—concrete, and up ahead—concrete, but it wasn't cheap, badly finished concrete; it was the well finished, smooth, unchipped, grey concrete. It almost looked like marble. It seemed like a man had built this world, and not a clever one, but a straight, boring one. The only excitement in the design was that he may have used a colored ruler to measure things up!

As I flew along, I was slowly deflated at the disgusting sight of the place. Every building I saw was concrete. They were all the same size, and they all had a hemispherical roof, like mini, concrete mushrooms. There was no grass, no nature, or anything of any sort of color or appeal anywhere. Society was frozen solid with this sort of magical conveyer belt as the only means of getting from point A to point B. I then began to notice other lines of people travelling along in different directions. This was interesting. I wondered if people ever crashed. I wondered if people had to get personal insurance. I wondered if I had personal insurance! I quickly turned my focus back on my own personal travel. I mightn't understand it, but at the very least, I should pay attention. It was at this point I noticed how big my thighs were. I suppose if one is going to be travelling around like this all the time then your body changes. Quickly bored by the assessment of my movement, I looked to my side again. Oddly, I saw a person in what looked like a wheelchair. He too was travelling along at this speed in a different direction, however not through his wheels. His wheels had been retracted, and like us, he was just hovering over the ground, being propelled forward by this unknown force in a seated position.

I began to think that even though this poor guy had a disability, the travel methods around the area did not penalize him... He could and did travel around like any of the rest of us. While thinking of this, I wondered how people travelled long distances. Surely one couldn't keep this up for a one-hundred-mile journey. Their legs would be like tree trunks!

It was about then that I noticed there was something strange about the sky. I could see the sky, though I was looking through something—yes, it seemed like glass. It seemed like we had a glass ceiling lining the sky. Where did it end? When I wished for a world that was equal, this was not the sort of place that I'd had in mind. I wanted an open, free environment where money was not important and people could do as they pleased. What I had forgotten was that irrespective of what a culture omits, mankind will always form a system that allows them to survive, that allows them to organize and manage their environment. It appeared, in this particular land, my idealistic equality was being achieved by a regimented, formulated method of living where no one got more than another. This world had accommodated equality at the cost of individual success and ambition. If no one gets better, everyone is equal. The formula was simple.

Chapter 7

As I slowly became a little more comfortable with my speed, I looked ahead and saw the guy in front of me take a sharp right and then exit the main pathway, entering a building. It was one of those little, concrete mushrooms. As I approached the sharp turn, I prayed that the invisible conveyor belt would not rely on me to make the turn; however, I was prepared to try and jump if necessary. Thankfully, the turn passed off effortlessly as I too followed on into the characterless building.

Upon entering the building, all of the gentlemen present gathered into a circle and sat down. As the final guy entered and took the last natural place in the cosy circle, the lights went out. It was pitch black. This was followed by a noise and some slight vibration. We were moving in a downward direction. Again, this feeling of excitement and fear was becoming all too common. Slowly, light began to invade our little circle. From the entry of the light, I could confirm that we were moving in a downward direction. It was like being in an elevator, except in this case, instead of an elevator, we were in a room the size of a small house. By this stage there was light all around us, and not only that, but the ceiling and the ground we were sitting on were also the same color. It was a very strange sensation. I soon had no idea if I was moving or how fast I was moving. Suddenly there was a stop, and a man appeared on one of the walls of our enclosure. He was walking to us from a distance, as if this wall had some sort of three-dimensional capability. As all of our walls, floor, and ceiling were the same color, this experience almost felt like we were in another place, a pure, clean place where one would expect kind, wise people that would speak to us and make us feel better about ourselves.

The man on the wall wasn't an old man, but a youthful, strong-looking person who I knew liked the sound of his own voice. "Good morning, everyone," he boomed in the patronising way that I had been waiting for and expecting.

"Until you hear the next siren, we are here to speak about construction in the widest sense of the word. The future of this world rests in your hands. Let us start with energy. How do we make it and get rid of it?" he said.

This actually might be interesting; I thought to myself.

"Each of the buildings you see outside is the same shape and size. The buildings rise up from the ground like giant mushrooms. The cores of each building are used differently, and the top of each one is used for eating, sleeping, and exercising. So how can we make our energy from these buildings?" he asked.

The man on the virtual screen seemed to be looking at us; heaven knows why I was still looking at him. Best look down as quickly as I can before he asks me.

"You, tell me the answer," he said.

Now, goodness knows how this guy knew that he was being asked the question.

"Yes, sir, the outer material of each building has been designed to absorb and store the energy given off by the light and convert it to power. We also make use of turbines to generate energy. As every society has up to one hundred thousand people living inside its glass housing…"

Hang on; did this guy just say that we live inside glass housing? So if I look up, I will see glass separating me from the sky. And if I look to the side, I will see glass. Oh God, I am getting claustrophobic; I knew I'd seen glass earlier.

"The glass housing protects us against the dangers of the atmosphere and allows us to control the air and the CO_2 that we breathe out. Obviously, any oxygen that we need comes in through the big compressors that continue to pump air into our society. Any source of CO_2 that is generated is controlled and directed into the CO_2 underground pipeline. There are turbines all the way along this pipeline where the flow of CO_2 turns and enables us to create more energy from our by-products. The CO_2 eventually exhausts into an opening outside of the glass housing, where it is used to help trees, plants, and foliage to grow."

I was getting quite involved in this little presentation. It was fascinating—a completely regulated, controlled environment. Though, surely transport must play an uncontrolled part in the environment's pollution.

"So transport, let's talk about that. Doesn't that cause pollution? You, answer the question," the man said, who appeared to be looking at all of us. Then, as before, another guy shot up from his seated position.

"The transport system is a simple series of programmable, powered magnets. When you leave a residence, you enter your coordinates, stand on to the magnetic strip, and it will take you there the quickest way it can. It also senses other people and things travelling on the magnets. This ensures that you will not crash into anything. Therefore, the transport system creates very little pollution," the guy said, returning to his seated position.

"Accurate answer. And how about if I need to go on a long journey? You, answer the question," he said again, as if he was looking at the whole room of people. There was silence. I waited for someone to answer. No one was answering, and everyone else was looking at me. This was not good for me. Frightened to death I would be found out to be an imposter, I stood up quickly and said the first thing that came in to my head.

"We don't need to go on long journeys," was the best I could come up with—logical, but a complete guess.

"Correct, everything you will ever need is within these confines. It is only the chosen in the interests of equality that get to go outside of our housing. You will spend your life here. Any provisions, food, or materials that the society needs get delivered at the housing gateway every forty days. They are then spilt and distributed to the different dwellings as communicated. You will spend your life here developing our community and contributing to its harmony," the man said.

The by-products of this manufactured equality were becoming painfully clear. Everyone would all live similar if not the same lives, live in the same places, and do the same things. It was a feeling of restriction, a feeling of suffocation within one's own freedom. I felt like I was living at home again. I felt like I was five years old again where mom and dad would decide everything for me. Who would have thought that from the world I knew, where I aspired to fit in and be accepted, the one thing I would want here was to be different and unique! Perhaps a person's character needs space or chaos to grow; maybe it needs challenge to develop. The one thing I did know was that I would never find myself in a place where I was forced to be the same as everyone else. However, on the flip side, for my character's sacrifice, other people who may otherwise have been poor and without love and without family could enjoy the same sort of life that I would enjoy. Maybe this is the ideal world after all. There seemed to be no obvious suffering, no obvious pain, and above all else, an unrelenting, flat distribution of equality—a place that is so controlled, so contrived that the sparks of any indifference or free thought are quickly extinguished.

However, amidst this perfect world was numbness, an emotional detachment from people and application. It was almost as if people were not aware of their own lives. The guys I lived with could have been great guys, but I couldn't know that. I am not even sure *they* have enough freedom to know that. It has long been speculated that far off in the future, robots would begin replacing people and start controlling our environment. What I had discovered in this world was worse. People were replacing robots! They were living insensitive, android-like lives, programmed to obey and not to think, like robots. Of course, the makeup of all people was still the same biological form, but the people's mindsets were not human.

Their brains had been overcome by an extreme, societal power that supported obedience and conformity and punished initiative and free thought. In truth, it was not a mystery how this environment was formed, but shocking that the powers that controlled this place were happy for people to live their lives without experiencing the full spectrum of their emotions but instead live in this constant state of suspended, emotionless vacuum, where the only acceptable way of demonstrating how you feel if an emotion is triggered is to suppress it and remain passive. I sat there in this room with all of these guys, allowing my mind to go wild because I had a friend once whose story reminded me of this place. He talked about restrictions in his own life, and I never really understood what he meant. He was a smart guy who probably filled my head with all of this philosophical rambling, which I am supposed I am thankful for, as I now have the words to represent how I think. I wonder if you can't think something unless you can say it?

I was consumed with the prospect of this type of life for the rest of the day in our little learning room, and although I constantly looked aloof and detached, no one batted an eyelid at how I behaved. After the man on the three-dimensional screen finished talking about how everything was made, we dropped another level, where we learned something different. After this session we ate and then resumed classes again. As we entered the second part of the day, I began to notice that some of the men in the class, though they looked quite similar to me, were a bit older than me. Shortly after this thought, we dropped another level, where we were to be let loose in a massive expanse peppered with workbenches. Maybe this mightn't be so bad after all.

As the day drew to a close, we went back to our seating, and we rose to the top room where all of it had started. Everyone stood there as earlier that morning, and on we went, out the door, where there was a lady waiting to enter figures into the pad on the front of our clothes. I couldn't wait to get back to where I had come from this morning. I was so tired. Upon someone entering the figures on to the keypad on my chest, we were back on the magnetic runway. This time I felt a lot more comfortable and took the time to look at the sky and set my sights on the glass ceiling again. How very strange; no wonder there wasn't a speck of greenery in sight. It was all being grown somewhere else. As we travelled along our merry way, I began to question if in fact I was going back in the direction that I had come from that morning. Sure, everywhere looked the exact same, but we seemed to be taking longer. Suddenly, I noticed some of the men that were in the same room as me were exiting the travel path up ahead and going into another little mushroom house. Upon arrival, we all did as before: stand around in a circle and wait. I was hoping at this point a large plate of food would rise up from the center of the room. Perhaps if I wished hard enough, something would happen. Then, as before, we began to go in a downward direction. Soon the movement stopped, and we found ourselves at a load of workbenches again. I thought, *Yeah, okay, this might have been okay earlier on in the day, but I have had enough of this for one day.*

Soon a man appeared and explained our workload for the evening. I couldn't believe it. This was great! After a long day of extreme weirdness, it seemed like I had to spend my evening in another sweaty, odd-looking room. I then remembered that this is exactly the way it appeared on the timetable from earlier. I had just forgotten. Or maybe I just thought it wasn't possible they could ask any more for us! Well I was wrong. We were now working. Silently angry, but on the surface diligently working away at my station to instructions on the table beside me, I looked around the room. Largely it was as I expected, rows of the same work benches all neatly packed together. But what I wasn't expecting was another one of these posters on the wall to the side of me. Like our washroom earlier, it was very dimly lit, but I could read some of what it said:

"You are in an area with people of the exact same competency as you in your selected field. If you sustain or develop further into your competency, you remain; however, if you fail to meet the standard, you are moved."

This made sense, but what do they do, come down here and push you onto that magnetic strip and set you on your way? Because if so, I am thinking right now, that may not be such a bad thing. Directly below there was another piece of writing that included:

"The system appreciates your work. The system is your family. You are working with brothers." I didn't know whether this meant people didn't have families, or if they were just trying to suggest a good work environment. I guess I'd find out.

Disconnecting a little from where I was, my mind raced again. I thought that from what I had seen so far that it was obvious that there really was no sense of family here. Maybe women were chosen to breed and lived in a certain place for this exercise; maybe this was their role in society. The children were then taken and raised by other women selected for this application until they were ready for assessment and work. Maybe that's why everyone around me was so emotionally disabled; they'd never had love. Oddly, sometimes it is only from love that one can feel anger, ambition, stubbornness... Love is such a positive emotion, but it can sometimes be the root of all other emotions, both positive and negative.

Suddenly a siren went off, which I made me so happy. I was tired, and I think all of this silence and work was making me crazy! My mind was functioning like a philosopher half the time and a little girl for the rest. Quickly we all assembled, and the magic elevator rose to its original position. Thankfully, this time we were returning to our lodgings. What was weird was that as we all had the buttons pressed on our pads so we could get out and travel home, a good lot of other people seemed to be going to work. Maybe time meant nothing here. Maybe each house kept its own time and rules, because it could, there wasn't really that much tying us to anyone else's timetable out there.

Shortly after we arrived back that night, we were ushered to where we had breakfast, and we were asked to take our seats. I was tired, fed up, and needless to mention, absolutely starving. It seemed as if we had just put in the longest day in the history of time, busily using up each and every minute of the day to learn, travel, or work. Oh yes, there was no wastage today.

The food, like the place, was boring, but considering how hungry I was, it felt like I was dining on the fruit of the gods. I just hoped there wouldn't be a limit. Four plates of food later, I was lying in my bed, holding my stomach and wishing I hadn't eaten so much of the fruit of the gods! We were all instructed to go to bed immediately after we ate—no TV, no talking, not even a chance to vent the day's frustrations, just straight to bed.

Most of the other guys were already asleep, which was not surprising. All we seemed to do was eat, learn, work, and sleep, just as the timetable suggested this morning. I missed acting like a human. I missed wasting time and having a laugh, but strangely, there was something very satisfying about knowing my place, role, and purpose. I knew what tomorrow would bring, and in a small way, I was looking forward to it. I liked being a part of something, being a part of a team and having a distinct purpose. Although there was the trade-off that you didn't get much input into your purpose, you just did as you were told and tried to make the best of it. As my bloated, worn body lay there pondering the day's events, I heard a noise—no voices, no sudden bangs, just a murmur of little sounds willing me out of bed to further investigate. Whatever was happening was all very well orchestrated. The noise was almost melodic.

Unluckily for them, I was in a strange place, I'd eaten too much, and I couldn't sleep. I was curious. I wondered if it was Bala and Wen. At that exact minute, I got one of those very brief flashes. However, this time all I could see was a black-haired girl shouting and screaming in fear for her life until a man approached her from behind and then dropped her through the floor. I paused temporarily from my immediate investigation and wondered what this wretched vision meant. Upon scanning the extent of what my memory had deposited from the day, I soon conceded to confusion and went about my investigation. As I ventured out of bed and down to the place where we ate, there was not a soul to be found, yet the noise was right outside. Tip-toeing quietly through the large, plain dining hall towards the noise, my curiosity was quickly being tempered by the surmounting fear that seemed to double on my every step.

The room itself was completely dark apart from a small light faintly illuminating the window nearest the quiet noise. Slower and slower I edged towards the window, frantically weighing up if I really wanted to know what was going on that badly. Could this be the dark-haired girl that the man in my vision killed? Or was it just a burglar trying desperately to breach our little fortress? It was times like these when I wished my imagination was calm and rational instead of being colorful and grandiose, concocting the most outlandish explanation possible. With this state of mind, I was jumping to all sorts of horrible conclusions, each with its very own special piece of fear. Without my anxious imagination, I would probably be a picture of composure with no such terrifying projections clouding my judgement. *Please, imagination, calm down.*

When I reached the window, my heart was beating at about a thousand beats per minute. I felt my heart had stopped beating for a second, leaving the blood now to race through my body as a result of the pulsing fear, as opposed to the mechanics of my heart. As I leant towards the window to unveil what dark mystery lay at the other side of the glass, I noticed a reflection in the glass. It seemed as a consequence of the dim light touching upon the outside of the house, the glass was taking on a partial mirror-like quality from the inside. I then noticed that it wasn't just reflecting my image, but an image of something positioned right behind me.

To its credit, my imagination quickly tried to arrest my fear by suggesting that it may be just a chair or an object

I hadn't noticed; however, these explanations were soon undone. The reflection I could see behind me was moving. Now, as chairs do not move, nor do other inanimate objects, my imagination soon opted out, and absolute fear consumed my entire body once more. Incidentally, I had also just realized that the noise outside had stopped. What was coming? As it moved closer, I saw that it was a person. Creeping slowly from the darkness up behind me, I could see the outline of a person approach. I was too frightened to turn around. I felt a sick breathlessness overcome my body; I was paralyzed with fear. Then, very slowly, an arm reached out, and a hand was placed on my shoulder. The noise from outside suddenly started again, however, this time roaring and growling a little more aggressively. I turned around. The voice behind the hand then said, "You should be in bed." It was one of those women who served us food. Oh, what a relief; like a pilot after a successful, dodgy landing, my heart rate soon returned to that of a normal person.

"I'm sorry, I wanted to get a drink of water," I explained.

"Absolutely, let me fetch you one," she replied.

"I thought you were checking what was outside, because I was," she said, pouring water.

"No, I was just looking for some water," I said again, hoping not to raise suspicion. The lady nodded her head from side to side.

"The replenishers are approximately ten minutes late, which is terrible. When they didn't arrive on time I came straight down and walked around to make sure everything was okay.

"These large containers have to be delivered to each residence at a certain time. We have a timetable. They bring every residence the exact same food and exact same clothes. These containers cannot travel on the magnetic runways during the busier times of the day, so they travel at this time when fewer people are travelling. When they arrive, the container they deliver sinks slowly into a lower room beneath the surface, where we can access them. Meanwhile another container rises up to the surface with our waste and washing from the month before. So if they do not arrive on schedule, it throws me off, and it could throw us off," she said, very upset by this guy's poor time keeping. I think he was going to get in trouble. As she handed me the glass of water and opened the window to look outside, I realized that she had a name tag that I hadn't noticed earlier. It said "Cast Nine."

"Don't worry, I will deal with this Cast Five," she said to me.

"Thank you for the water, good night Cast Nine," I said reluctantly.

"Goodnight Cast Five," she replied slipping off in to the darkness once more.

That was a lot of information. This is probably how they manage to ensure everyone is equal, how they make sure everyone gets the exact same. It's also probably what "replenish" meant on the timetable from the bathroom earlier this morning. Though people still seem to do different jobs, I wasn't convinced of this equality just yet.

Maybe their equality was all about having the system find what you are good at, use your skill to the advantage of the system, and then give you the exact same as everyone else. And what's all this about Cast Five and Cast Nine? Was the whole residence called Cast One, Cast Two, Cast Three…? It certainly seemed so, and if so, how boring! For an extremely developed, organized world, they made the interesting parts of life so plain.

Ironically, though everyone continued learning and developing everyday, they made sure you didn't learn enough to develop an identity or uniqueness; if you did, you would become more than just a standard component, and you would be harder to use. Yes, I had to give them credit; there was something very clever about their society. It was a complex system of moving parts operated by a collection of blank, standard, replaceable components. I was learning to accept that my existence was to be a standard, replaceable part. I didn't feel like a person, but I felt equal.

Chapter 8

The following day, I awoke with the same shriek of the same siren from the day before. This time the day began exactly as the day before—wash, exercise, and food. Again, as we soon finished our food, there was the sound of another alarm, and before we knew it, we were back at the same building as the day before. Once I have done something already, I am minus the excitement that helps me get through the unknown, though in the comfort that nothing horrible is about it happen.

As we did yesterday, we gathered into a circle and began to sink into the ground. The same slightly amusing man then appeared on the walls and began to preach to us on the different types of electronic signals we could send and receive. This was an area I'd always found quite alien; however, it was suddenly making a great deal of sense. It was like listening to a different language that I had always known how to speak. So, while I enjoyed my newfound fluency, I sat there and listened intently. What was different from the day before was that I kept feeling a sort of prickly feeling on my backside and legs, but I dismissively put the feeling to the back of my mind and focused on all this new information.

Later that afternoon we were once again set loose in a workshop, where we were given a task and asked to complete it in a certain timeframe. As before I followed the instructions on my bench, except this time, there were video cameras on the walls focusing in on me from all over the room and red, laser-like lights shining on me for most of the duration. The lights certainly were not there the last time, and the cameras—well, I wasn't sure where they were pointing during my last task. I just never thought they were on me. When the exercise was complete, a siren rang, and as before, I made my way to the circle. Unfortunately this time, quite abruptly, I was stopped.

Two metal claws came flying down from the ceiling and grabbed both of my arms. Although I was powerless to do anything, I still struggled fiercely, having about as much impact on the metal arms as a mosquito does on a truck. I was terrified, flinching from the grip of the arms like a freshly caught salmon in a net until I felt the prick of a needle slowly pierce my arm and send me quickly off to sleep. This was getting ridiculous. These sharp rushes of adrenaline would simply have to stop, or I may have a heart attack at a very young age.

When I woke I found myself in a bright room. There were seven large, black pillars in front of me, each marked with a yellow symbol in the center. Although I could not move freely enough to step forward, I could tell that there was a person on either side of me in a similar comatose state. They both seemed my age and were also just slowly coming around.

"Roto Ten," said a robotic voice that oddly seemed to be coming from all around us. The guy to my left shook and looked to attention.

"You have been two months in Roto residence, and you have been deemed unsuitable; you shall be re-assigned," the voice said.

The boy looked shaken yet motionless, and as quickly as he received his verdict, he was he sucked up towards the ceiling and into a thick, white cloud.

"Cast Five...," the voice said.

Ahhhh, I was regretting the fact that I had discovered my name from the day before. Dreading the possibility of being sucked into the heavens, I stood as strongly as I could manage and looked to attention. What did they inject us with? That was powerful stuff.

"We have been monitoring your behaviour in the residence of Cast, and your skills and competency seem to match this sector. For now, you shall remain with Cast."

Looking forward to the only sight visible—the pillars—I gave a brief sigh until, like my Roto colleague, I flew up into the air and found myself on a magnetic runway back to my house. I would have hoped that by passing their test I wouldn't have to be whisked up into the air like that; perhaps I could get issued with a more elegant exit from their forum. That can be just a little feedback for them if I ever end up back there again.

So it seemed that I was not at this house by sheer coincidence; the powers that control the place had been trialling me in this area and measuring my suitability—or the Viscent's body that I was occupying. If I was successful, I would stay; if unsuccessful, they would put me somewhere different that would better match my competency and, more importantly for them, somewhere I would be of better use to the system. I found it odd, I found it sad, yet it made perfect sense.

As nightfall came, we made our way to our beds. I found that the longer I spent in this place, the more questions I had. What did these pillars represent? Who was the dark-haired lady that I saw drop to her death? Where were Bala and Wen? I was homesick and beginning to despair that I would be trapped in this hellish place forever. As I lay there tenderly gripping my pillow, I thought of my family. Did one get to have a family life in this place? It seemed not. I yearned for people that would make me feel like a person again, not just a component that provided a function on a day-to-day basis.

I wanted to feel vulnerable and comforted. I wanted to feel that people cared for me. The odd thing was, in a place that had people monitoring my career, feeding me, and sharing my living space, I had never felt so lonely. It goes to prove that a little attention with a lot of feeling is much better than a lot of attention with little feeling. It seemed that from the moment you showed any sign of free thought, they would separate you from anything resembling comfort and continue to test you. They may not know you or want you, but they would use you. What

I was used to was the reverse. I may not have liked the place or environment I was born into, but I would use it for my gain. I was accustomed to using my environment to get what I wanted from it. I would harm it, abuse it, pollute it, yet never really show any remorse for it. It wasn't so much fun when the boot was on the other foot.

The next morning, like any other, was initiated by the siren, some healthy exercise, food, and then out the door for another day of monitored learning. I wasn't sure if there was anything special about remaining as "Cast Five," but I certainly didn't want them to rename me. It seemed like keeping my name was about the only control I could exert on my existence in this world.

As we quickly approached our destination—our little, concrete, multi-level, underground learning hub—something very startling occurred. The magnetic conveyor runway came to a halt, leaving us all standing there like a series of badly spaced dominos. This had not happened over the previous couple of mornings. I was somewhat panicked in respect to what was about to happen. A voice then hit the airwaves and said:

"Defiance—Defiance—Code five four five four—Subject continually acting against designation. Defiance—Defiance."

This chant continued to harass the silence as we all just stood there waiting for something to happen. I wasn't sure what we were waiting for, and I was quite perturbed that everyone else was so calm. Honestly, if this defiance was in reference to me, I was going to be angry. I was getting very sick of all these rules and regulations.

Then something truly spectacular started to occur. Very slowly, all of the buildings within our colossal, glass enclosure as far as the eye could see began to slowly sink. While this was happening, parts of the glass hemisphere began to blacken. It seemed to blacken in stripes. The lowest circumference to the ground level went black, the next level up clear, the next level up black. It was as if night and day were controlled for us. Then, at the highest point of our glass hemisphere, a circle of light began to form and focus a more intense beam of light on the surface of the ground directly below. I caught up with the visual clue drawing my eye-line to this magnificent beam of light, I realized that the focus was on a piece of earth that was slowly beginning to rise up from the surface. It was about the size of half a tennis court, with its sides rounded so not to impair anyone's view of the platform as they looked up into the air. It rose until everyone from all around could see the top of this newly born platform. It was about as high as a four-story building, and with this light beaming down on top of it, the platform ensured that whatever was about to happen would be in full sight for all to see.

Once all of the changes were completed, we were left with a very chilling environment. All of the buildings that were once the primary occupiers of the area were gone... vanished and replaced with a bare ground covered with thousands of people, complete with a striped lighting shining down on everyone through the glass. And then there was the center piece—this bright light beaming down from the center of this enclosure onto an empty, waiting stage. This was now the only standing structure in our little world.

Suddenly the constant hark of "Defiance—Defiance..." stopped and the faint cry of a lady's scream was heard struggling from a distance. I immediately felt terrified for this woman. This did not seem like a very positive gathering. I noticed that some people were now beginning to move in the direction of this mysterious stage. Now, although this whole event could have meant the end of all human kind, like the sheep I had become, I followed on and moved closer to the stage. As I approached, I was scanning furiously to see if I could identify the cry from earlier. I put my left hand to my left eye as before in the world with out money and kept scanning but saw nothing. I couldn't see Bala or Wen anywhere.

As people collected and stared at the platform, there was a little chatter going on. I found this very strange, so whatever was about to happen must have been big because for as far as I could see, people just did not chatter around here. At that moment the siren sounded once more, followed by:

"We find the accused under code five four five four guilty of non-conformance in a prescribed area. The penalty for this crime is death."

As the announcement uttered these fatal words, a dark-haired lady appeared at the top of the platform. My heart stopped beating when I saw this girl. She looked so much like my sister Lucy it was shocking. She was dressed in a long, white gown, hands tied behind her back, and bands around her legs. Her hair was tossed and she had the look of a scared, angry, desperate girl. I felt so sorry for her. What was weird was that, although we were in a different world, it seemed as though my sister had an identical twin in this place, the only difference being the color of her hair and she must have been older than my sister. I wonder what this girl's real name was. Maybe everybody has a counterpart in every world or universe out there. Then it struck me that this girl could be Wen. If it was I would have to do something fast, so quickly I raised my hand to my head, but nothing. The sacred, distraught girl who looked like Lucy was not Wen. I was relieved, and I felt guilt for feeling relieved. This poor girl was in trouble.

"The accused shall get to speak one last time—please listen," the voice said coldly.

The girl had a severely bitten gag removed from her mouth. She was breathless from all the panic, but she regained her composure, stood upright, and prepared to address the silent audience.

"People—Please, this is not the way..." She tried to plead to the crowd.

"Defiance—Defiance." The girl was again forcefully gagged and locked into a transparent glass box. As she stood there struggling, her once desperate gestures now turned to shear panic, going from side to side in the glass box, looking pitifully upon anyone who would make eye contact.

"Please begin with the disposal," the voice said. And with this command, another striking sight emerged at the top of the platform. A man in a long, black, hooded cape rose from behind her and went over to the side of the glass box where there was a lever. The girl pressed herself to the glass, pleading with this new, mysterious figure not to do what he or she had been ordered. The dark figure turned to face the crowd, bowed, and proceeded to fully remove his hood. On the removal of his hood, the large man stood there. He looked as big as a prize bull and just as rough. As he looked out onto the crowd, scanning the area, the animal-sized man put his left hand to the left side of his eye. *No, no,* I thought. *It can't be.* Quickly I put my hand to my left eye, and sure enough, the man on the top of the platform was either Bala or Wen, the big brute of a guy, had the silver glimmer under his left eye. He was a Viscent.

As the angry-looking beast looked over in my direction, the big man raised his right hand to fix his hood, but in doing so raised three fingers in my direction. It was Bala, and he could see me. I knew it was Bala, that dumb three finger thing was actually becoming useful. Then as Bala looked out to the right of me, he raised his right hand again with three fingers, again pretending to position his hood. I looked in the direction of where he was looking, and I saw a girl, with her hand up by the left side of her eye. *I see you, Wen.* Overjoyed, I slowly made my way over to the girl who I thought was Wen. Thrilled on the inside but silent on the outside, I realized that Bala seemed to be the executioner. This took considerably from my happiness. How could Bala knowingly take the life of another person?

Bala stepped up to the lever that controlled the girl's destiny and looked at her. He took a minute to focus on his responsibility and then pulled the treacherous lever. The girl fell uncontrollably through the floor, roaring and wailing until her cries were no longer heard.

"Wen, it's me," I said softly. The girl turned towards me with her hand up to her left eye. There were tears in her eyes. She had been crying.

"Zach, it's good to see you," she said.

"Are you okay," I asked quietly, just below the soft chatter volume everybody else seemed to be talking at.

"That was a girl from our residence; her name was Birth Three. Our residence is responsible for bearing the next generation of this hemisphere's population. Every two years, you become impregnated. You then have the baby and give away your young to another residence to be raised, taught, and tested. Birth Three was really unhappy, so she started to miss classes and then tried to run away. It was then she was told she would be dealt with," Wen said, again looking up at the platform.

"The disposal is now complete. Please find the nearest magnetic strip and it will take you to your destination," the voice said, as if nothing had occurred.

As I was still absorbing the magnitude of what had just happened, Bala terminating one of Wen's residents. I turned to Wen and said, "We must stop this. We must..."
"We can't, Zach," Wen replied somberly.

I stood there, staring into space, haunted by the memories of what had just happened and thinking hard on what we could do.

"Yes, we can. This place relies on the dictation of that infernal audio system. If I could somehow block it, would you be able to tell the people that they have a choice in life and that things do not have to be this way?" I asked in great hope.

"Well...yes...but who will listen to me?" Wen replied.

I sighed sympathetically and said, "They will have to if you are up on that stage."

"That stage...no...no...if you think..."

"Look, if I thought there was another way..." I said, almost tearing up.

"Do you know what you're asking me to do, Zach?" Wen said angrily.

"Wen, you know Bala won't pull that lever, he just won't..." I replied.

"Oh, shut up. Shut it, Zach...You have put me in a really awkward position here..." Wen said as she stood there trying to determine the right thing to do.

Wen's manner was now straying from anxious to childish and back to angry. Though considering the circumstances, I thought she was processing the proposition quite well.

"Wen, look at me. This is our only way to make a difference. Trust me, in two days, you need to defy the confines of your role. They will then choose to 'deal' with you. When you are up there, I will jam the signals and make sure they cannot order you to your death..." I said confidently.

"Oh, very good, it sounds great when you put it like that, Zach," Wen said sarcastically.

"We have to try, Wen. We just have to." I said.

Wen looked away for a second. The once elevated platform was sinking into the ground again. The buildings were rising up to their original uniform height, and the place was once again to be filled with light. What a completely unfitting aftermath for an execution of such cold proportions.

Wen just stood there staring into space as the last of the little clusters of people who were talking were beginning to break up.

"Yesterday I had a vision that placed me on top of that stage. I didn't know how or why, but I knew you would have a part to play in my getting there," Wen said with a tired, strained look on her face. "I trust you, Zach. I only hope you are as confident in yourself as I am in you." She looked at me intensely. "Two days, Zach. Come up with a way to jam the signals, and I will speak to the people." She turned and marched off into the distance. Although this was exactly what I wanted from her when I started the conversation, now that Wen had agreed so passionately, I questioned whether I had even thought it through. To be honest, a lot of what I said after I saw that girl plunge to her demise was just an angry rant. Maybe I shouldn't have been so forceful with Wen. Unfortunately, it was too late for considering the options; there was now a plan in place, and I had approximately two days to save Wen and introduce a bit of humanity into this dead world. The clock was ticking.

Chapter 9

The following day I resumed my daily routine as normal. However, little did my roommates know, today was different; today I was trembling at the prospect of not being able to produce the goods that Wen would depend on. Thankfully, as I found out again later that day, all of the electronics stuff was really suiting me. It was as if I had been secretly studying it for years, and it was only now that I was choosing to use my special gift. I was enjoying the application of my skills. I was enjoying being good at what I did. Unfortunately for the girl yesterday, she didn't seem to derive the same joy from what she did. I was fortunate; luckily, my abilities matched up with what I wanted and with the skills of the Viscent's body I had taken over. It must be hard when what you are best at does not match what you want to do. Do you try to do your best at what you enjoy doing or do you enjoy the success of doing something you don't like doing but something you excel at?

As I worked away that day with my assigned exercise and my secret, special project, I had a good feeling that what I was trying to achieve might work. Granted, I would be making a ridiculous amount of assumptions in the creation of my little device, but what else could I do? I'm sure Wen would want to hear something a little stronger than, "making a ridiculous amount of assumptions," but, amidst my ranting fury yesterday, this is as good as I could do. As Wen quite rightly pointed out, hopefully, I am as competent in my ability as I suggested, and I am not confusing my confidence with my arrogance. Because up until a few days ago I didn't even have confidence, never mind arrogance!

As another day passed by, we slept and rose to deliver another day. Every day I was beginning to feel like an impostor. Here they all were politely feasting on the same food around the same breakfast table, duty bound to their nominated task, while I sat there secretly hatching a plan to free them from the oppressive monotony. Then all of a sudden I panicked. What if they don't want to be set free? Maybe they like this. I put my spoon down and looked around the table. The last thing I wanted to do was make things bad for people. I could only hope what I was doing was right. At this point, I wasn't so sure myself. I had lost my appetite.

As the siren rang to signal the end of another breakfast, we rose, prepared for the day, and set off on our magical runway. At this stage I expected Wen was probably already acting out, so I knew I only had a couple of hours to put the finishing touches on my prototype. I wondered if Bala had his vision. I wondered if he knew what was about to happen. I wondered if he would dispose of Wen.

When our stint in the workshop came around, I dived straight into my secret project in an effort to quickly complete the final part of my little gadget. Thankfully the cameras and lasers were not on me now. They had been focused on other guys for the last two days, which allowed me just enough freedom to construct something on the side of what we were there to build. Then, before I had anticipated, the alarm sounded. *Oohhh for God's sake, Wen, you could have at least given me a few more hours.* Upon the sound, we were all ushered to the surface. I grabbed the final version of my first attempt and made my way outside. God, I hoped that this would work.

As before, when I arrived outside, all of the buildings began retracting into the surface. A towering platform began to rise up, and an intense light began to shine down on the elevated area. Very slowly, parts of the glass dome began to get shaded out as before, and it wasn't long until all was completed and thousands of people stood on the bare, unruffled surface, staring at the illuminated platform. Once more the scene had been set.

I fixed my gaze at the top of the platform. As before, a woman was being dragged, screaming. It was Wen. She looked terrified, yet still had that glint of determination in her eyes suggesting she wasn't quite beaten yet. She was forcefully pushed into the glass box when a voice announced, "The accused shall get to speak one last time—please listen."

Wen found me in the crowd and focused on my position. They say the eyes can speak in ways our words will never master... how true. Wen looked at me with intense vulnerability and anger, pleading with me not to let her die without even uttering a word. The gag was then removed from her mouth to speak this one last time. Wen looked out at the masses, picked a point in the distance and began speaking as if she were talking to herself.

"I am not a murderer or a liar or even a cheat. I have a warm heart, a caring nature, and my only wish is that people are happy. If you—"

"Defiance—Defiance..." the voice said, interrupting her speech. A large figure rushed to Wen and reclosed the door to the lethal glass box. Wen did not struggle. She did not fight. She just stood there, continuing to look into the distance; she looked lifeless.

"As a consequence of your remarks, your disposal will now start. Please begin." I glanced down at the little gizmo I had put into my pocket and stared at it as if the more I hoped it would work the more likely everything would be okay. I bloody well hoped so. As I began inputting a program into my creation, the tall, dark figure appeared. My glance at the top of the elevation was prolonged when I noticed that it wasn't Bala. My blood ran cold and a bead of sweat quickly formed on my brow. Wen was going to die, and if there weren't going to be announcements before the assassination, I would not be able to affect the proceeding. This looked bad. Should I shout? If I shouted, then would we both die? I was panicking, and this extreme sense of urgency was not helping my frame of mind. Not knowing what to do, I continued to work on my gizmo in the blind hope that it might work.

Slowly, the man in the black hood approached the glass box. He stopped for a minute and looked straight at Wen. I was too late. Wen was a goner...We had failed. As the man placed his hand on the lever, another man in a black cloak appeared. This was strange; this hadn't happened the last time. Wen looked at both of the black-hooded men when *bang*, the black-hooded man that had just come on stage punched the executioner, knocking him to the ground.

The crowd gasped as the man took off his hood...it was Bala. Although I was eighty-five percent consumed with panic and anxiety, at this point, fifteen percent of me was filled with deep joy. Bala had done it! He had saved Wen...for now. The next step was up to me. I quickly went back to my device, keyed in the last digits, and hoped for the best. Right at this time, the voice boomed "Defiance—Defi—" Good God, my prototype was working! The voice had stopped. I had managed to block the signals!

Bala quickly opened the door to Wen's enclosure and took off her gag. Initially they hugged. Even from the distance I could see the warmth and longing both had for human touch and care. I ran to the foot of the platform and scaled the ladder at the back to be with my friends.

Meanwhile, Wen turned out to the crowd again, smiled, and said, "As I was saying earlier, everyone here today is an individual; we all like and dislike different things. What is important is that we have equality and we respect one another; however, this should not be achieved at the cost of our freedom and character. If there is one shred of doubt today that you are doing the wrong job, or that you can't be yourself, speak now. They cannot kill us all. The powers that control us need us to be weak. They need us to be dutiful and obedient, irrespective of their requests. The fact is, they need us to be weak in order for them to be in power. They need us to require control in order for them to have control. Well, it doesn't have to be this way. We can stand together now and do what we know is right. If we show our own desires, strength, and character, we can be the ones that take control. Do not be afraid. I understand this oppression is all you have ever known, but believe me, now is your chance to have a say in your own life. You need to ask if it is better to risk death and strive for victory in this one chance we have to unite today, or if it's better to risk feeling dead for the rest of your lives. The probability of long, slow death and never really living is much worse than whatever would happen to you now if you speak up. *Now* is the time for the strong to speak... this is our time!" Wen said, waving her fist.

The crowd was silent, but heads were turning as if Wen's words had stirred some sort of sleeping desire in each and every one of them. A gentle mumble soon replaced the silence. It seemed, for the first time ever, they began to imagine a different type of existence. As the discussions continued and grew in volume, I looked at Wen and Bala smiling at the impact of our little exercise. However, our joy was short lived as the gentle mumble was drowned out by a creaking noise.

Soon after the noise, seven beams of light came from above, all around the central reservation where Wen, Bala, and I were standing. This quickly wiped the smile off my face. We had no other plan in place to deal with anything else. We were now completely at the mercy of whatever was about to happen. Each beam of light was like a spotlight illuminating seven pieces of ground around Wen. Suddenly the creaking stopped. The silence had returned, suffocating any sort of uprising that appeared to be forming from a few moments ago.

Then, very oddly, what seemed to be the same black pillars I saw when I was assessed came down from the sky in a very controlled manner. Once all had landed, the pillars began to move. *Strange,* I thought to myself, *though nothing stranger than a lot of other things here.* A hand emerged from each pillar and pulled back a hood. When the hoods came back, I could see that my seven black "pillars" were seven middle-aged, strong-looking women with long, white hair. From the elegant, stark contrast between their coal-black cloaks and snow-white hair, I wasn't sure if I was excited, afraid, or slightly attracted to the older ladies. One of the ladies turned in my direction; she looked at me with her clear, blue, piercing eyes and said, "You shall be punished for today."

"What? I didn't... I didn't do anything," I whimpered.

"You blocked our air waves. You made us powerless. We are the keepers of this land, and it is imperative that we maintain equality at all times," the lady said.

The lady then turned to Wen. "You shall be punished for today," she said.

"I did nothing wrong," Wen said strongly, making my response look as wimpish as it was.

"You ignited a flame, a desire amongst the people that I am about to extinguish," the lady said.

Wen tried to reply, "But I thought that—"

"*You shall be punished*," she interrupted.

Finally, she looked across at Bala.

"You shall also be punished. You are an embarrassment to your cause."

Bala said nothing.

"You make a mockery of our equality, and you shall pay," she said, walking closer to Bala.

Bala, still looking at where he was standing, began toe-tapping the ground, and as the lady began to turn to me once more, Bala said, "Why do you need power if we are all equal?"

She scowled at him.

"Why do we have to be so strictly equal?" he said. "Why have your people lost whatever life they ever had?" he asked calmly. "Why are you doing this?" he said, finishing his requests.

The cold, old lady, clearly ruffled by the comments, frantically searched her person until a gun was located. She took the gun out, aimed it at Bala, and said, "You are a disgrace."

The other ladies began to walk over to the lady with the gun. There was a dead still in the air as her stiffly extended arm pointed right at Bala's face. She cocked the trigger, and a loud click echoed across the people. Bala looked back in the direction of Wen and me. He wasn't frightened; he wasn't upset. In fact, in the midst of this impending threat on his life, he looked at me and smiled. He then found Wen and winked, as if these actions would constitute his final words. He then looked squarely back at the woman, eyeing her as she did Bala, almost inviting her to pull the trigger. What bravery.

As the other ladies approached, the black swarm closed in on their gun-happy friend like bees to honey and stood around her. At this point I thought they were all going to pull a gun and exterminate Bala. Then there was a loud cry. It was Wen. "Hey!" Everyone looked at Wen. "Well, if you are going to kill him, then you better kill me too. There is far too little hope or opportunity in this place to even begin to know what it is like to be alive." She went over by Bala's side, held his hand, and stood firm. She was such a little terrier.

As moved as I was by this brave exercise, I feared the brave, mad, little terrier had inadvertently forced me to take action. So far being friends with Bala and Wen was forcing me to be bigger than I was, and although I think I would have eventually ended up doing the right thing, stepping up and being as brave as they need me to be, did we have to do things so dramatically all of the time? So, clearing the girlish whimper from my throat, I said, "Yeah, if you are going to get rid of these guys, then you may as well get rid of me too." When I made my way towards Wen and Bala, all eyes were on me, watching me closely as I too situated myself in front of Bala. It seemed that the bravery and selflessness Bala and Wen demonstrated was contagious.

Once in front of Bala, I turned and gave him a manly slap on the back and then looked to my side and, getting eye contact with Wen, winked at her as if I knew all was going to be okay. In return Wen grabbed my hand, and Bala slapped me on the back. "We were wondering where you were," he said, shaking my shoulder as Wen also smiled squeezing tightly on my hand. However, as quickly as the moment arose, we wiped the smiles from our faces and proceeded to look forward once more to the gun that was now only a foot away from all of our faces. God, I felt like an impostor. It felt like Wen and Bala probably had more courage in their baby toes than I possessed in my entire body. Anytime I ever tried to do something half-brave, I was terrified. I was lucky. How many people get to stand side by side with their heroes? They showed me what being a hero is, doing what is right no matter how terrified it makes you feel.

The lady walked a little closer, and cocking her head to one side, kept looking at Bala as if he was still the number-one enemy. Her long, white, straight hair went from one side of her back to the other. I could now confirm that it was a lot more terrifying over here than it was where I had been standing. The lady stopped and said, "Why are you not pleading for your lives? Why are you not terrified?"

Bala, in an almost patronizing way, looked across at me and Wen as we looked at him and said, "When you have experienced real friendship, a real sense of belonging with other people, you don't need a role to define you. You can be safe in the knowledge that people value you for who you are. When you appreciate this, everything else seems manageable... even death." He smirked again as if to egg her on, inviting her to do her worst. I was glad the lady asked Bala. If she'd asked me, I probably would have started crying.

The lady cocked her head to the other side, thinking deeply of Bala's last comments. A voice from the crowd then said, "I want that." Then another voice said, "I want to feel that somebody cares." And then another and then another until there was a gunshot. The crowd once again fell silent. I looked quickly to see if she had shot Bala. Thankfully she had only shot into the air to get attention.

As the trail of smoke cleared from her gun, the other ladies huddled around, whispering to each other. After a couple of minutes, the head angry lady emerged and said, "Difference has caused so much fighting and bloodshed. Difference has caused so much separation and segregation. Having a community full of different individuals scares us." She lowered her gun and looked at the faces of the other ladies. "We have only ever wanted this to be a safe place. We never meant any harm to anybody by the world we tried to create. We just wanted it to be the same for everyone. What we forgot was that even though we did not split you into different societies, job levels or classes, we still split you up. I suppose anytime you have a collection of people in one area, they are going to want split into groups. Maybe we forgot our goals along the way. We're sorry," she said on behalf of the women. "And we promise to make this place less restrictive. We promise to listen a little more than we have done." The woman then turned to us and said, "Thank you, thank you for reminding us of what we set out to achieve. It seems as if we had forgotten the objective by trying to achieve it."

I looked across at Wen and Bala. Unfortunately, my emotions were soon to overtake my manliness. I grabbed them and held them tightly. I closed my eyes. It was the kind of moment I never wanted to end. Wen was weeping a little, while Bala, though visibly relieved, seemed a stronger person from the day's events. I thought about the girl that had died a couple of days before, the girl that looked like Lucy. I wished she could be here to enjoy this wonderful moment.

I turned to the lady and said, "When you … dispose of the people, where do you bury the bodies?"

She looked at me grimly and said, "Follow me." A couple of minutes later, we arrived at a doorway into what appeared to be a doorway into the ground. It was like a grave with a front entrance. I looked at it sadly.

"Is that where she is, the girl from a couple of days ago?" I asked, thinking of the horrible act of her removal from this world.

Lowering herself down on one knee, she began to pry the door open. I was very glad the lady had taken the time to show me the girl's resting place; however, opening the door to a dead person's grave was crossing the line from being helpful to a little weird. As I leant forward to stop her in all her strangeness, the door swung wide open. It was awful … though not as I had expected. The girl lay there completely still, completely unblemished, just as I remembered her on that horrible day.

The lady rose again. "Let me tell you a secret. We never actually dispose of anyone. We merely suspend them." I smiled as the once embodiment of evil said, "She is going to be okay." It was then explained that after a few weeks of a person being kept in this suspended state, they would awaken them. After the reawakening, they would categorize the person again in the hope that the time spent unconscious would dilute their personal desires. While I was shocked at this sort of inhumane process, it was a lot better than actually killing them. I was so happy, so uncontrollably happy that the girl was going to be okay.

"Maybe one day you can visit her?" the lady suggested.

"But that would mean us being together and mixing," I said.

"Yes, Cast Five, there are going to have to be some big changes around here, big changes."

She put her hand on my shoulder, and like a mother and son, we walked slowly as she explained her future plans for the colony. I smiled to myself until that dreaded pain in my head set in...it quickly became worse and worse until...

Chapter 10

When I woke, I felt a cold, wet feeling from my knees downward. Worse again, when I tried to move my legs, they were completely stuck to the ground. It was like there was some sort of giant magnet pinning me to the ground. On closer inspection I could see that I was standing in a small pool of water. It was only the size of a small pond, but deep enough to come up to my knees. Anxious and alarmed, I looked around for more information regarding my predicament. In contrast to the clear, blue water I was standing in, there was a carpet of hot, yellow desert sand surrounding me. To my immediate relief, further on in front of me on my left was Wen. Like me, she too was in a pool of water up to her thighs, though did not seem completely conscious yet. Up ahead on my right, I spotted Bala. He hadn't seen me, though like me, he too was becoming very vexed upon discovering that he was stuck to the ground.

"Bala... Bala... you okay?" I asked.

"Yeah ... but this water is freezing," he replied.

I laughed as a dark shadow passed over our bright yellow sand. I had already survived one drama today. Wasn't that enough? Eventually, the mysterious shadow ceased moving and steadied itself to a finite stop. It had positioned itself right in the center of Bala, Wen, and me, casting a shadow of a large disk onto the yellow sands below. I looked over at Wen briefly, and it appeared that she was waking up. She too was a little miffed at her immobile state but soon conceded to her impairment.

"Bala," a voice called, "and Zach, you have both lived in your selected worlds. You have experienced how a world must operate in order to conform to the one overriding, governing principle that you wished for. As you witnessed, the side effects of these conformities can sometimes be ugly. No care, no community, and perhaps, in some cases, an absence of any obvious happiness." It always seemed quite tense whenever we met with this mysterious voice. There were the orchestrated silences, long, rambling speeches, and the occasional life-altering question. Though, above everything else, what was beginning to frustrate me most was not being able to see who we were talking to. I mean, all I had to focus on was this round shadow on the ground; so much for eye contact!

"You have all done well in identifying how to help these worlds. You have been very successful in your efforts and completed the first two tasks in these first two worlds as a team. I am also pleased to see that your abilities are developing through your experiences," the voice said.

Abilities? I am not seeing the evidence of abilities developing!

"In Bala's world you touched each other and you all got to see parts of the past that helped rectify the present. In Zach's world you did not need to touch, but had your respective visions separately and then had the foresight and trust to act on them. However, you still have a long way to go," the voice warned.

Just as the voice finished this sentence, there was an abrupt drop. The base in the pool I was standing in lowered. The water was now up to my waist. I looked over to Wen and Bala, and they too had their bases drop. Additionally, despite the best efforts of any of us, none of us could move an inch. We were stuck. This concerned me a little. If the base continued to lower, I would drown. Surely this wasn't another test.

"I mentioned earlier that there are Viscents of other worlds; however, I should mention again that not all of them have good intensions."

"What do you mean 'do not have good intensions'?" Wen asked curiously.

"As I have said before, you are the three that have been selected to represent our world. The role of every three from each world is to improve their own world. However, the journey of each three can differ. While some may be sent to different worlds for periods, others spend the rest of their lives in the world of their origin. What is consistent is that everyone strives to make a positive impact. However, there are a collection of others that have not been selected for good. They have been picked by the dark powers to ruin, sabotage, and wreck all that we try to improve. We do not know much about these powers. We never have. All we know is that they are out there. Unfortunately, they do sometimes succeed in undoing the good we have created and, I regret to say, taking the lives of those who try to make these positive changes. Recently, the three chosen ones from the world of the timid were destroyed after an ambush by these destructive forces. In the world of no money, it is suggested that the reason this world took such a negative twist is because an evil Viscent sent the Bronson family to different hospitals and broke their spirits. It is also possible that some of the guys you fought in the world of equality, Zach, were not regular guys. These may have been one or more evil Viscents. There was definitely one if not more of them out to kill you during the exercise sessions. They were out to cause damage to this world by destroying you.

"There is a strong chance you will encounter some of these forces again, and when you do, it is imperative that your powers be more developed so that you will be well equipped to battle them," our Evall warned. I was not that surprised to learn of what Evall had just shared with us, but for Bala and Wen, I could see in their eyes that they had not yet been as exposed to this evil as I had been.

As I stood there waist deep in freezing water, struggling to feel my own legs, I was growing less and less impressed by my new role. I was only thirteen years old. I hadn't even made that many mistakes yet. I wanted to be at least old enough so that when I died, I'd have a couple of regrets! But with blind power comes blind responsibility and blind danger. What else should I expect? I couldn't believe that I had encountered some of these guys already. I wondered in the future if they would gang up on us individually or if someone had been assigned to each one of us to take us down respectively. I was scared by the confirmation of this information, but felt strong with the knowledge that I couldn't pick two better people to be scared with. I was confident nothing would stand in our way.

Just then, the base dropped once more. We were now all standing in water up to our chests and necks. If this happened again, we would die. Suddenly, I wasn't as confident as I had been five minutes ago. Maybe we were about to meet our inevitable doom.

"You simply must continue developing your skills. You may depend on them sooner than you imagine. From the movement of water on your bodies, it is clear that time is running out. This next trip shall be your last and final visit. If you succeed in this place, you will return to your world with the real opportunity to make it a better place," Evall stated.

That sounded good—the first piece of good news all day.

"However, if you fail, it will mean that either your enemies have destroyed you or that you have failed to complete your task, meaning that you will never return to your world again," Evall warned.

That reminder, on the other hand, was not good.

"So please, let us prepare for your final trip. Wen, what kind of world would you like to visit?" Evall asked.

I could see by looking at Wen that she had the answer to that very question ready and waiting.

"Because of all the impersonal places we have been to, because of the rigidity of each society that we have visited, I want a world with no hatred, no evil, just love and care. I want to go to a place where there is nothing but love," Wen said. What a girly request. As I raised my eyes to the heavens, the water suddenly rose a little further. It was now well over our heads. I couldn't breath. I tried to move, but I couldn't. I was going to drown...help...hel—

Chapter 11

I woke to the joyous singing of a little group of very happy-looking people. With both my hands holding my head, I sat up from my lying position and took my place in the nest of this strange group.

"Happy, happy, happy, happy smiles."

"Happy, happy, happy, happy smiles."

What in the name of mercy was going on? It was like waking up in a nursery rhyme! Oh no, now I remember. I was in the world of love. Flipping heck, Wen, this seems like a ridiculous place!

"Hey… hey there, rosy cheeks, you want to sing our song?"

No, I did not want to sing his song and… *Did he just call me rosy checks?* Perhaps I misheard him; yeah, maybe he was saying, "Hey there and welcome, would you like to sing along?" Yes, that's probably what he said. Still a little weird but better than what I first thought he'd said to me.

"Happy, happy, rosy, happy cheeks," the man sang as he strummed his guitar. Son of a gun, I was right the first time. He did say rosy cheeks. This guy was beginning to annoy me. I think he was openly mocking me, sitting there playing his guitar, smiling away at the fact that he thought I had rosy cheeks. In fact, he was staring right at me, singing this stupid song.

"Rosy, rosy, rosy, happy, rosy cheeks."

Just when I thought it couldn't get any worse, the entire group of twelve began chanting this song. They were all smiling and clapping as if my rosy-cheeked face had some sort of majesty about it. Maybe it did?

My experience in the world of love so far was highly offensive. Though admittedly, the song about my face did have a catchy ring to it, and the attention was great. The grinning man with the guitar might have been an idiot, but boy could he get a crowd going.

"Happy, happy, happy, happy smiles."

Phew, as eventful as that was, I was glad the limelight was finally off me.

"Rosy, rosy, rosy, rosy, cheeks."

Maybe not—it seemed the group was now exclusively singing about me and looking at my face. I certainly did not think I had rosy cheeks. I don't care how many are singing the song! As I smiled passively back to the glaring crowd, I went to get to my feet.

"Hey, hey, so what you gonna do today?" the hairy man with guitar asked. As he was the one with the guitar, by him talking to me, the song had stopped, and he had focused all of the attention of the group on my response.

Nice one, you big hairball. With the added pressure of this audience, I paused for a second and thought to myself that I wanted to be careful my response did not trigger another song. I suppose the first thing to do is try to find Wen and Bala, and after that, attempt to figure out how his place works. *Damn it, is everyone still looking at me?*

"Ahh, I'm gonna go for a walk or something," I said plainly.

"Good for you, my friend, good for y-o-u. You get those big, strong legs moving and that red face puffing." Everyone started clapping and cheering at me as if I'd just announced I was pregnant!

"Ahh … by the way, do you think I have rosy cheeks?" I asked, wanting to stamp this out once and for all.

"Yes, you're like turkey at Christmas," he said, laughing, riling up the others and actively encouraging people to laugh at me.

That didn't even make sense. Turkeys are white. Is he comparing me to the face of a turkey when the turkey is being chased? Either way I was offended, I was very *offend*ed, and in trying to remain calm, I said, "Excuse me, but I do not have rosy cheeks, and for the record, I'm not sweating." "Welly, well, well … Yeah, man, look at you. Aren't you a big man, setting us straight." The guitar guy laughed.

"I don't want to come across as negative … I just want to clear up the whole rosy cheek thing. I just don't think it is a nice word or an accurate description in my case," I explained.

"Ah, you're cute," said some other random man.

I paused in shock as I deliberated yet another word that I wasn't comfortable with. "I'm not cute, I'm... I'm just not cute, okay?" I said, stressed a little by the weird additional attention.

"Yeah, you are," he said.

"Ah no, I'm not," I replied.

"Yeah, you are," he said.

"*Aaahh no,* I'm not." *What is this, is he trying to infuriate me?*

"Coo chee choogi coo," some other guy said.

"Oh, for goodness sake," I said wearily. My patience was wearing thin.

Then a girl stood to her feet and looked at the crowd. She began clapping slowly, chanting, "Cutie, cutie, cutie..." And it wasn't long before the whole group was at it. This was not the terrific start to my day I had imagined. Conceding to the crowd's insatiable appetite for my humiliation, I gave a frustrated smile and raised my hand as I walked out of the circle of shame. To their credit, I did get an enthusiastic cheer as I marched my cute, rosy face out of there. As soon as all these challenges were over, I was going to have serious look in the mirror; maybe I do have rosy cheeks!

As I pondered the imperfections of my complexion, I noticed the absence of something I would classify as pretty essential. I wasn't wearing any pants! I mean, what is this world? I wanted pants! In their place all I donned were a small, dirty, white pair of shorts. They were neither trendy nor functional, and compounded by this new paranoia about my appearance, I was distinctly unhappy.

On top of that, I had the benefit of a dirty white t-shirt, so at least there was some shred of normality about my outfit. In a mild state of shock, I looked around to see what my counterparts were wearing. To my disturbed relief, most every other man around was also wearing a pair of shorts and a t-shirt of different colors, while the women were wearing baggy blouses and knee length dresses. It was like everyone in sight was on holidays, had lost their luggage at the airport, and instead had to wear other people's clothes from the 1980s!

I was also surprised by how warm it was. I turned back one last time in the direction of where I had come from and said, "It's very nice weather we are having at the moment; is it always this hot?" Unfortunately, most of the singers—or my excitable, new friends—overheard my simple question. They all laughed, and the hairy man from earlier started strumming his guitar and singing:

"It's always hot when you're sitting on your bot."
"It's always hot when you're sitting in your house."
"It's always hot…"

I stood there in exasperation with my hands on my hips, looking at this clown. I was tiring of our one-way banter. Although a big effort had originally been made to disguise my frustration, I had now, unfortunately, outgrown these concerns, and my annoyance was in full view. Unexpectedly, I then received a firm slap on the backside. Granted, these shorts were always going to draw the wrong sort of attention, but there was no need for such a firm whack. I turned quickly to eye the most likely perpetrator. Oddly, the perpetrator was standing right behind me, waiting for me to discover her. She stood there with a big smile on her face and said, "It's always hot inside, silly. When has the weather ever changed in here?" She laughed as she went back to the circle of mockers.

Confused, I scanned over the inside of our containment and realized that we were in fact inside a giant warehouse. It must have been about a mile wide and as long as the eye could see. The ceiling was noticeable, but as I had been so preoccupied by my immediate surroundings, I hadn't even noticed. There seemed to be people everywhere. They sat in circles laughing, joking, and sleeping. Who would have thought that being lazy could be so rewarding? However, amidst this volume of life, there was a wretched stench. There was a smell of dirty people, feet, and rotten food. Furthermore, although there was an immense volume of life, it appeared that some people had little life left in them. Although they may still be smiling, there was little enthusiasm or spirit behind a lot of these ill smiles. Something wasn't working for them.

So with my clenched, disgusted face and my disgusting shorts, I set off in search of my two allies. On passive observation, most of the groups were not families but random collections of people sitting together. They seemed like caring people, fun people, people who could show and accept love. People take this ability to give and receive love for granted; however, as we had seen from our past two experiences, emotional availability cannot always be taken for granted.

Deep in thought, I continued to walk through the masses when I heard a yell. *Please don't let it be some-*

one from the singing group. Not the guitar guy, anyone but the guitar guy. I looked in the direction of the friendly cries and saw two guys beckon me towards them. As I raced over as quickly as my shorts would allow me, I could see that whoever was calling really was genuinely eager for me to sit with them. Both were quite skinny in appearance. One was wearing a polka dot T-shirt with conflicting bright yellow shorts while the other wore a blue T-shirt and striped, black-and-white shorts. What a sight. I think I could hear their clothes screaming at me before I could see them. The guy in the yellow was cross-legged, and on approach, he gleefully patted the ground beside himself, selecting my resting place.

"Hey there, why don't you come and join us?" It seemed his excited face was the perfect match for his excited voice.

"Yeah sure, what you guys doing?" I seemed to be improving with my ability to meet strangers and come across as if I had known them for years. I wasn't sure if that meant I was becoming more socially competent with different people or more superficial. Either way, it was a necessary part in this journey that I had no choice in.

"We are absolutely fan-tastic," the guy in the black-and-white shorts said, rocking back and forth. However, rocking himself to a slow stop, he looked at me and said, "We did get some bad news this morning." Mr. Yellow Shorts also stopped smiling at this point and put his hand to his forehead, rubbing it anxiously.

"What, may I ask, was the news?" I said.

Mr. Black and White looked at me sympathetically and said, "One of our friends passed away." I recoiled a little from the heavy news and put both hands on my head.

"That is absolutely terrible news. Good grief, are you both okay?" I said sympathetically. I was beginning to wonder why they'd invited me over; I would imagine they would want to be on their own.

"Oh yes, we're fine again. It's just that this morning wasn't very nice. Maizey was a ripe old age and had a very long and fruitful life," Mr. Yellow Shorts said as both guys looked at each other in support of this statement; however, their big smiles were threatening to reappear at any second. "What age was she?" I asked.

"Maizey was the big thirty-nine when she passed away... I mean, what more could she have wanted?" Mr. Black and White Shorts said.

My face went pale, and my jaw dropped a little. "That's a bit young, isn't it?" I got a strange look back in response to this question, as if I had just asked where babies came from.

"Thirty-nine is a massive age; most people around here do not see a day over thirty," Mr. Yellow Shorts said.

"But why... why don't people live longer?" I stuttered back in amazement.

"Because medicine has not come on a lot, and, well, people should die naturally, don't you think? Not use all of these chemicals and things," the guy replied.

What a different perspective they had on life.

"Yes, but surely you would have wanted for Maizey to live longer? Surely you both must still be hurting?" I asked curiously.

There was a slight pause as both looked at the ground. Then with a smile on his face, Mr. Yellow said, "Sure, it would be nice to still have Maizey, but you shouldn't wish for what you don't have. We do not have a lot of medicine, so it's best to deal with death positively than deal with the causes or results negatively, don't you agree?"

Mr. Black and White then chipped in, "You see, while we loved Maizey dearly, now that she is gone, mourning her would be for our own selfish needs."

"Yeah...but that's okay, isn't it?" I asked as I tried to resurrect my own values from the spoils of this conversation. They laughed.

"Of course not. How could we be happy for anyone living if we continued to invest our emotions in those who are no longer with us?" I was told.

It was strange that in such a loving place they could be so cold about death. Though, I suppose that is why so few people are really that sad. They all seem to have an equal amount of love for a high volume of people; hence, if someone dies, they will not be missed that much. In contrast, in the world I was used to, most people only had a small group of very close friends and family. This may be why it was so much more upsetting if they died. I missed this closeness. I suppose it made sense. Because they were in such a massive enclosure, they always had the ability to meet new people and increase their friend count. From my experiences so far here, I would not have guessed this was how they would have dealt with death in the world of love. And although it was nice to feel so wanted by so many, really I wasn't that special to anyone. I was just another smiling face.

Still deep in thought, I was awakened when a dog burst into our little circle. My two new friends were all about the dog, laughing and joking as if Maizey was the dog! As Mr. Black and White patted our new canine addition, he looked into space and, with a confused look on his face, said, "What do you think dogs dream about?" I smirked. There were echoes of my very own Bert and Henry in this odd line of enquiry. Maybe these two guys were the Bert and Henry of this world.

"Ahh, maybe they dream of their food or their dog partner," the other replied, reaching out to the dog with his hand as if to confirm his statement.

"So you think dogs are capable of love?" Mr. Black and White asked as if he had Mr. Yellow one move away from checkmate.

"Of course they are. Dogs are one of the most loyal animals you will ever find," Mr. Yellow said.

"So you think because they can love their owner, they are capable of falling in love with another dog?" Mr. Black and White asked as he considered the information. I stared on from the sidelines of this debate; however, I was now confused and a little bored of it. I would imagine if the dog understood what we were talking about, he too would be bored, if not a little embarrassed.

"Hmm... Good question. So I suppose... if they are capable of love, then they must be able to show emotion," Mr. Yellow said.

I thought it was time to join the conversation before the dog did. "Have you ever seen a happy dog?" I immediately got a decisive nod back in my direction.

"Most certainly, I have seen many a dog happy," Mr. Yellow replied. From the prompt response and obvious momentum of the debate, I decided to go all the way with Mr. Yellow.

"So, if you have seen happy dogs, have you ever seen one smile?" I asked.

"Ah... no, actually. I don't think so. Why? Don't you think they smile?" the guy in the yellow said. How did this come back on me?

"I don't know. I'm not exactly a dog expert, am I?" They laughed as my efforts to exhaust the conversation seemed to be working.

"Though I think I saw a bird laugh once." Mr. Yellow seemed to be off again.

"How on earth could you have seen a bird laugh? They've got beaks," I said, confused.

"Ohhh," Mr. Yellow said in response. "So you're a bird expert but not a dog expert, is that it?" They laughed a little again, though I was growing weary and frustrated by the proposal that a bird could actually laugh. If they could laugh, then I would feel decidedly worse about all of the turkeys I'd eaten throughout my life; I don't think they were laughing!

Although very weird and slightly frustrating, it was nice to have some light-hearted conversation and forget my responsibilities every once in a while. But it was time for me to get back on track and start searching for Wen and Bala again.

"Listen guys, I have to go," I announced as I got to my feet again.

"Ah, don't go. We're going to try and make the dog laugh," Mr. Black and White said. Unfortunately, I couldn't tell if they were serious!

"Ah, sounds great, but I have to go," I said as I took my first step away from them. "Well, great talking to you, buddy. See you again," they said as their waving ovation saw me off from the area.

I enjoyed that. I'd felt something warm, something very special about our little time together. Was it a connection? I wasn't sure, but whatever it was, it had revitalized me. I looked back one last time; however, to my disappointment I found the most awful sight. They had just called some other guy over and were chatting and laughing with him as if *he* was now their best friend. In truth, they were just being open and friendly with everyone. I was being petty and jealous. In a way, I felt that in order for someone's friendship to mean something to me, they needed to not to be friends with everyone else. They needed to have enemies and have people they didn't like. Otherwise, their lack of screening criteria to accept me as a friend would mean there was nothing special about me. I'm just a regular, average person, no different from anybody else. Does this mean the value of a friendship is a measure of how exclusive your friendship is to that person? Maybe the more exclusive your friendships are, the more likely your friendships will survive. Perhaps those with many friends don't need to work on individual friendships because they have so many others to choose from. Maybe it goes back to having to be able to hate in order to be able to love. And without the existence of hate, love is wholly empty. Or, in simpler terms, was it that I am extremely insecure and need them to like me and only me in order for me to feel special? Unfortunately, the latter, selfish explanation trumps any of the other explanations. God, I think these tight shorts were having an effect on my brain.

Chapter 12

It was difficult to tell what time of day it was inside the big structure, but more and more people seemed to be lying down. I hoped it was nearing night time, as I was growing tired, both physically and emotionally. Feeling a little dreary from the environment, I decided to run back and forth for some exercise. As I did so, a group gathered and began clapping. I tried to ignore them for a while but then a song started up. This was too much for me; my run had been ruined by the excessive support I seemed to attract.

"Thank you, thank you," I said to everyone, waving them away.

"Thank you," said a small man standing right in front of me.

"Okay," I replied.

"Thank you," he said again, smiling.

"Its fine," I said, trying to end this situation. He just stood there looking at me, staring like he had never seen anyone run before.

"Thank you." Oh, come on, man. Give me a break. What is this? It isn't even funny, or being happy; this is just weird. Then from the side of me I heard another person approach me, not another one I thought.

"I didn't think lizards got tired from running," a guy said to me. Immediately I put my hand up to my left eye and saw the silver glimmer; it was Bala. Taking no chances, he put his right hand up with three fingers.

"You don't have to keep doing it when we are this close, Bala, but it did work out pretty well in the world of equality," I said, correcting him and complimenting him.

"Thank you," the man said again.

I looked to my side, and the man was still standing there. "I wasn't talking to you... sir," I said, wondering why he was still here.

"Let's get out of here," I said without even letting Bala speak. It was great to have found him, to have found someone that wouldn't always be happy and smiling. It was exhausting being happy all the time.

As we walked side by side, reflecting on the events of the world of equality, I began to notice Bala was also dressed strangely. Stopping for a moment and pulling away from him to get a good overall view of how he looked, the smile on my face grew wider and wider. I was surprised I hadn't realized already, but suddenly I caved in and burst into laughter. He looked like someone had dressed him up as a fairy, a fairy in a sleeveless top, silver shorts, and brown sandals. What a sight. The top was hot pink, stopping just short of meeting the shorts. All Bala was missing was a magic wand, and I would have asked him to grant me a wish.

"Bala, I forgot to mention, what on earth are you wearing?" I said proudly, knowing I was dressed a little better than he was.

"All right Zach, very funny," he muttered back, knowing he was dressed a little worse than I was.

"Do you want to swap clothes?" he said.

"No." I laughed. Though on further assessment of my own clothes again, they were nothing to be proud of. This killed my buzz; I was enjoying that for a second.

"There you are," a voice called in our direction. We both looked to the back of Bala when Bala turned to me, putting his hand on his head.

"Not again," he said, shaking his head from side to side.

"We were playing tag, silly, when you ran off, but you brought a friend, and what are friends? Friends are welcome," the man and his two friends said together as they seemed to get around the back of us in the blink of an eye and begin ushering us like sheep. It was about then I noticed where we were heading, towards a team of people running around, giggling their heads off. It looked like all was lost until, by some miracle, the guys ushering us got distracted by a dog, which allowed us to make our getaway.

"That was close," I said, walking briskly away from the excitement.

"Tell me about it. I had a whole hour of that earlier," Bala replied, running his hands through his hair.

"So is this your family while we're here?" I asked.

"No ... don't you know?" he replied.

"Know what?" I responded.

"There are no such things as families around here; it is just a tightly knit community that allows you to stay with whomever you like, whenever you like," Bala explained.

"Really," I gasped.

"Yeah, it seems a pity, not having an immediate family, but great to be part of such a bigger circle of care," he said as he scratched himself through his silver shorts. I suppose he was right. Maybe this was a positive set-up. So with no-where to go, and no obvious plan or vision to guide us, Bala and I decided to find a space on the ground. We desperately wanted to find Wen, but this place was so exhausting, and we needed to formulate some kind of a plan. In the end we stayed in that space all day and continued to chat into the night about what we had done so far and how it had affected us. We were both eager to find Wen, which we would do first thing in the morning. Morning time would mark the beginning of our mission to locate Wen. I only hoped she wouldn't die of laugher when she saw her two weirdly dressed fellow Viscents coming towards her.

The next morning we woke early. I was starving, though there was a distinct lack of food anywhere. As Bala regained consciousness, I noticed that he didn't seem as big as he had the day before; maybe it was my imagination, but he seemed smaller. I looked into the space in front of me when I recalled something in my dream. I turned to Bala.

"You know, I had a really vivid message in my dreams last night."

Bala looked at me, scratched his head, and yawned. He didn't seem that concerned.

"I saw Wen. She was lying down with a certain degree of pain, though imparting something of great value to me."

"Oh … God, you had your vision," Bala said as he suddenly broke from his animal-like state and engaged his human anxieties. Now I had his attention.

"Did you have your vision?" I asked.

"Well no, I don't think so, though I did have a dream about some sort of creature that was half fish, half monkey." I put my face in my hands.

"No, Bala. I expect that was just a dream … and a weird one, at that."

We continued talking about this mythical, dream-world creature for the next half an hour as we walked in search of Wen.

About two hours later, we had progressed almost halfway down the enclosure and had seen nothing.

"Did you say you saw her lying down?" Bala asked curiously.

"Yeah, why?" I replied.

"Well, maybe we haven't been looking hard enough at the people lying down. I mean, what color clothes was she wearing?"

Just then there was a loud roar in our direction. We looked over to see a scattered-looking woman running towards us. We both thought about running away from her, but then looked at our shorts and thought the discomfort of running away outweighed our fear of the woman. The lady was wearing a big, flowery dress. She had big, wide, crazy eyes and tossed, crazy hair. She grabbed us both by the arm and pulled us back to where she had just come from.

"Hey, you guys." She giggled.

"Hello," we both said at different times.

"We're playing a game of huggsies. You wanna play?" she said, barely containing herself enough to ask the question.

Oh, I had been down this road before so immediately stated, "Unfortunately no, in fact, we have to…"

"*Yes*, I've got two more here," she roared back to her fellow players.

I repeated, "Sorry, I said no. We actually have to—"

"They're a bit shy, but lovely," the woman said, beaming with joy.

I looked to the ground, shaking my head from side to side. *Not another game.* I turned to Bala. He looked like he was in a state of shock.

I asked Bala, "I did say no there, didn't I?"

Bala, in his glazed state, said, "To be honest, Zach, after the lady's shouting, everything else is a bit of a blur."

I really couldn't believe it. Not again, bullied into a game of "huggsies" by a crazy woman. How embarrassing. I was not wearing a happy face.

Suddenly, Bala and I found ourselves in a circle with about fourteen other people. I was still looking down, shaking my head from side to side. Then, very sharply, person one ran over to person ten and gave them a massive hug. They then put up their hands to score the hug. I put my hand up as it seemed that's what the majority were doing.

"Score eleven for number one," the crazy lady said. I turned to the person beside me and asked, "If we all vote, the maximum score is fourteen, is that right?" The lady nodded happily back at me.

"So tell me, what is this game up to?"

Her face lit up. "It's up to one thousand."

I felt faint. How depressing, how utterly depressing. This was ridiculous; it was going to take hours. My head dropped again. I appreciated this was probably the wrong attitude for huggsies, but I wasn't sure if I could take it. I glanced over at Bala, and he seemed to be warming up. I wouldn't imagine that I was going to pull a muscle, but being a complete beginner, who knew what could happen.

A couple of minutes later, an enthusiastic number five ran over to Bala. By the nature of his diligent preparation, Bala had completed the warm up; however, his face revealed that he wasn't ready for the real thing yet. His face was like that of a man whose brakes had just failed while sliding on ice towards a tree. The moment seemed to be playing out in slow motion. Number five soon reached Bala, threw his arms around him, and gave a good, loud, audible hug and ran back to his original position. It got a tremendous "Ahh" from the crowd and may have even been the hug of the day. Unfortunately, because of Bala's poor reciprocation to the 120 percent number five was giving, the scores were not good—six out of fourteen. I smiled a little. However, my comic relief was short lived as it seemed my turn was soon to be upon me.

As the game wore on, I got more and more into it, and I began to hatch a hugging strategy. I thought I would identify the smallest guy in the circle, run over, pick him up, and spin him. The old pick and spin, an elaborate trick that I hoped would translate directly into points. On execution, it went even better than I had anticipated. I even threw in a grunt at the end for good measure. There was a moment when I thought I had lost my balance and I was going to end up on top of the little man, but it all came together quite smoothly. My score was an impressive eleven out of fourteen. Disappointingly, Bala was one of the guys who didn't vote for me, but considering how I reacted to his efforts, I wasn't surprised. How childish! When Bala's turn came around again, he predictably went down with a cramp. I mean, come on, a cramp in a game of huggsies? How pathetic. I went over and volunteered to drop out and attend to Bala and his fake injury. Thankfully, the game did not suffer. Who would have known that you can have hug-subs in a game of huggsies? Not me.

"What are you playing at, you big, girl's blouse," Bala said as he dusted himself off and rose to his feet.

"I was getting into that game," I said, sounding slightly ashamed by my interest in hugging. "Just 'cause you're not as good a hugger as me. Come here, let me show you," I offered jokingly. Bala had already turned his back on me and was walking.

Without even turning back to look at me, he said, "Oh come on, Zach. What has got into you? Let's find Wen."

Slightly ruffled by the coarseness of his response, I walked tall after Bala. "Let's then, Bala. Let's find her... and when we do, let's see who is the better hugger," I said in an effort to make light of my earlier embarrassing antics. It was like that game had hypnotized me. This time Bala didn't even reply. Funny how you can get so worked up about something you don't care about purely on the tone of the other person.

As we marched on in silence, I was secretly reliving the hugging brilliance I'd displayed just before we left. I was ashamed of the pride I had in this stupidity, but man, I was in the zone! It's not my fault I was that much better than awkward Bala. Poor Bala. Maybe one day I would teach him.

"Bala," a weak voice cried. Bala and I stopped and scanned the area. It sounded like Wen, but we couldn't be sure.

I was panicked; the voice seemed troubled and distressed. I was looking left to right frantically until I saw a hand, from only feet away from us, slowly rise from a lying position, raising three fingers. It was Wen. "This way," I said to Bala. As we approached, our prayers had been answered. It was Wen, though she looked terrible.

"Lucky for me you guys talk loud and talk about stupid things. I thought I heard you two bickering," Wen said, and she was right on all counts.

"Wen, you okay?" Bala said. I was far too breathless and anxious to speak.

"Yes," she whispered back with a faint smile. She was lying on her back with a blanket over her. There were black bags under her eyes, her skin seemed red and dry, her hair greasy and tossed. What was most disturbing was how weak she appeared—so very weak.

"Now, listen to me, both of you. I am only going to say this once. I had a vision last night, and it concerned you both. Bala, you need to find a gateway out of this enclosure. The gateway is a massive structure. There you will find a girl, a desperately hurt girl, a girl that needs your help. You must rescue this girl and bring her to me. If you are not in time, she will die," she said firmly.

Bala looked to the ceiling and then down to the ground. Suddenly the game of huggsies didn't seem so bad.

"Now, Zach, I don't want you to panic. I just want you to listen carefully." I wished she hadn't said that. I was now going to panic more and most probably miss absolutely everything she said.

"I am dying, and all I saw last night is that you will soon have the opportunity to do something that will save me. I don't know what that is. All I can ask is that you do what is right," she said.

I looked over at Bala. He was still staring into space, trying to digest what was just said to him. I, on the other hand, was, as I predicted, panicking and unable to absorb the gravity of what Wen had just said.

"Now go, both of you. Go quickly, there isn't much time," she said.

Bala and I rose to our feet immediately and got on our way. We just didn't know where. It was like beginning a race but not knowing which direction the race is in. What we had was a mission. However, instead of a note, we had a briefing from a good friend of ours. And instead of the note that would self-destruct, we had a girl that would self-destruct if we didn't act soon.

"A gateway," Bala said nervously as he looked all around him. For a brief second, my panic subsided, and I began to think logically.

"Bala, as we don't know where to start from, let's just go to the nearest wall and walk around the enclosure." Bala nodded. The plan was simple and might possibly work, but if we started off in the wrong direction, we might be too far away from the girl to save her by the time we found her. It was a gamble. We made our way to the nearest wall, straight past the laughing and joking. Both of us were noticeably anxious. Bala was leading. He was determined to find the girl. Then suddenly there was a loud bang behind us, followed by a huge gale. There were pieces of rubbish and debris flying everywhere. Bala and I turned and saw that the gateway into the enclosure had been flung open. The power of the wind was fierce, huffing and puffing, jarring both of the doors to the back wall. People were screaming and crying, and very quickly, there was a distinct absence of love and calm about the place.

Bala and I raced towards the gateway, dodging and jumping over the moving obstacles as they came hurtling towards us. When we reached the gateway, there were a number of men trying to push the gates closed. "Where is the girl?" Bala shouted to me as we sized up the situation. The gates were made of metal, about thirty feet in height and twenty feet in width. It was like each gate was the size of a basketball court. I wondered how they ever moved the gates in the first place.

Bala and I joined forces with the other men trying to push the gates out and back into position. However, our efforts were futile. The gates were not moving, and as the men were tired and malnourished, hope was quickly fading. Then, amidst the groaning and shoving, there was a brief lull in the gale's persistence. Suddenly, all that could be heard was a girl's cry. Bala looked at me and backed away from the gate. His eyes were popping out of his head. He understood that if he did not succeed, this girl would die. Then, briefly again, I heard her cry. It was coming from behind one of the gates. Thankfully, the gates had not completely slammed up against the wall and were stopped by some broken wood. This girl seemed to be trapped amongst the rubble. Unfortunately, this rubble, this messy collection of broken wood and random objects, would eventually yield to the unrelenting force of the wind and slam right back on the wall, squashing everything behind this door. By this stage it would be too late, the girl would be crushed

From her agonizing cries, she sounded about ten years old, pained, and scared. We then spotted her mother at the side, shouting to the little girl, promising her everything would be all right. Things may not be all right, and Bala and I knew that. With a real focus, Bala and I returned to the door and pushed it harder than ever before. Our faces red, our muscles tensed, we simply had to move this gate. Then there was a crack of some wood, and the gate moved farther back on the wall. We waited to see if the girl was still crying or if this was the final, fatal movement of the gate that would finish the helpless girl. The mother's cries went from anxiety to mourning. We feared the worst. Then, tensely, there was another cry from the girl, though this time a little fainter. We all gave a slight sigh of relief as the mother's cries increased in volume as she celebrated the better of two evils.

Bala was getting frustrated. His gaze darted from side to side, and a vein protruded from his forehead. I could see that he thought that he would fail. He put his head in his hands and said, "We just have to save her, we just have to." He seemed to be getting angry. It was hard watching him unravel like that. I decided to go back and do all I could: push with all my might and hope for the best. It was now or never.

Nothing was happening until, shockingly, the gate moved by the slightest margin. I pushed again and noticed another movement. The odd thing was, there was no one else helping me; all of the men seemed to have given up. Surely this wasn't all me. I realized that I now did thirty press-ups in the morning as opposed to my usual twenty, but surely the difference in strength wasn't this staggering. It was strange because as I pushed and I pushed against these horrible winds, the gate got easier and easier to push. While again realizing that there was no one helping me, I thought, *There is something odd afoot here. How is this happening?* Thirty press-ups or no thirty press-ups, this was not normal.

Out of the corner of my eye, I then noticed something. At first I thought my imagination was playing tricks on me. I had to look again. Maybe I was dreaming, so slowly I stopped my pushing and stepped aside. It was Bala, except not as I knew him. Bala had grown to a height of about thirty feet, his muscles were like giant whales, his legs like giant tree trunks, and his hands like racket ball courts. He was enormous. I was shocked—so shocked that I fell backwards and watched the monstrosity shut both gates. He seemed to be closing these doors with relative ease against the full force of Mother Nature's venom. Each step inched the gates closer and closer to their original position until *boom*—they were closed.

Once Bala had finally managed to push them shut, there was a tremendous *bang* that resonated throughout the building. This was followed by a silence. Bala took his hands down from the door and turned to face me. It was only me and him. My heart was racing. Was he still the same Bala, or was he going to eat me? He put both hands on his head, and as he puffed from all of his pushing, he said, "Maybe this is what they meant when they said 'special abilities.'" Phew, thank God he wasn't going to eat me. It was still the same Bala. Quickly recovering from his exertion, he turned to find the girl.

He turned back towards the large heap of rubble. There was furniture, wood, and instruments all piled up with a whisper of a girl's cry still emanating from the center. Bala began sifting through the pile with great urgency, gently lifting each piece in case he hurt the girl. Then all of a sudden, Bala lifted a piano up from the area that revealed the small, short-haired, blonde girl crunched up in a ball. Bala lifted her carefully and looked at her as he held her in his open palm. He said, "You're going to be okay, little girl."

She was still crying very softly and weakly, yet still managed to say, "Thank you, giant man." He smiled at her as giant tears began to gather in both his eyes. However, the cries of the mother soon brought Bala back to reality, which prompted him to turn quickly and bring the broken girl to Wen before it was too late.

Chapter 13

A couple of minutes later we arrived at Wen's side. She was now very pale, though still managed to smile weakly as we placed the girl down by her side. I was scared. Wen looked frail and vulnerable. She was nothing more than a shadow of her usual self. It was horrible seeing someone I admired so much be so helpless and fragile. As soon as Bala placed the little girl down, he stood back, trying to be as inconspicuous as he could. Unfortunately, he was now about as inconspicuous as an elephant, but it was Wen's turn now—she had to take it from here. Wen rose up slightly from her lying position and leant on one arm. She looked at Bala in shock and then at the girl sympathetically as the girl drifted in and out of consciousness. Wen whispered, "I'm not sure what I'm supposed to do."

Panicked, I darted from the shadows and said, "But you said all Bala and I had to do was bring her to you."

"I know, Zach. I know, though I never got to see why or how I help this situation." It seemed like we had turned up for a game of football with out a football! The outlook seemed dismal. I threw myself to my knees. I was so tired, so emotionally battered from all this death and pain. Wen, in her weak, saddened state, just stroked the girl's hair and looked at me sorrowfully, saying, "I'm sorry."

As I looked away I couldn't help but notice a change in Bala. He seemed to be shrinking. Though as he shrank, people began appearing. The smaller he got, the more people appeared. I scratched my head. When Bala was back to being his regular size, the place was once again packed. About thirty to forty people must have appeared. It seemed like in some odd way, Bala absorbed all of the people down by the gate earlier and focused all of their energy through him. I was shocked. I wondered what else he could do. Could he do the same with animals? He was now back to his normal size and lying on the ground. It seemed this transformation had taken a lot out of him.

Drawn between him and the little girl, I had begun to climb to my feet when Bala jumped up quickly and also ran over to Wen.

"I know why I had to bring the girl to you, Wen," he roared across to her as he ran in her direction. "Your role is to rid her of her pain and suffering, Wen."

With a confused look on her face, she looked at the girl and asked, "But how?"

I then remembered that day at the park, when Bert, Henry, and I saw Wen break up a dogfight and appear to heal the dogs. "Wen, do you remember that day in the park when you were reading your book and you seemed to help those dogs. Maybe you have something in you that can help people heal," I said, trying to encourage her.

"No, I have just always had a way with animals. As soon as I touch them, I can feel them and usually help them, but with people, no, I have never even tried," she replied as if she thought it wasn't possible.

By this time, the girl's mother was right there beside Wen. Her very presence was creating an enormous pressure. Wen then edged a little closer to the girl and placed her hand on the girl's chest, closed her eyes, and concentrated. A couple of tense minutes later, Wen lifted her hand saying, "I'm sorry, but this just isn't working." She looked defeated. The girl's mother cried, weeping bitterly as if her daughter had already passed.

The atmosphere was thick with frustration and sadness. The people looked exhausted; it seemed the girl was dead. With tears welling up in my eyes, my sadness converted to defiance in the hope that one last effort might be enough. I marched over to Wen, knelt on one knee, put my hand on her face, and looked her in the eye, saying, "If anyone can make something magical happen, Wen, it's you. You are an inspiration. Wen, you are my inspiration. You are so strong, so smart, and so courageous. I believe in you more than I believe in anyone... Listen to your heart and your instincts. You can do this," I said as I looked to my side and saw Bala look at Wen, nodding sincerely at everything I just said.

Her pale, sad face blushed momentarily. We both looked at the girl, and with one last, desperate attempt, we placed our hands on the girl's heart. As before, there was nothing until suddenly, I was thrown back from the girl, and a bright light began to form around the heart of the girl. In that brief second, just before I went flying backwards, I felt an enormous flow of energy enter my body. I wasn't sure what was happening, but Wen was doing something. The light got more and more intense until, as abruptly as it had started, the light disappeared, and Wen fell back on her back.

There was an eerie stillness in the air. People were beginning to question whether Wen was helping or trying to cause harm. Then, very slowly, the little girl moved her right arm. She was lying on her back, but began bringing both arms to her eyes to wipe them. Her mother ran to her side and held her tightly as if she would never let go again.

As the little girl lay in the arms of her mother, she looked over her mother's shoulder at Wen and said, "Thank you for making the pain go away."

Wen turned to me, took me by the hand, and said, "Well done."

"Nonsense," I said. "It was all you, all you..."

She looked down for a second and then turned in my direction once again. "I'm not sure how to say this, Zach, but while our hands were over that girl, I felt the most horrible feeling pass from her."

"Yes, me too." I recalled a very sharp, dark sensation.

"And I have a strong feeling that this negativity was passed to you. Now, as you are still okay, it must not be affecting you directly, but you must be aware that you are holding something very dangerous and very powerful. You will need this darkness, but beware of its danger," Wen warned. The elation of saving the girl soon began to wear off as I began to consider the implications of Wen's fatal warning. I was worried, scared, and... worried.

As the crowd began to disappear and people forgot the earlier drama and returned immediately to playing games, Bala, Wen, and I sat there, talking. We sat there all night, reminiscing about the excitement of our most recent adventures. The three of us were sitting around a bucket, a bucket filled with wood that we set alight and used for lighting, warmth, and comfort as we talked against the background noise of the crackle of the fire. All we could see was the light from the flames against each other's faces as we spoke about the mystery of these emerging powers—Bala, with some sort of growing power, and Wen, with some sort of healing power We then began talking about this particular world of love. Wen said that she thought this would be the perfect world. However, as we had discovered in every other place we had been so far, there were negatives and side effects to every positive. And though this world had a very positive atmosphere, it was dirty, smelly, disorganised, and there was never a ready supply of food or medicine.

It was perhaps the perfect place to spend time in the short term but lacked a future and long-term plan. The shortage of food seemed the most pressing problem that needed addressing. Wen had heard earlier that the next day there might be some sort of trial where you could win food for the community. Though this path to better nutrition was laced with terrible danger and possible death, we began to think one of us should go. Everyone else in this pack of professional smilers would be too weak to go. It had to be one of us. As the fire's final cinders surrendered to the evening's dark, we all lay there, anxiously thinking that this may be our final rest before our ultimate rest.

The following day we were up early. Who would have guessed that Wen snored? Turns out she wasn't perfect after all. By day she was a demure, striking, gentle-looking girl, and by night, a fog horn. I looked across at her as the masses began to surface and make their first movements of the day. "Morning, all," Bala said, throwing both arms up in the air and stretching. "Did you hear that noise last night?" Bala said. Wen and I looked at each other, both of us with confused looks on our faces, but me knowing exactly what noise he was referring to! "I never looked up, but it sounded like someone was trying to start a car," Bala said as he looked over his shoulder, checking for the arrival of a car. I laughed a little to myself as I saw Wen also check around her for this mysterious car. I could have told Bala that this car was around four foot tall and had long, black hair, but I thought I would save it for another time. "No, maybe it was my imagination," Bala conceded as he climbed to his feet for another stretch, this time a full-bodied one.

With a couple of body stretches later and the lack of any sort of car anywhere, we began talking with some of the people about the nature of these food trials. With all of the talk about the noises or snoring of last night, I had completely forgotten that I might die today. *Excellent, back on track. Let's get an idea of the potential dangers that lurk ahead.* Slowly, we began to discover that there were three trials. One person would have to do all the trials and have to win them all in order to get food for everyone for a month. One person was sent to do these trials every month; however, recently the results had not been good. Out of the last six men that were sent, none had survived—this is why everyone was so weak and hungry. I was aware that I had not done anything exceptional yesterday, yet my two friends had been magnificent. They were heroic in unknown, uncertain circumstances; it was now my job to do the same.

So with a little more thought and a whole pile of nervousness, I decided that it was going to be me. Bala and Wen seemed to have completed their visions and were brilliant in both the world of equality and the world without money. Now surely it was my turn to show them I was serious about being a Viscent...for better or for worse. So with the temporary momentum of my current madness, I sought out whomever it was that needed to be consulted on this decision and stepped into the ring. As a result of recent events regarding these trials, it transpired that I was the only one to volunteer for the exercise out of the whole community. This worried me horribly, but as I was soon consumed by the chanting of the crowd, my inhibitions were drowned out by my insatiable vanity. The whole community seemed to assemble and clap as they made a human pathway from where we were standing to the corner of the enclosure. As I walked proudly, waving as if I had already been triumphant, I saw all of the people that I had met over the past couple of days. There were the two guys I had spoken to about dreaming dogs. There was that crowd who'd invited us to play huggies... how could I forget! And of course the first people I met, who seemed to still be chanting something about me being "rosy of the posies." I wasn't sure if this was intended to insult me or inspire me, but as they all seemed to be smiling, I just smiled back.

Then, amidst the celebrations, I saw an older man sitting over by the exit I was approaching. He waved me over to his side. With the high volume of people and noise behind me, it seemed every step I took towards the old man was happening in slow motion. He took my hand and said, "I am the oldest in this community, my son." I gasped.

"Wow, what age are you?" He looked at me.

"I am fifty-one years old," he replied. I didn't know what to say; that was still so young.

"Well... Good for you..." I said.

"Yes, son. I have had a great life, and my heart is full of love, but what I have learned in my years is very relevant to your trip. I fear a great deal of these people will not last another month. With the trials growing increasingly challenging, if you do not come back with food and medicine, it could mean the worst for our kind," he said.

I turned and looked at the people as the old man placed his hand on my shoulder. He shook me by the shoulder, saying, "Look around. As soon as people get sick, they either die or weaken. You have to bring change," he said with an almost desperate look in his eyes.

"I'll do my best," I replied.

He straightened himself quickly, his desperation soon turning to a stern glare as he said, "You'll have to do better than that, son...These trials are something wicked. All I know is that each trial tests a different part of your character, so be the best you can and think. This is going to expose you for who you are, as opposed to who you think you are. Prepare to be positively reassured that you are the person you think you are, or horribly disappointed that you are much less than the person than you thought you were. You are in for a chilling end if you do not measure up."

I felt his stare melt me as his eyes pierced my own. He then looked to the ground, tapped me on the knee, and looked away from me. It seemed our time together had ended. I too looked at the ground, wishing I was the man I thought I was and a whole lot more. I suppose like any crisis situation in life, it brings out a person's true colors.

Well this was a crisis situation, and I hoped to God my colors were bright enough. In a selfish way, I began to wish that I'd known this information before I'd volunteered. Maybe I wasn't the right person for the job after all. I then felt a warm hand on my back and another catch me by the hand. It was Wen and Bala. Fortunately, I wasn't holding hands with Bala but instead got a firm pat on the back from him as Wen gripped my hand. I looked at them as if this was the end, and in many ways, it seemed like it was. However, as I freed myself from their anxious hold, I placed my hand on the door out of this place, pushed it forward, and stepped outside. "Forever," a voice called out from behind me amongst the buzz of the crowd. I looked back one last time, it was Bala, he had one hand on Wen's shoulder and the other in the air with his three fingers in the air. He smiled and nodded, as did Wen, before she noticed he was doing the three finger thing again and turned to him, raising her shoulders as if to ask, "Why do you keep doing that?" I hoped I would get to hear his answer, I thought, smiling to myself as I raised my three fingers in return.

Chapter 14

I was surprised at just how good the land looked outside. Sure, it may be subject to freak gales that could blow in the doors of our enclosure and kill people, but the land certainly seemed fertile. God, I sound like a farmer. Off to the distance on my left was another giant enclosure, where I guessed another community resided happily. On the right there was a cave with a pathway worn from the exit of our enclosure to the entrance of this cave. Putting one and one together, I gathered that this was where I would face my destiny. Bravely and reluctantly, I marched into the wide-open space through the heart of the rugged greenery down this man-formed footpath, as the dense foliage on both sides flanked me all the way up to the entrance of my doom.

When I entered the cave, it appeared the only way to proceed was to crawl down a small tunnel on my left. I hoped that this crawl through a tight, confined space was one of the trials. I hated narrow spaces—they made me feel like I couldn't breathe—but I continued and pulled myself along until I saw some sort of light. My knees and elbows were getting a little sore, but with a glimmer of light ahead, my energies began to double. There is nothing like hope to give me a bit of motivation. As I reached the end of this rabbit run, I entered a massive opening. It was a colossal opening with a never-ending ceiling and was as wide and as long as the light would allow you to see. It was lit by the number of voids or cracks in the roof of the cave. They were like lasers coming down from the ceiling but spreading wider as they neared the ground.

As I walked forward a little, I could feel the damp, cold air on my skin. It felt like the inside of a frog's house...if frogs had houses. On my right there was a wall that would soon end and leave me with the massive area in front of me. At first, all I did was follow the wall with hope that it would give me some indication of where I should be going. I was getting scared again. At any second something could jump out and eat me alive— my mind was conjuring up all sorts of possibilities. With my heart beating faster and faster, I ran my finger along the grimy wall as I continued to look out for potential dangers lurking in the shadows. Then I felt something on the wall. At first I thought that it was just some peculiar marking; however, under closer inspection it seemed as if there was a message carved into the wall.

I stopped, rubbed the suspect area, and tried to see if I could read something. It was too dark. I couldn't see a thing. I tried again, but it was no use; the beams of light from the ceiling fell nowhere near this part of the wall. I walked back in the direction I had come from and thought to myself. I then looked at one of the beams of light and decided to move a little closer to one of them to further inspect the situation. As I did, my toe hit something quite solid, and I fell flat on my face. It felt like a body. Again, my heart began racing as the surges of adrenaline pulsed through my body. Engulfed by fear, I rolled slowly and crawled gingerly in the direction of this mysterious solid. I reached out nervously to feel what it was. My fingers seemed to fall on a material of some sort. My initial reaction was that it was a piece of clothing, but as I let my fingers feel a little further, it seemed to be nothing more than a bag. I passed a momentary sigh of relief as my paranoia returned to just common fear.

I dragged the bag towards me and went in the direction of one of the rays of light to see what I had found. I sat down, put the bag between my legs, and began opening the straps. For a second I thought that perhaps this was the first challenge; however, as I was soon pulling out a cup, a plate, a coat, and a pair of shorts, it seemed nothing more than a survival pack. How ironic. I doubt its owner would have left it behind if they had survived! Before my mind could go off on another fear-packed mental tangent, I looked back at the wall and tried to figure out how I could read the message. Staring solidly at my intended target, I fiddled with the metal plate that I had pulled out from the bag. Then very quickly I saw a flicker of light out of the corner of my eye. Freezing for a second, I quickly realized that I was responsible for the flicker. The plate had briefly reflected the light from the ceiling's beam and thrown it onto the wall. I said nothing, though inside I was screaming with joy. Maybe I could throw the light on the part of the wall I wanted to see. So with a little messing around with the metal plate (I wished I'd packed a survival pack) I began to try and direct the light where I wanted. Initially, it felt impossible, but after a while, to my amazement, it worked. It looked like there were a couple of lines etched into the wall. The message read:

"Anger fights the fires of love, of which you will deal with three

Where the biggest sleeps the soundest and the smallest shouts and screams

Beware of those who wake and those who kill and chew

So when the wave of anger wakes let it not wash over you"

The first action this cryptic message yielded was a firm scratch of my head. However, there was an arrow next to the message that at least showed me what direction to start walking. The direction of the arrow made me walk in line with the wall. I walked nervously, trying desperately to make some sense of the clue the wall had given me. My hand was still scratching the top of my head, and if the pondering went on much longer, I may have even started rubbing my chin.

Fortunately, as soon as I cleared the wall, the message did not seem so cryptic anymore. I looked to the right as I walked out from the wall and saw my first trial. Amidst the massive, open space in front of me, there were three paths. Each path was about the length of an airport runway, a couple of meters wide, and all the paths were separated by water. Towards the middle of each path, there was a link that tied all the paths together briefly before they separated again into their original three. However, my gasp was not at the size and length of the paths but at what was on them.

The first path was peppered with a number of very large, sleeping beasts. Each one was about the size of a horse but a lot more gruesome looking. They had three legs, big teeth, two strong-looking arms, and a large eye on each side of their heads. Fortunately, all of these eyes were closed and sleeping now, so I needed to keep very silent. Although their bodies seemed slimy and wet, they seemed to be all kinds of different colors.

The next footpath had a range of much smaller beasts. They were around the size of a large dog but shaped much differently. Their bodies mainly consisted of a head, which looked like a giant beach ball. They had four little mouths around the circumference of the head and hundreds of large spikes coming from their small bodies. From the look of some of the spikes, it seemed like they rolled around on their prey and then retracted the spikes, feeding off the living agony of whatever they rolled on.

The last footpath had a series of giant leach-like creatures on it. At first all I could see were their backs, which were all sorts of pretty colors, stripes, dots, and circles. However, on closer inspection I discovered that one of the creatures was on its back, exposing an underbelly layered with teeth. What the hell was I to do? What did the message say again? There was definitely something about fire and anger. I thought to myself, *The only thing that can combat anger is calm, so maybe if I keep my head, I might keep my life.* Now for the path. Well, from the message, the small ones wake easiest, and if they wake, everything else will be on me in a second. And while the largest are the heaviest sleepers, if they wake, they will rip me to shreds. They will be all over me like kids on a bouncy castle! I stood there, perplexed, though after a little more thought, prayer, and guessing, I made my decision... It was going to be the path with the biggest creatures. Hell, if I was going to get beaten, I may as well get beaten by the biggest.

Carefully I began my wretched journey, creeping slowly through the fearsome beasts. My heart was thumping like an African drum, so loudly I thought one of them was bound to wake. These things smelt awful! Despite the stench, I tippy-toed onwards as softly and gently as my large feet would allow. Then there was a noise from one of the beasts I passed. Terrified, I turned around slowly. Mercifully, it seemed that he was just turning over. I sighed in relief. Step by step, I inched farther and farther forward until I successfully reached the quarter-way mark. Although this was not physically draining, I had just about used up a month's supply of fear in getting to this point. There was a still long way to go.

As I edged closer to the midway point, I hit a problem. Right across the entire width of the path were five beasts lying side by side. Grimacing, I scratched and shook my head from side to side with despair as this new information was revealed. I put my hands on my hips and thought, *This is going to be interesting*. Not sure why, but at first glance it seemed like the guy in the middle was in the deepest sleep. He wasn't snoring the loudest nor did he look the stillest, but from the awkward position he had fallen asleep in, he had to be sleeping the soundest. My only options seemed to include, getting into the dark, mysterious water between the paths and go around this obstacle, go back on the path I had just travelled from, or climb over the beasts. I thought I'd take my chances with the big, smelly beasts and try to climb over one of them.

I approached it slowly and stopped at its foot. Gently, I placed my foot on his and then brought my other foot on board and put it on his calf. He was now holding all of my weight. I stopped for a second to see if he would notice anything; luckily, he didn't. So, with the tiniest bit of confidence, I proceeded and slowly stepped onto his thigh. As I did this, I heard something; it was a noise from the water. I thought nothing of it. Maybe it was a stone falling into the water or something. Either way, I had my own problems at the moment. Then again there was a noise from the water. However, this time I did see something. Rising slowly above the water's surface was a hand. It extended its fingers as much as it could and then made a loose fist and disappeared. The hand was a part of something that was very much alive. Temporarily I was paralysed. I shivered as a hot and then cold flush churned from within my body and then slowly made its way to the surface of my skin. It was like the devil had just caught hold of my heart and squeezed it. What was in the water?

Was it the guy whose backpack I found? Was it a signal? Should I go into the water?

Quite shaken by this new discovery, I shook myself and continued stepping over the body of the beast. I couldn't possibly enter the water without knowing what was in it. Then once again the water stirred, except this time it was a loud splash. This was followed by another splash as a creature rose up from the water and passed straight over the top of me and straight over the footpath I was standing on. I was stunned. As it passed over me, it went through one of the beams of light from the ceiling. Remarkably, it was half monkey and half fish with big, strong arms and an angry face... and it was covered in blood! It turned out that the light was so bad in here that the surrounding water was not water... but blood. Who would have thought Bala's abstract ramblings earlier had substance to them? The large arms then grabbed out to try and get me, but fortunately they missed. Suddenly, I realized that not only had I identified something else that could kill me, but also that this something could wake the rest of these beasts. As it continued on its failed flight path, I feared the inevitable—another large, loud splash that could wake everything and everyone. I was standing on a giant man-eater, surrounded by things that would want to kill me. I was not happy with the situation.

I looked again as the monkey-fish continued over the footpath right to the surface and then splashed into the blood. The next second seemed like a lifetime as I stood precariously on top of the beast. Then, slowly, all of the giant leaches on the furthest path began to shout and scream, roaring and screeching like their lives depended on it. My worst fear was about to come true. The spiked balls in the middle path then began to chant in a very deep groan, almost harmonizing with the leaches. The next to wake were the beasts. Well, they certainly were the deepest sleepers. Not one had woken yet. If I'd known they slept this soundly, I would have run over the lot of them!

In order to take advantage of these deep sleepers before it was too late, I continued walking over my beast until *bang*, I slipped, and suddenly I was lying face down on the back of the beast. As I had both my arms around its neck, I was directly facing the large eye on the back of its head, which was about the size of my whole head. It then opened its giant eye slowly and looked directly at me. I was terrified. I hoped for a brief second that he might not be able to see me; though as I was about two inches away from his direct line of sight, I figured my wish for a blind beast was an ambitious one.

What happened next was pretty much what was bound to happen. The beast's eye widened in anger. It roared loudly, jumping straight to its feet. It was like holding on tightly to a foghorn with bad breath, but I had to hold on; it was my only chance to survive this. He was angry, very angry... jumping around and moving, trying desperately to get me off his back. As scared as I was, I was experiencing quite a weird sensation. Usually when you hold on to someone's back, they cannot see you. Unfortunately, as these creatures had a giant eye in the front and the back of their heads, I was staring right back at this fellow the whole time he was trying to shake me off his back. This must have been aggravating him even more as he continued to twist and twirl in an effort to loosen my grip. By this time the cave was like an orchestra of angry roars and moans, and anyone that was asleep was now most definitely wide awake. The leaches, the spiked balls, and the beasts were all moving everywhere, and all the time these monkey-fish were jumping over the footpaths, trying to drag something into the water. I was pretty sure this was the end.

I had let them all down: the enclosure, Bala, Wen...everyone. I then felt something on my leg that quickly stunned me back to reality. I looked around as I clung firmly to my guy and discovered it was another one of the slime-ball beasts. He was licking his lips in preparation for his tasty treat. As he came closer, he was quickly wrestled to the ground by another one of the beasts, pinning him down and looking back at me as if I was now *his* prize. I hadn't been this popular for a long time. At this stage things were getting frantic. As I nervously peered beyond the eye of the beast, I saw three to four spiked balls coming towards my beast. Suddenly, he stopped trying to shake me off as I turned into his secondary concern. As they hurtled towards us, I held my breath. From nowhere, a number of leaches ambushed one of these balls and brought it to a stand still. Another was grabbed by one of the monkey-fish and pulled into the pool of blood. Another one of the spiked balls was grabbed by one of the more stupid beasts, but there was still a spiked ball that was nearly upon us.

Closer and closer it came until, quickly, the beast stepped to the side and kicked it off the footpath. An effective defence, however, it had left my beast injured. Disastrously, the beast fell to one knee, and I thought it was only a matter of time until one of the many other predators got the better of me. In this time of desperation, I began to think of all the advice people had given me so far. To be calm, be myself, and to not let fear or anger get the better of me. I thought of the heroics that Wen and Bala had displayed so far, putting their own lives in danger in the name of what was right. A tear welled up in my eye as I thought that, and although I admired their bravery and courage, above all else, it was their friendship I valued most. I wiped the tear to one side and decided to do what they would do in my position. I knew what they would do before I even had to ask the question; perhaps the real question was if I would be prepared to do the same? I nodded my head as a signal to myself, deciding yes, I would do the same. I would be prepared to jump from the beast's back and try as best as I could to get to the other side. I couldn't just stay there, clinging cowardly to the beast. In a matter of time they would come get me anyway. No, I was going to die trying to do what was right. How could I rest in peace if I didn't?

So with that in mind, I climbed up onto the shoulders and then the head of the beast and jumped proudly into whatever lay ahead. Perhaps it was the magnitude of the decision, but for a couple of seconds, it seemed like my leap was lasting forever. My eyes were closed, and my arms were outstretched, waiting to touch or fend off whatever would stand in my way. However, I then strangely began to feel this tingly feeling through both my hands. I opened my eyes upon landing and discovered that, amazingly, my hands were radiating some sort of fire—pushing all that was in front of me out of my way with the powerful flames coming from my hands. Surprised, shocked, but thankful, I didn't waste time questioning this wonderful development but furiously pointed my hands in the direction of the door at the end of the footpath. The power from my hands was amazing. This must be my Viscent power, and it seemed that as long as I pointed my hands at the ground, this impressive fire from my hands made sure that the path would be cleared. Though, all it would take is for something to knock me to my feet and it was all over. This was a very likely scenario as I felt a thunder of followers tail my every step. Large masses of beasts teemed towards me, and the monkey-fish increased in number, flying overhead, getting closer every time.

The noise was also horrific. What had started as an orchestra of shouting and bleating had turned into a chaotic cacophony of shrieks and war screams denoting a certain level of savagery about the night. There was sweat pouring down my face as I puffed my way onwards down through this curtain of ill-will. Then I felt the fire coming from my hands weaken a little. I wasn't that far away from the end, but I now had to jump over leaches and sidestep the spiked balls. I simply could not clear them with my hands anymore. Worse again, about ten meters from the end, my powers failed completely. All that was left in front of me were a couple of leaches and two spiked balls. They were coming straight at me. Again, all I could do was continue running and hope I would know what to do. Step by step, our crash into each other became more and more inevitable. Then, just at the point of impact, I stepped on two of the leaches, dived straight over the spiked balls, and landed head over heels, rolling up to the exit. I picked myself up, rushed through the door, and locked it behind me as I felt the volume of followers behind me pile into the closed door at my back.

"Phew," I said as I wiped my forehead. I sat there exhausted and wet with a cold sweat, trying to take in everything that had just happened: an array of killing beasts, a new power, and my life flashing right before my eyes about fifteen times! I was exhausted. The second task had better be an easy one, like a game of cards or something!

Chapter 15

I looked around to see where I had ended up. It was very dark. All I could see was a steep staircase in an upwards direction right in front of me. I got to my feet with the little energy I had left and began to ascend the staircase. About twenty to thirty steps up, from the little light that was in the area, I thought I could see some more etchings on the wall. As I continued, I reached the point where I suspected there to be a message, and sure enough, there was writing on the wall. It said:

"Force can be your crushing
Force can be your end
Force can be a blessing
Force can be your friend."

As in the earlier task, the message was so cryptic, my discovery of it seemed pointless. I scratched my head again, then my chin, but to no avail; it seemed neither my chin nor my head had a clue what this meant! Ah well, maybe it would make more sense in a while. It did appear that I would encounter some sort of force, but the appearance of it and what I should do about it were presently not clear. I began walking again until I reached another door at the top of the staircase. I had climbed a massive distance up to the top of the stairs to this door inviting me to walk through it. I just hoped the next task had nothing to do with heights. I hated heights. I took the door handle nervously in my hand, turned it, and pushed. What happened next was unexpected. Just as I turned the handle on the door, a trapdoor opened up beneath me, sending me crashing uncontrollably in a downward direction. Thankfully I wasn't falling for that long, and my loud, girly whine was brought to an abrupt end as I tumbled onto my landing area. It was a rock, a big rock about the size of a tennis court. The sides of the rock were not touching anything. It seemed to be suspended in midair. As I walked nearer to the edge, I realized that we were not the only rock island in this massive expanse. They were everywhere, and what was scary was how far down the drop was between the rocks. I couldn't even see the bottom of this place!

Still scanning the sheer vastness of the almighty enclosure, I spotted the doorway out of this endless and bottomless place. This was the good news. The bad news was that it was about one hundred and fifty meters away with many rocks and voids between it and me. It appeared impossible to get to this stupid doorway. I detached myself from the glorious insides of the place and quickly thought back to what I was there to do. How on earth was I going to get over there? And what on earth is going to start attacking me? Wonder and amazement were soon to be replaced by depression and concern; yes, I was back to reality again.

I stared out into space, hoping for a little inspiration. Unfortunately, my inspiration was soon to arrive. In the distance I could see something large and dark coming in my direction. Was it a bat, a person, a ghost? It got larger and larger until all I could see was a giant rock flying in my direction. As it got nearer, it got larger and faster until the huge boulder was soon to be upon me. I dived to the floor quickly and then, *bang*. It ploughed right into the side of the platform I was standing on and knocked some of the rock away. Just when I thought the panic was over, there was another *bang* and then another. It turned out there wasn't just one rock trying to crumble the platform; there were four, one on each side. I also began to notice that the rocks were swinging back in the direction they had just travelled in, like pendulums going back and forth, crashing against anything that got in their way. These things were ripping the place apart, and I knew that if I didn't get off the rock soon, I would be crumbling to my death.

I sat in the middle of my rock, momentarily blanking out the constant thunder, and tried to think. The clue on the wall seemed to suggest that the force could be my friend—that I could use it to my advantage. With my head resting in my hands, I looked at the continuous onslaught and noticed that the rocks were so big and so powerful that every time they struck something, it took a second or two for the rock to start to go back in the direction it had come from. I closed my eyes and thought, *If only I could jump aboard one of these moving rocks, its pendulum movement away from the rock I was on would take me to a different rock.* I understood my plan was ridiculous and highly dangerous, but I decided to go for it. I quickly looked to see which one would be my ticket out of here. It appeared that the moving rock on my right would swing towards the rock that was only one swing away from the exit. "Let's do it." I sighed. I didn't think this was a good plan, but it was all I had. As I nervously eyed my chosen rock, I took a number of steps back like a bull ready to charge. On its approach, I ran in its direction defiantly and, on impact, took an almighty leap of faith. If my timing was one bit off, I would have a long fall ahead of me. My acrobatics through the air seemed to take forever. However, I thankfully landed roughly where I'd intended, and I smiled in disbelief. "It worked!" I said aloud. What a dramatic finish to such a simple plan. Though, as it began to move again, the rock was quickly going back in the direction it had just travelled from. This reminded me of the second part of the plan that I hadn't entirely thought through yet—disembarking. As I departed from my rock I quickly gathered speed, and it wasn't long before I was holding on for dear life. The speed was such that I was fast approaching the next rock. I poised myself so that just before impact, I could jump. On collision with the next rock, I jumped—this time it wasn't so graceful. Barring an awkward landing, the first part of my plan seemed to be going very well. When I looked over at my next rock, I noticed it was soon to be upon me. So, wasting no time, I got up, brushed myself off, and once more ran in the direction of my next ride.

This time, perhaps because of the luck of my first attempt, I jumped with a little too much haste and only just managed to stay aboard the moving target. That was a little too close for comfort. The rock then began to swing away from the second rock I had landed on and towards the direction of the exit door's platform. Then disaster struck. The platform that led to the exit door was *gone*. All that was left was a doorway into a cliff-face. Consequently, the rock hit nothing as we swung to its full stretch, flying straight over the exit door. As anticipated, I then began to swing back in the direction that I had come from. I was soon to crash into my most recent departure platform. *Bang*. What do I do now? This was the only swinging rock that went near the exit door; it was either this way or no way. I conceded that the only way to do it was to jump from the rock while in flight and hope to land exactly on the doorway's edge. This was a very high-risk option, but there were no alternatives.

The rock soon began to swing back towards the exit door. As before, it gathered more and more speed as it swung. I needed to time it perfectly. Poised, I bent my knees and eyed my target like a cowboy about to lasso a bull. Closer and closer, I could feel a bead of sweat run down the center of my back. Then, without the inevitable impact of bumping into another rock, I jumped, soaring through the air like a bird on its first flight from the nest. I kept my focus on the door and hoped time would take me there. My legs and arms were like jelly. I seemed to be getting closer to the door...but...but I wasn't going to make it. Desperately I reached out with the hope that I could cling on to something. As I neared, I completely missed the door, but miraculously as I fell past my target I reached out and somehow managed to grip onto the bottom of the doorway. I was tired, but I had to dig deep. I simply had to hold on to the doorway's threshold. This was too tough, as I just hung there wondering if I even had the energy to save myself. But then, maybe it was adrenaline or maybe it was someone praying for me, but I got this surge of relief that allowed me to pull myself up, turn the handle, and climb through the doorway. This was a lucky escape. I screamed to myself in sheer elation. I had been very, *very* fortunate. I felt that I should really be lying at the bottom of the big, black void right now, but instead, somehow, I'd managed to survive.

As I lay there puffing, my chest moving quickly in and out, I mumbled, "Two down, one to go." I was shattered. If the final task were to arm-wrestle a five-year-old girl, she would probably win. I was so very shattered. Slowly, the frequency of my puffing began to lessen, and I began to regain control of my lungs. I lifted my head and sat back against the wall to size up what was next. I dreaded to imagine whether the worst was over or if the worst was still to come. I looked to the wall for clues to inform me of what was next to come, but there was nothing. Oddly, I saw where a message had been etched into the wall; however, it appeared someone had purposely scratched it out. Who would scratch out the clue, especially when I never really understood them until it was too late? If someone was out to sabotage me by preventing me from reading clues I didn't understand, then they were not very clever saboteurs. On the other hand, maybe for some strange reason, over time this one had gotten scratched out.

I looked ahead again, and there was my final door. I was very nervous; the last time I'd tried to go through one of these, the floor had fallen from under me. I reached forward to catch the handle and slowly turned... nothing. It seemed that this door checked out okay. It actually was a real door. I stepped through the doorway and peered around. It was a very wide, long room with a low ceiling. The floor was completely flat. It was a light brown in color, and the room almost seemed to be lit from the ground upwards. I could see the floor very well, though apart from that, visibility got worse as I raised my gaze from the floor.

On second glance, I saw that the doorway was straight ahead, roughly one hundred feet away. I looked around, nervously waiting for the catch... nothing. Was it going to be this easy? I went to take a step forward when, "You will fail, Zachary," a calm gentleman's voice announced. "You are afraid of failure; you are afraid of failing yourself and afraid of failing others. It is your fear that drives you and destroys you. What happens when you are no longer afraid? Will you cease to exist? What happens if you get too afraid? Will you cease to persist? You are weak, and you know what happens to the weak, Zachary. They are crushed." And right then, a large boulder dropped from the ceiling, slamming into the center of the room.

"I am one of the sworn *others* you have been warned about. I am here to stop you. I am better than you, faster than you, and wiser than you. Tonight is the night you die," the voice informed me. Another boulder dropped from the ceiling over to my left. I couldn't see where the voice was coming from, but slowly, it began laughing and said, "They say that if you are pure of heart, you will know what path to take in order to avoid all of these little, dropping rocks. But unfortunately this will be the least of your troubles, as tonight you will be facing me. I have been doing this for a long time, Zachary... I have been *around* for a long time. I was around with Bronson when, in the world of no money, he mysteriously got sent to the wrong hospital." He laughed to himself. "I was around when the world of equality began to turn bad. I got someone to infiltrate their precious leadership and give all the wrong advice." He laughed and then, slowly ending his laugher, he said, "I even had some of my colleagues pay you a visit on your first exercise morning in this world to see if you could fight... to see if you could survive."

In the distance I saw a man appear. From where I was standing, he seemed a large man, wide, one half of his head with long, blond hair, the other half with long, black hair and both sides acting as curtains to a long, pointed, sharp, evil face. From the intimidating speech, it seemed I had two problems: the large, dangerous rocks and the evil-looking man. How was he going to hurt me? The man began tapping his foot. "You have some serious power within you, Zachary, some serious juice... but luckily for me, you don't know how to use them yet. This is why you're mine, Gerbils. You are all mine... 'cause unlike you, I know what I stand for, and I know what I have to do to get what I want." The man stopped momentarily. "This is why your life must end. *Die, my friend,*" he said, raising his voice. All I could do was listen to my heart and hope that my heart would be good enough. Sweating furiously, once again I took two steps to the left, but then *bang*, a rock fell three steps to my left and my mysterious, ill-wishing adversary began beating his chest.

"I am ready for you. Do your worst," I said, terrified inside.

Regardless of what would happen, I had to struggle on. I took another few steps forward and a couple to the left again. All throughout, rocks were falling but none of them near me. It seemed the faster I moved, the more rocks fell. Although this was the third task, and I was exhausted, my heart was pumping fiercely, and my eyes were popping out of my head with anxiety. As I edged my way along, the man began making noises. I wasn't sure what he was doing, but the noises soon grew louder and louder. Although he did not move his position, he was making a range of exaggerated movements with his head, hands, and legs. It was like he was working himself up to explode. I wondered what his power was. I looked up briefly to view him and saw these frantic movements build and build until they suddenly stopped. He stood completely still with both arms down by his side, his chin nestled into his chest, and his eyes glued on me with a wide grin spread across his face. It looked so creepy; his eyes were burning through me. Then, unexpectedly, a massive boulder fell from the ceiling and hit him squarely on the head.

His head, body, and expression didn't even flinch; instead, he continued grinning at me and whispered, "I am going to kill you." I could see from his eyes that he meant it and, from the little reaction he'd had to the boulder, that he was capable of it. He then began making the noises again, his grin slowly turning to serious concentration, all the time focused on me. He began walking, and more rocks began to fall. The noises he was making again got louder and louder as he stared at me the whole time. His walk then broke into a ridged run in my direction as he chanted a fearsome war cry. Faster and faster he ran, and as he proceeded to get closer and closer there were rocks falling everywhere. I was terrified, and his earlier war cry had now turned into a scream, until he took one almighty leap forward from the momentum of his run, stopped himself suddenly, raised his arms above his head, and landed, saying "Hhheeeaaa—ccccccoooc-coooo—ratatttttticccchhaaa." As he landed, a massive burst of black cloud came flying out from his chest and flew in my direction. How was I going to protect myself from his evil magic?

Out of pure fear, I instinctively crouched down and clenched my hands together, bracing myself for the absolute worst. A few moments had passed, and I felt nothing. A little surprised by this, I opened my eyes slowly to see what had happened. I was standing in a black bubble.

At first I thought this was a result of my new enemy, but then I heard a voice; it was Wen. "Today when you helped me with that girl, I gave you something to help you on your way. Pain cannot infiltrate pain; hence, when I absorbed that girl's suffering, I passed a little onto you so you could use it in a time of need. However, only use this as a last resort. The effects are only temporary, and you will not feel well after it." *Now she tells me.* It appeared that I generated this black bubble through the pain received from earlier; this bubble was protecting me. I did not use this as my last resort but inadvertently had selected this course of action as my first resort. I was in trouble. This guy looked angry; the guy looked like he was going to strike again. While staring back at my failed assassin, I thought back to what he had said to me earlier about my fears.

He intimidated me, and some of what he had said was true. But what if his power depended on my insecurity? What if, in order for him to feel big, I had to feel small, just like in the world of equality? This angered me. Whatever the answer, I was about to stand up to him. Perhaps this was my final trial, using the faith in my own abilities to protect myself from these ubiquitous dangers. Though the scenario was grave, it was time for me to start showing a little belief in myself.

The dark bubble soon began to fade. I stood there firmly, ready for whatever he had. Boulders were now readily falling between us as we locked eyes, ready to do battle. "Are you ready to die, Zachary?" He smiled, tilting his head to one side. He then stepped forward and flicked his chest, chanting the same "Hhheeeaaa—ccccooooccooo—ratatttticccchhaaa" as he had before as another black ray came from his chest, hurtling towards me. This time I wasn't afraid. So with much rage and even more hope, I outstretched my hands, looked at him, and roared, "Aaaaahhhhhhhh."

To my surprise, a powerful jet of fire came from both my hands, nullifying the treacherous advances of my merciless attacker. He persisted a little more, but I gritted my teeth and reproduced this almighty fire. I was euphoric, angry, and terrified all at the same time. We were locked in battle, both our faces clenched, oblivious to the constant pounding of the rocks falling all around us.

And then nothing. He and I stopped right at the same time. We were both puffing; my hands were shaking and stinging from all of the fire. He smiled uncomfortably and, wiping his brow, said, "Maybe I will have to do this the hard way." He began walking, first slowly and then very quickly. He started to gather speed in his robot-like run. His arms were pumping, and his body was almost throbbing with determination. At first I put out my arms in a fury to unleash my fire, but it was to no avail. It wasn't working.

As I was standing there sizing up my options, I put my right hand down to one side. I then clenched my hand and brought it back up to my stomach. As I did this, a rock on my right-hand side moved a little on the ground. I moved my hand again, and sure enough, the rock moved again. *Maybe I could throw one of these rocks at him,* I thought to myself. It seemed from earlier that my

Viscent power was the ability to control fire, somehow, but I also seemed to be able to move that rock. Confused, but with this new potential ability in mind, I looked out to a rock in the foreground and tried to move it with the power of my hand, but it was no good. It seemed I could only move the rocks closest to me. As the guy was almost upon me, all I could hope for was that a rock would fall near me so I could wave my clenched fist and the rock would hit him. It was a tall order, but I was out of options. Nervously I waited there, shaking in pure fear as this maniac closed in on me. He looked so angry, punching the air as he travelled in anticipation for my blood. By now he was only about fifteen feet away, rocks hitting him as he travelled, but he smashed through them as if they didn't exist. He was roaring as he had been earlier and pumping his arms in rage. I knew it was either now or never to do something. Nine, eight, seven, this was it... five, four... and then, out of the corner of my eye, I saw a rock fall to my right. It seemed time had slowed down as the rock steadily made its way to the ground. On impact, I snatched my right hand from my side, bringing it across my body. In doing this, the rock flew across the air in the direction of the movement of my hand and knocked the guy to the ground. The rock hit him on the legs and threw him completely off balance. The rocks were no match for him as they hit him from above, but hitting him from the side was very effective. It worked, but I had no time to enjoy it. I had to run because the guy would be on his feet in no time. I was not ready to fight him.

The rocks were still pounding the earth randomly as I zigzagged forwards all the way to the door up ahead. The rocks were only just missing me, and worse again, my evil attacker was on his feet again. He gave an almighty roar and then proceeded to chase after me, shouting and screaming. I was puffing; it wasn't long to go now. All I could hear was *thump, thump, thump,* supported by a loud growling sound coming from my attacker. Eventually, I got to the door. I quickly went to open it, but it was locked. I panicked... this guy was closing in fast, and if he wasn't mad before, he was furious now. "Ahhhh," he roared as again he closed in. Twenty, nineteen feet, eighteen. I tugged desperately on the door, shaking it, and banging it until, suddenly, it opened. As I looked around, my evil opponent was only feet away so I dived desperately through the door in order to get to the other side as fast as I could. Swiftly, I slammed it in his face, stopping him right in his tracks. In full anticipation that the hulk would quickly beat the door down and me with it, I pushed myself against it in the hope that my final, feeble, exhausted efforts would in some way keep the monster at bay. As I continued to push, all I could hear from the other side of the door was a series of heavy thuds and a muffled voice saying, "You're mine next time, Zach, you're mine..." He was laughing. "Though what's funny is that I am not who you should be afraid of... I am not even the most powerful. There is a price on your head now, Zachary. Good luck." He laughed as his voice grew fainter.

I didn't care whose I was and I didn't care what the price was. I was finished... I did it. I was looking down, puffing and panting, trying to get my breath back when I saw a pair of sandals in front of me. I looked up. It was a man.

"Do not worry. He can't hurt you; that door has two very special features. It is a cast iron, reinforced door on hinges that make its movement seem effortless, but more importantly, it is a product of love, built by the sweat and community that this world was founded on. Love is not weak because you can't see it; when running from the forces of evil it is the most powerful weapon you can possess," the sandal man said. Well this made a lot more sense, as the thought of my little muscles holding back this hulk really wasn't making sense.

"On a lighter note, well done on your achievement, young man. You truly are an inspiration," he said.

"Thank you... thank you very much," I replied.

"Now are you ready for all of the food?"

I looked down at the odd-looking sandals again before throwing my eyes to the sky and said, "Can I ask why you never give them seeds or the means to produce their own food?"

"Because, young man, this is a chore, a task; they do not need this distraction," he said defensively.

"Sir, your people need a constant source of food and medicine... You really cannot live on love alone." He stood back.

"Excuse me?" he responded.

"Look, I'm sorry. I know this is the sole foundation of this entire community, and it is love that can make everything feel like paradise. However, it cannot alone make a place look like paradise... You need to help your people... you need to help your paradise," I said as sensitively as possible.

He looked at me with a sorely disappointed look on his face, though it appeared like he was recognizing things were not perfect. He then walked away with his head down, looked back briefly, and said, "You will have your seeds and medicine. Perhaps my utopia needs a little help after all." He gave me an embarrassed smile and said, "Thank you." It was at that moment I think I completely blacked out. The magnitude of the last couple of hours had finally gotten the better of me.

Chapter 16

When I awoke, I was in the comfort of someone's living room. I was sitting in a very cozy mustard armchair, and what seemed to be Wen and Bala stood at the fireplace warming their hands. There was soft music playing in the background, and a very slight hint of vanilla flirting with my sense of smell. I jumped to my feet onto a carpet that felt like a kitten's fur and immediately ran over to my two pals.

"Wen, Bala... you're okay." My face was beaming, I was so happy to see them.

"Zachary... oh, well done..." Wen said.

"Yeah, well done, Zach. You did ace..." Bala yelled.

"Yeah, as soon as you completed your task, there was a massive delivery of food, medicine, and seeds, and not just that, but the tools needed to sow the seeds," Wen added.

"We did it," I said proudly.

"Right, we did it. We are the terrific three," said Bala.

"That's a silly name, Bala, terrific three... Surely we can do better than that," said Wen.

Bala took a step back to size up little Wen. . "Well, you come up with something then, clever clogs." And on they went bickering until...

"On your own you will be nothing, but together you could be unstoppable. Please be seated," a clear, soft woman's voice commanded. Up until now it was a man's voice—how strange if it turned out that it was a woman that had been giving us our commands all this time. As we took our seats, Bala and I sat on the couch, and Wen settled on the mustard armchair. All of the seats were facing inwards towards the fire when a door opened behind us. Our heads turned, but the chairs were so high we still couldn't see a thing. We were dying to know who it was that had been controlling us all this time. Who had sent us on these missions? Who was Evall? The footsteps stopped behind us; she was there—but we were all too frightened to look.

"Are you wondering what I look like?" she asked playfully. "You know exactly what I look like, don't you?" Oddly, it was that last word she said that reminded me of someone I knew. I looked across, and Wen and Bala were also straining to picture who this familiar voice might be.

"This is not the first time you have dealt with me; in fact, I deal with you almost every day." She began to walk around the left side of the room to circle back into our enclosure. It was a small woman dressed in a long, navy, silk cloak with a hood and a white scarf. Her head was down so she was still not identifiable. She then raised her right hand and pealed back the hood.

"Mi… Mis… Mrs. Malkin! Mrs. Malkin is Evall," I said with astonishment. Bala laughed a little while Wen's jaw remained wide open.

"Hello, you lot," she said warmly, and her wrinkled smile immediately comforted us. She looked down on all of us as we sat there gobsmacked and said, "Isn't it strange that people who you only ever have the slightest encounters with in your life can sometimes go on to have such a major influence on your life's path? A stranger, a teacher, a co-worker, or in your case, your shopkeeper! I am extremely happy with your work. Not only have you helped everywhere you have been, but you have all begun your own separate journeys of self-discovery," she said as she smiled again and opened her arms to us.

"Bala, you have discovered the gift of consumption." We all looked a little puzzled. "That time when you grew in size, you absorbed every single person around you in the world of love and added all of their strengths together. If you absorbed more people, you would get bigger again. You can also absorb animals, birds, even ants, as you discovered when those bullies were picking on you. However, you have a gift that without control will kill you, but with discipline will make you almighty," Mrs. Malkin said to Bala as his eyes gazed in amazement at the prospect of what he could do.

Mrs. Malkin then turned to Wen. "Wen, you have the power of feeling—the most complicated of all. You can use, sense, manipulate, and take feeling. As you demonstrated with Zachary, you saved his life, and as you demonstrated with the little girl, you saved her life. But be cautious; as just as you can save life, you can also take it. I can teach you more about your power and tell you how you appreciate the fullness of this gift, but you alone are the one who needs to feel this power and grow into it," Mrs. Malkin said with a motherly concern and consideration for Wen's development.

And then, finally, Mrs. Malkin turned to me. "And Zachary, you have the power of the elements. Astonishingly, you can control the elements as defined by the Oranthium code: water, fire, and earth, all basic in concept but magnificent in practice," she said, looking at me and smiling. I thought about the world of love when I did have to use my powers—what it felt like and the limited control I had over them. It was amazing that all of this time I had this power within me and I didn't even know it. I couldn't wait to learn more about how to use my power. I also thought about the man in the world of love. When I had to use my power against him, he said that he had caused trouble in the world without money, the world of equality, and even had someone try to destroy me in the world of equality. However, he never mentioned anything about the strange doctor I had my visit with in my own world. Who was that person, and was he out to hurt me? As I ran over this in my mind, I decided to ask Evall, or Mrs. Malkin, if she knew anything about this.

"I have a question," I said as I looked up to speak with Mrs. Malkin. She awaited questions from any of the three of us after just telling us a little more about our powers. "Before I met you as Evall," I said, "I paid a visit to the doctor; however, I think I was tricked, and I don't even think it was a doctor as he had me doing strange things with rocks, and it turned out not to be the doctor I was there to visit. I also assumed when I learnt more about being a Viscent that this may have been someone out to cause me harm or kill me, like an evil Viscent! But the doctor did not hurt me, and the evil man I fought in the world of love never mentioned the doctor. I am confused to who this fake doctor could have been. Do you know anything about the identity of the strange doctor?" I said with a very confused look on my face, which was also met with confused looks on the faces of Bala and Wen, both, like me, eagerly awaiting Mrs. Malkin to respond. Mrs. Malkin walked away a little and paused; she remained silent. "Mrs. Malkin," I replied, "are you okay?"

She turned again and looked at me sympathetically. "As you know, I am this world's Evall, and we are all a part of this much wider Viscent community known as the Oranthium. From the moment I learnt of your powers, Zach, I have suspected that the senior members of Oranthium would be watching you." She paused again as if she was trying very hard to select the correct words to use to convey what she wanted to say. She took another breath and said, "You see, as you know, no two living Viscents can have the same power, meaning that the powers that you all currently have were once possessed by other Viscents that are now dead." Bala, Wen, and

I nodded, even though I wasn't sure if this had already been explained.

"In your case, Zach," Mrs. Malkin said, "every single Viscent that has had the power of the elements has had a very special destiny. Some of them have been the leaders, commanders, and heroes of the Oranthium, while others have been equally as effective but for all the wrong reasons. Some of your predecessors with this power have been evil, malicious murderers, who were some of the most ruthless Viscents that ever existed. On top of that, the power of the elements is actually three separate powers: the ability to control water, earth, and fire. There are only five Viscents with a power that allows them to control more that one thing. You are one of these five, and it is because of this that all Viscents before you with this power have been brilliant or treacherous."

I was shocked. I had a sick feeling in my stomach and throat that made me feel that, irrespective of what I thought, my destiny was predetermined. Mrs. Malkin then walked a little closer and said softy, "So you see, Zach, it is possible all of the most powerful, evil, *and* virtuous members of Oranthium are watching you and weighing up whether you are someone who can lead them or someone they need to watch carefully!" I gasped. "So really, Zach...that doctor you met in your world, if it wasn't an evil Viscent, it was probably a very senior member of Oranthium, trying to learn more about you before they decided whether you are an asset they can groom for the greater good or a threat they need to take care of," she said in as comforting a tone as she could. Up to this point I had only been worried that the bad Viscents were out to get me; now I had the concern that the good Viscents were also out to get me. This was a lot to take in, and pretty depressing. I wasn't sure if I could even do anything about it. All I knew now was that I could not afford to trust anybody.

In an attempt to break the silence, Bala then tried to make things positive again.

"So we did good, Mrs. Malkin?" Bala said like an eager puppy.

"Oh, you did very well, Bala, very well. Though it is strange... when I asked you whether the world you lived in was perfect you all said no. However, when I sent you to these worlds to live in, the first thing you would always try and do is make it like where you have come from." She smirked as if we had behaved like predicable school kids.

"Though on all counts, you were correct in what you did. You did not enforce any of your principles but in fact facilitated the evolution of a better balance to the extremes you encountered," Mrs. Malkin said.

"So... what next?" Wen asked tapping her knee impatiently.

"Well, I will begin by honoring my original promises. Firstly and most importantly, I am proud to announce that you have successfully passed the Trials of Oranthium. You completed the three tasks in three different worlds, so for as long as you live, Zachary, you will have a mark of the house of *Soll* branded into the underneath of your right arm," Mrs. Malkin said to me, reaching out to encourage me to turn my arm over. Responding to her advice, I pulled up my sleeve. I turned my arm over, and sure enough, a symbol, or a kind of tattoo, appeared between my wrist and my elbow. I didn't know what exactly it meant, but I knew that it implied that the house of *Soll* accepted me. I smiled, staring at it like a small boy who just won his first medal.

"Bala, you too will find a symbol for the house of *Mant* in the same place, and Wen, you will find the marking of the house of *Rove*," she said, looking to them as they too searched for these new markings. I looked up, still smiling, and looked to Wen and Bala. Rubbing at their own new markings, they both looked up eventually and smiled back at me. It felt good.

"What do these symbols or houses mean?" Wen asked.

"All will be explained at the Oranthium, a place that you will be visiting very soon, my young ones," Mrs. Malkin said smiling. But then, in a matter of a half-second her expression changed, and she looked at us sadly.

"Your powers are now developing and will always be a part of you. Your branding will always be visible, and you will always be a part of these houses, but with these immense powers, please never forget that *none of you are invincible*. You are still just very fragile people with a lot of power." She then looked back in our direction. "But you are different. You will stay together, stick together, won't you? This is very important," she pleaded as her eyes filled with unwanted memories. "Now, for my second and final promise, you get to make a wish that will change your world forever. Now wish wisely," she warned.

We all looked at each other with great concern, covering our arms again, getting back to the wish we had been promised. From our experiences to date, we discovered that whatever kind of wish we asked to have, there would be imperfections. It just seemed so risky that by trying to do well, we could initiate something quite terrible for our own world. We could destroy our world.

"What do you think, Zach?" Bala asked.

"Wow, I don't know. I thought I understood what was good and what was bad, but now, well I'm not so sure. Maybe every imperfection in our world could be a consequence of us doing something else perfect. So to wish for a certain imperfection to go away may mean that we get rid of something that *is* perfect."

Bala scratched his head as I scratched mine. That had seemed a lot clearer in my head than how it came out. Wen came from her chair and sat between us. She looked down at the ground, toeing a piece of the fluffy carpet with her foot.

"We have the potential to cause such an uncontrollably blind domino effect of damage. All from trying to cause positive change... ohh, it's such a gamble... but such a great opportunity to do right," Wen said.

"Yes," said Bala, agreeing with Wen, but none the wiser on what to suggest. There was a short silence when Bala said, "Look, maybe we should just not wish for anything."

Immediately Wen and I nodded, saying, "Yes, it's too risky, definitely."

Until Mrs. Malkin said, "Actually you do have to make this wish, otherwise you cannot truly finish." Again Bala scratched his head, then Wen jumped to her feet and looked back at Bala, and I and went over to Mrs. Malkin and whispered something in her ear. "So is this definitely your wish?" Mrs. Malkin confirmed.

Bala and I jumped up. "What? No, no, hang on, Wen, what did you say?" Bala and I asked.

Wen smiled and said, "Look, guys, you trust me, don't you?" Nervously, Bala and I looked at her and nodded. "Don't make me use my emotional power on you guys," she said as she laughed. As we laughed back, slightly concerned at this strange show of decision by Wen, Bala and I stepped away anxiously.

"Okay then, Wen, your wish on behalf of the group shall be granted," said Mrs. Malkin. "Now the next time you wake up, you will be back in your own world. Do you understand?" Mrs. Malkin said.

"Wait...is that it...I mean, will we ever have another mission or trial?" Bala said with a slight whimper in his voice. Mrs. Malkin walked over to the chair where Bala was sitting down.

"You are now very valuable to me. You are very valuable to your world. You have discovered your abilities. You have a number of counterparts out there that want you dead. You will be in danger for the foreseeable future. Therefore, it is imperative that you keep your gifts secret. I need you alive, as I will need you again. Keep this group secret. Keep this work secret," she advised. She leaned forward in her seat towards us. "This is just the beginning…" And slowly, we drifted off into a deep sleep.

When I woke, I felt an enormous sense of success and safety now that I was back in my own world. I lay there in silence for a moment, smiling to myself before I got back to the world I had left before these trials, and curious to see if I would notice what Wen wished for. With curiosity getting the better of me, I opened my eyes. Alarmingly, my comfort was soon replaced by a deep concern. I could feel the adrenaline assault my system. What had the other Viscent who occupied my body done while I was gone? What did Wen wish for? Had Wen turned? Was she now one of the evil Viscents? I looked around again, scanning all that I could see. What on earth had happened while we were gone? This was not the place I left, something had gone wrong.